TwoKinds

Book One

Thomas Fischbach

TWOKINDS VOL. 1
by Thomas Fischbach

TWOKINDS © and ™ 2022 by Thomas Fischbach

Cover and interior illustrations by Thomas Fischbach.

Published by
Keenspot Entertainment
Los Angeles, CA
E-Mail: keenspot@keenspot.com
Web: www.keenspot.com

Keenspot
CEO & EiC Chris Crosby
PRESIDENT Bobby Crosby

ISBN 978-1-932775-64-8

TWOKINDS VOL. 1 Manga Edition
Second Keenspot Printing, April 2022
PRINTED IN CANADA

Dedicated to my father

Cliffton Morris Fischbach

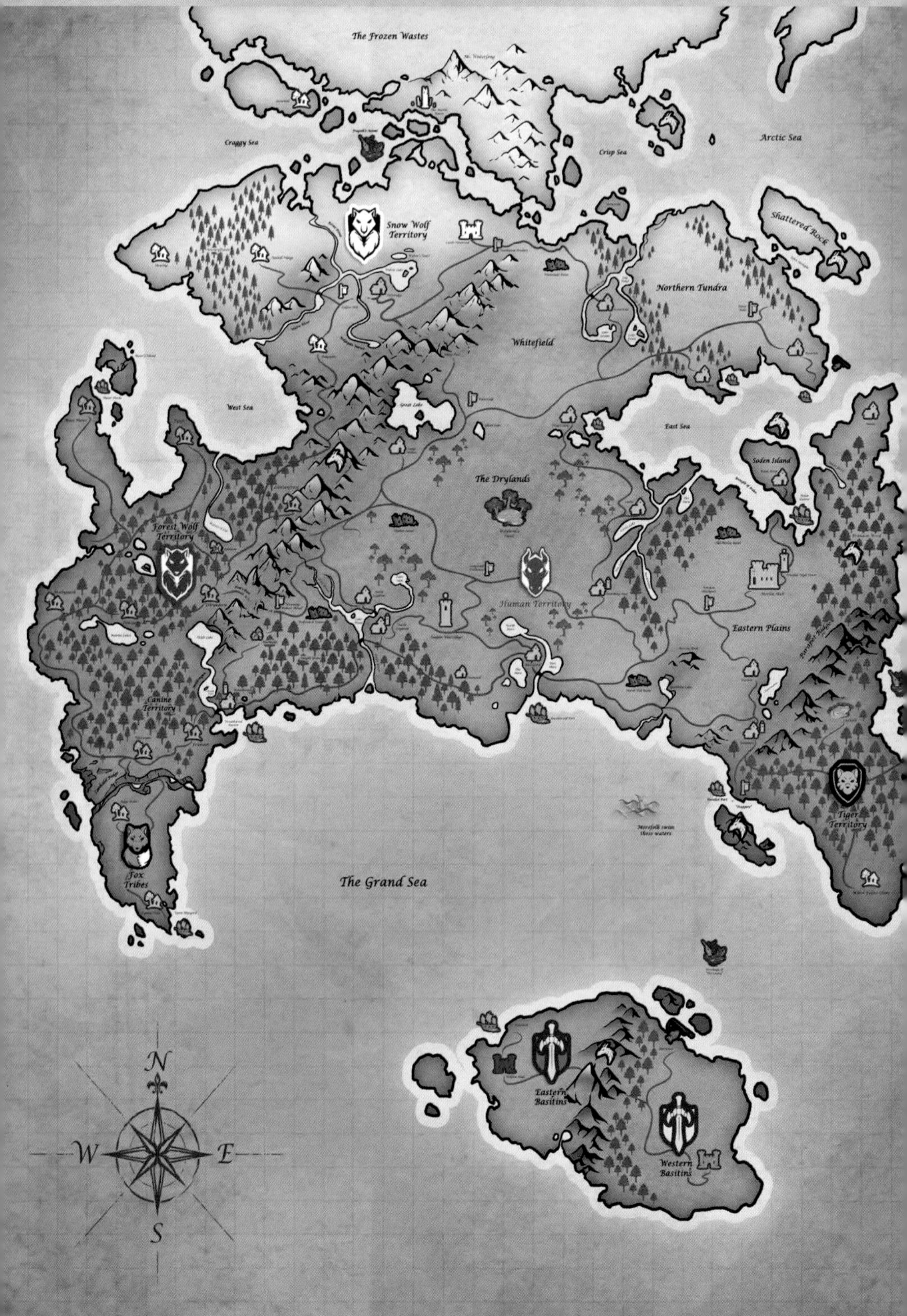

The Frozen Wastes
Craggy Sea
Crisp Sea
Arctic Sea
Snow Wolf Territory
Shattered Rock
Northern Tundra
Whitefield
West Sea
Great Lake
East Sea
Soden Island
The Drylands
Forest Wolf Territory
Human Territory
Eastern Plains
Canine Territory
Tiger Territory
Merefolk swim these waters
Fox Tribes
The Grand Sea
Eastern Basitins
Western Basitins
N
W
E
S

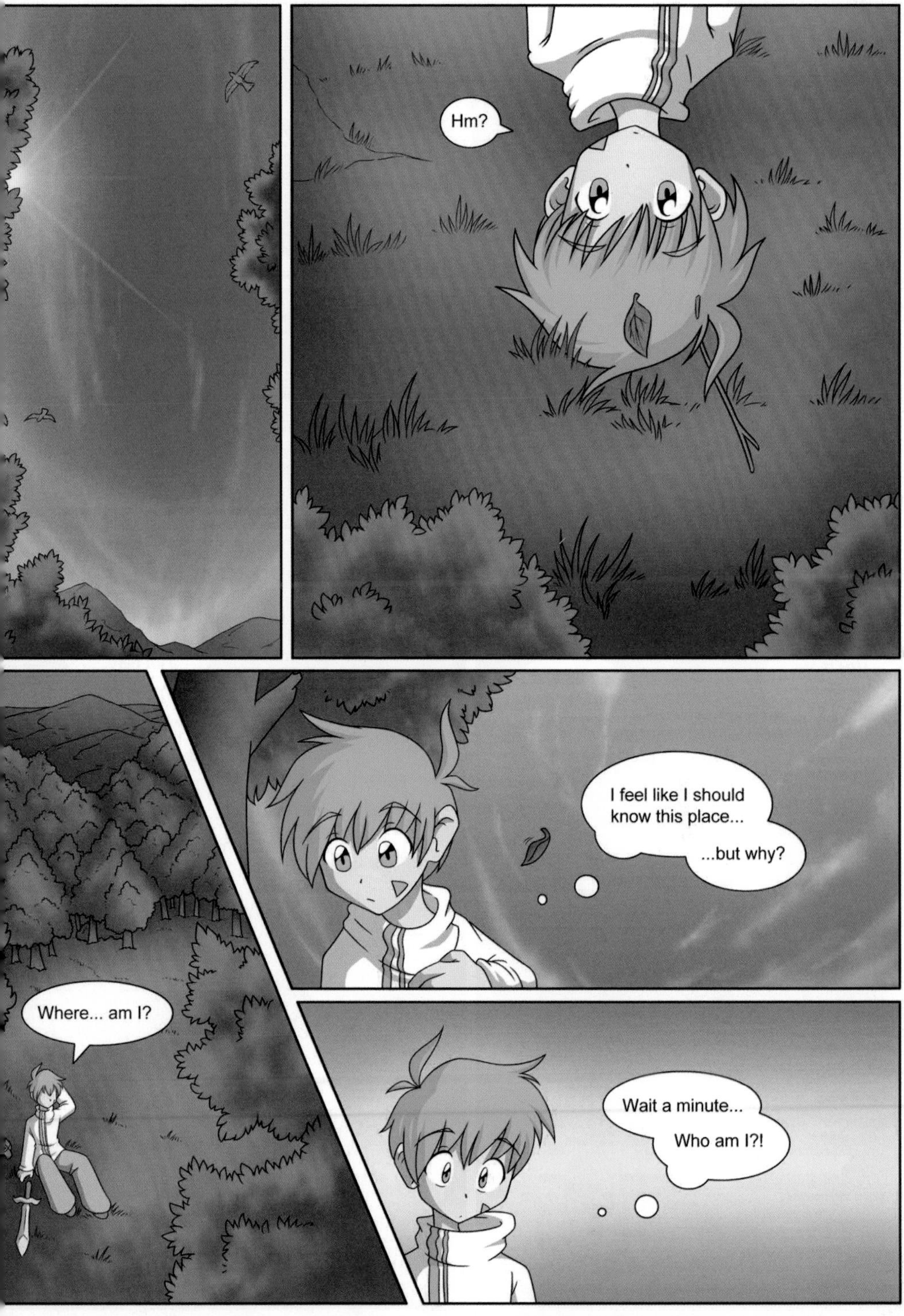
Hm?
I feel like I should know this place...
...but why?
Where... am I?
Wait a minute...
Who am I?!

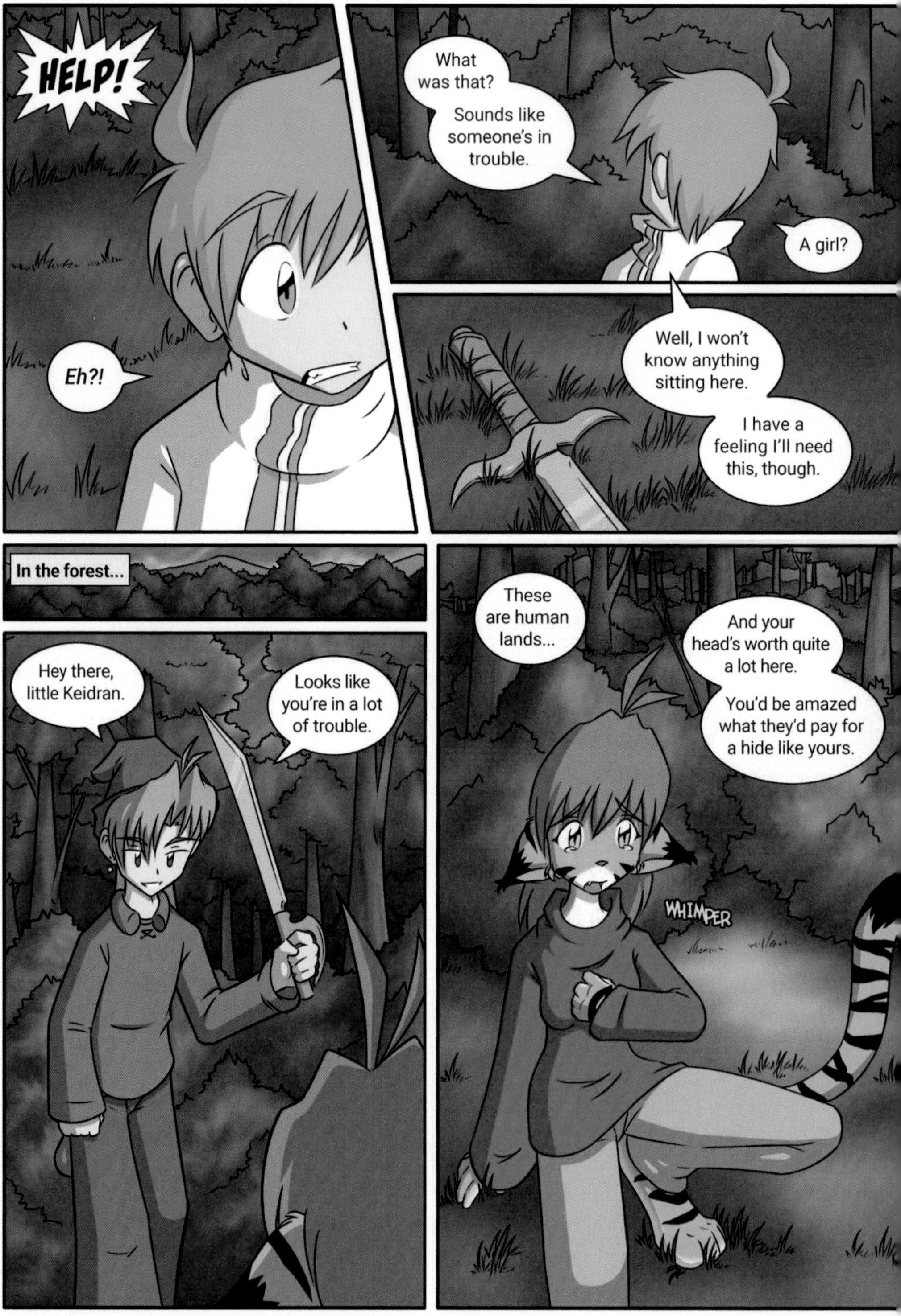
HELP!
Eh?!
What was that?
Sounds like someone's in trouble.
A girl?
Well, I won't know anything sitting here.
I have a feeling I'll need this, though.
In the forest...
Hey there, little Keidran.
Looks like you're in a lot of trouble.
These are human lands...
And your head's worth quite a lot here.
You'd be amazed what they'd pay for a hide like yours.
WHIMPER

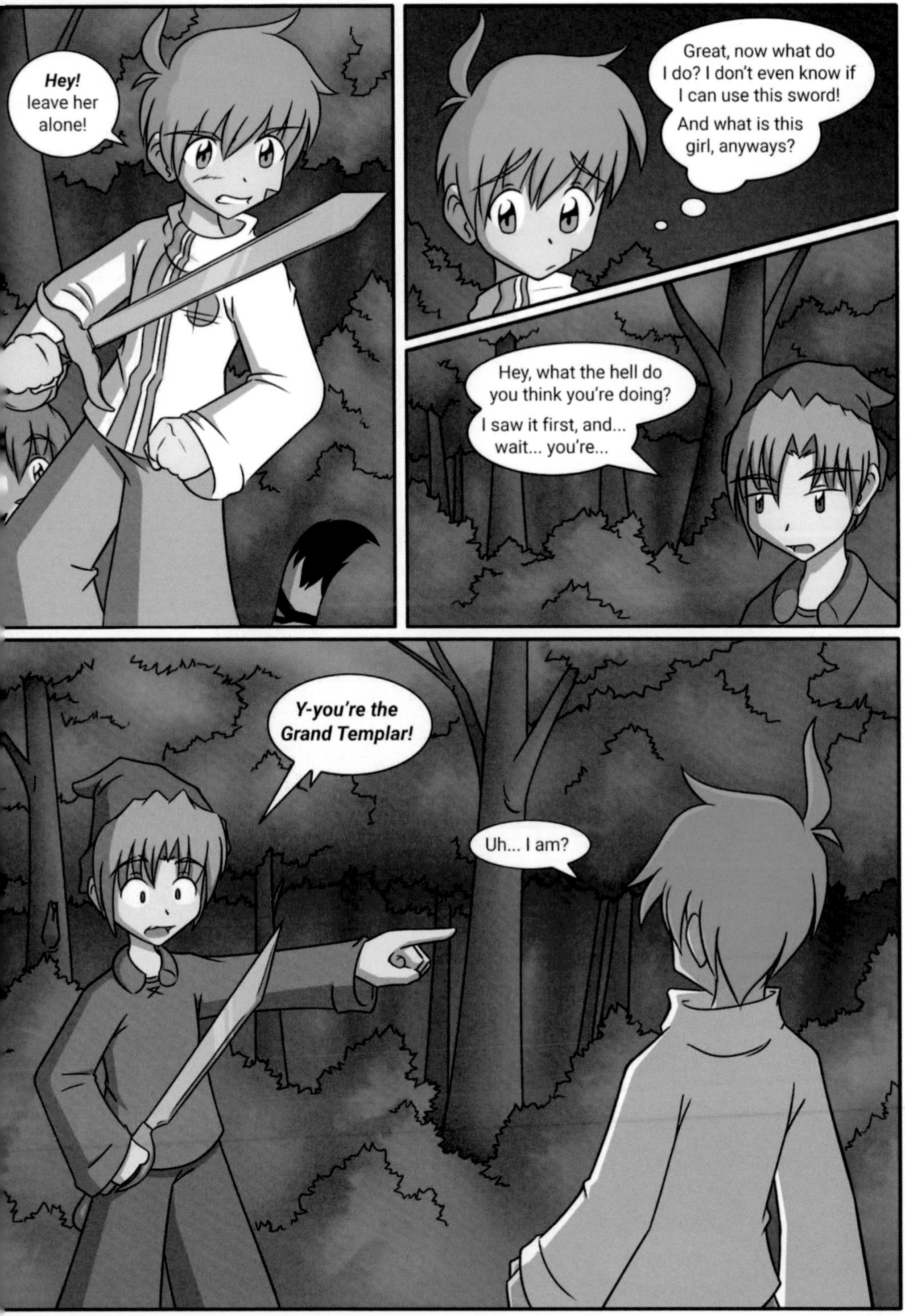

Hey! leave her alone!
Great, now what do I do? I don't even know if I can use this sword!
And what is this girl, anyways?
Hey, what the hell do you think you're doing?
I saw it first, and... wait... you're...
Y-you're the Grand Templar!
Uh... I am?

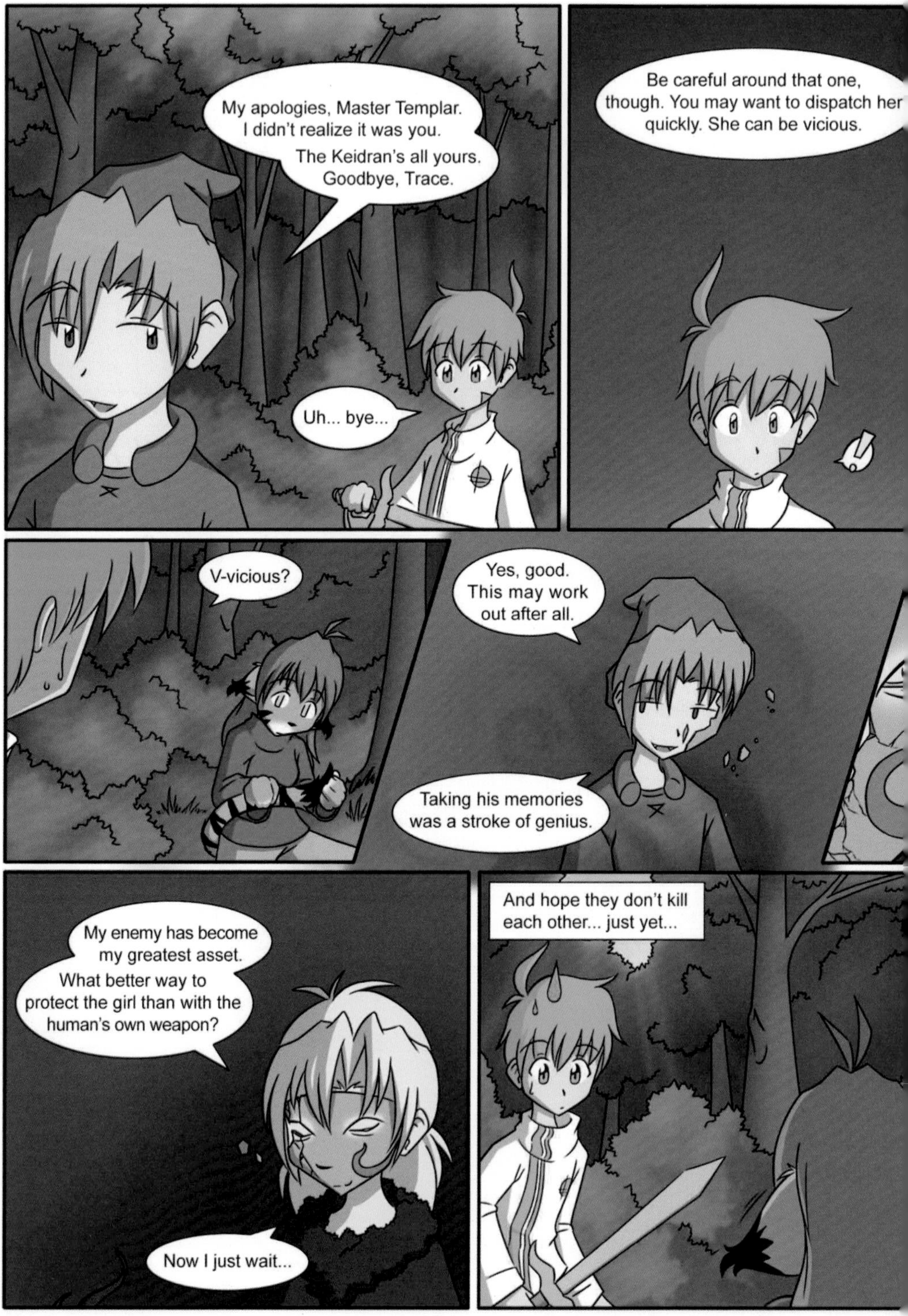
My apologies, Master Templar. I didn't realize it was you.
The Keidran's all yours. Goodbye, Trace.
Uh... bye...
Be careful around that one, though. You may want to dispatch her quickly. She can be vicious.
V-vicious?
Yes, good. This may work out after all.
Taking his memories was a stroke of genius.
My enemy has become my greatest asset.
What better way to protect the girl than with the human's own weapon?
Now I just wait...
And hope they don't kill each other... just yet...

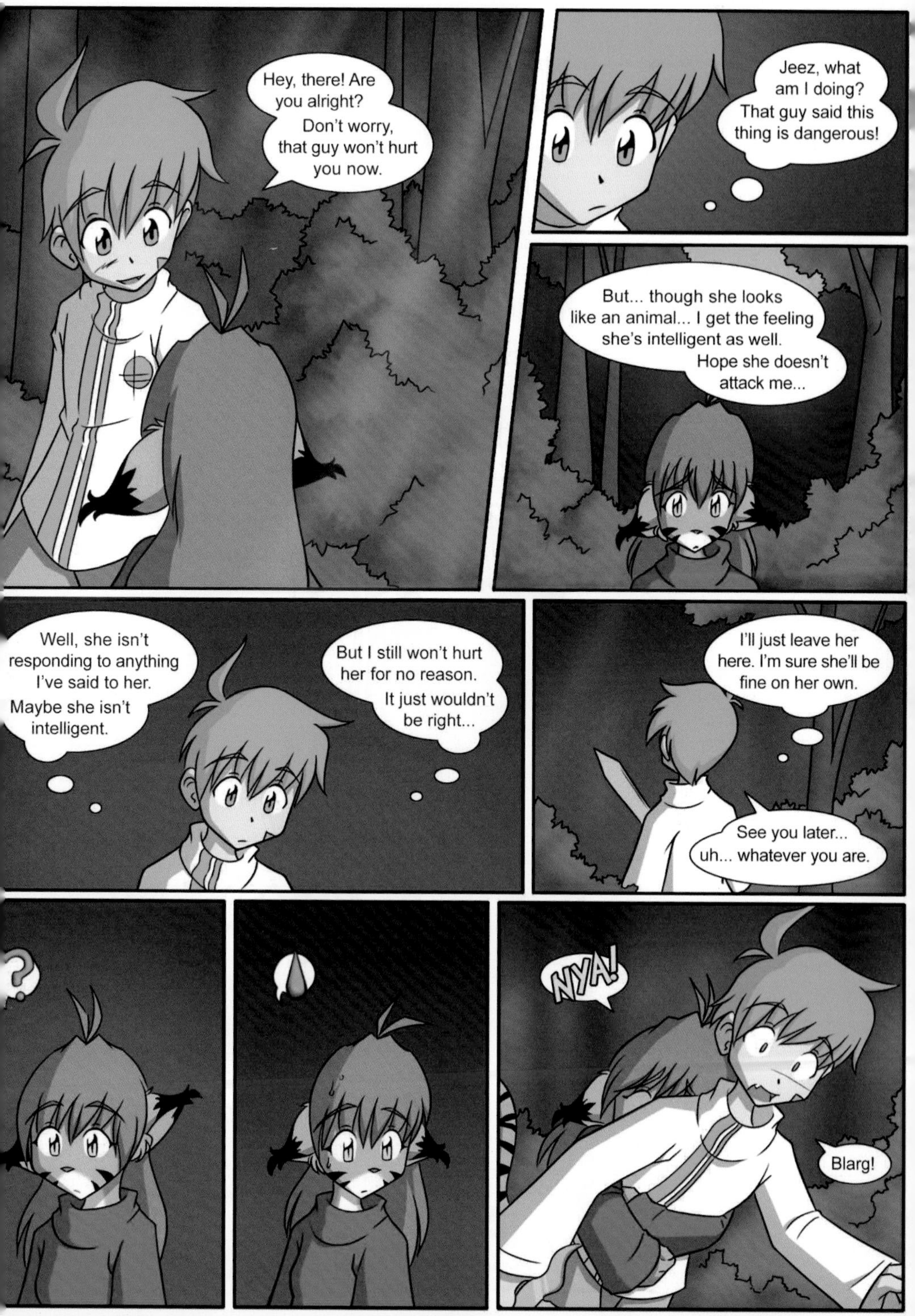
Hey, there! Are you alright?
Don't worry, that guy won't hurt you now.
Jeez, what am I doing? That guy said this thing is dangerous!
But... though she looks like an animal... I get the feeling she's intelligent as well.
Hope she doesn't attack me...
Well, she isn't responding to anything I've said to her.
Maybe she isn't intelligent.
But I still won't hurt her for no reason.
It just wouldn't be right...
I'll just leave her here. I'm sure she'll be fine on her own.
See you later... uh... whatever you are.
?
NYA!
Blarg!

TwoKinds

Chapter One

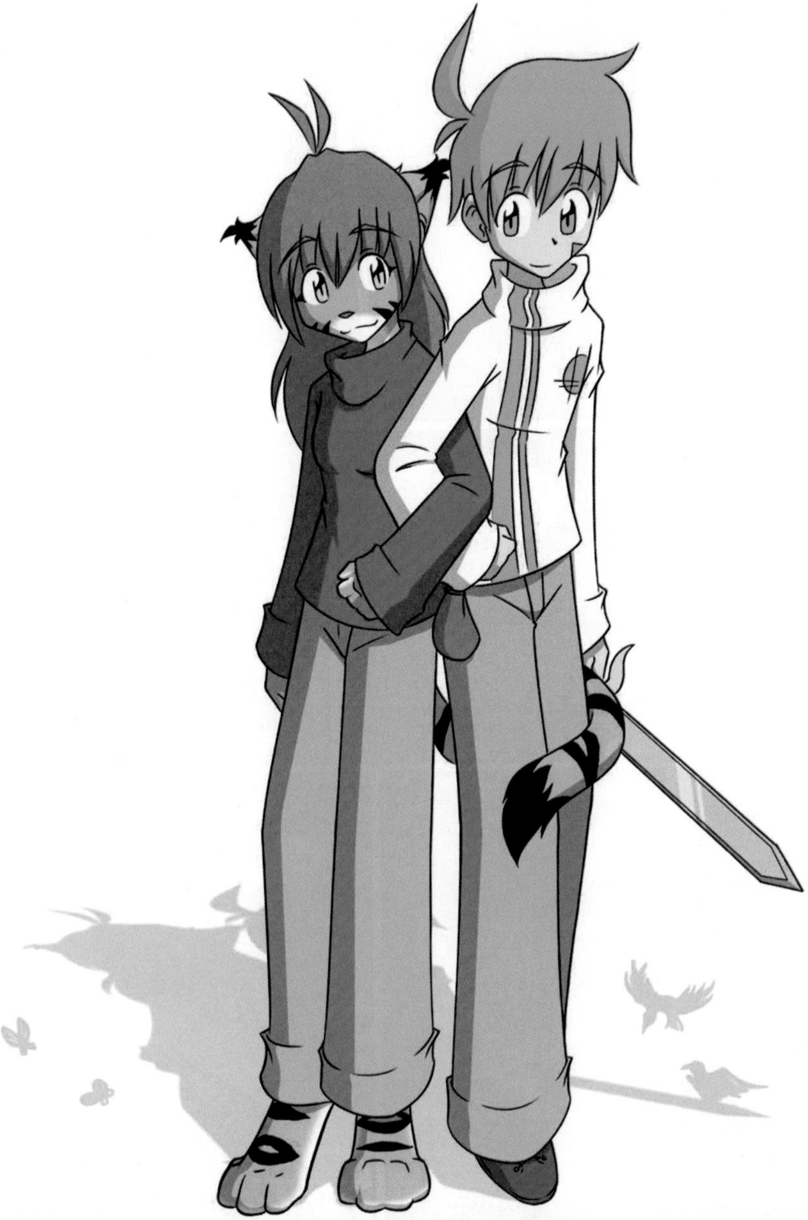

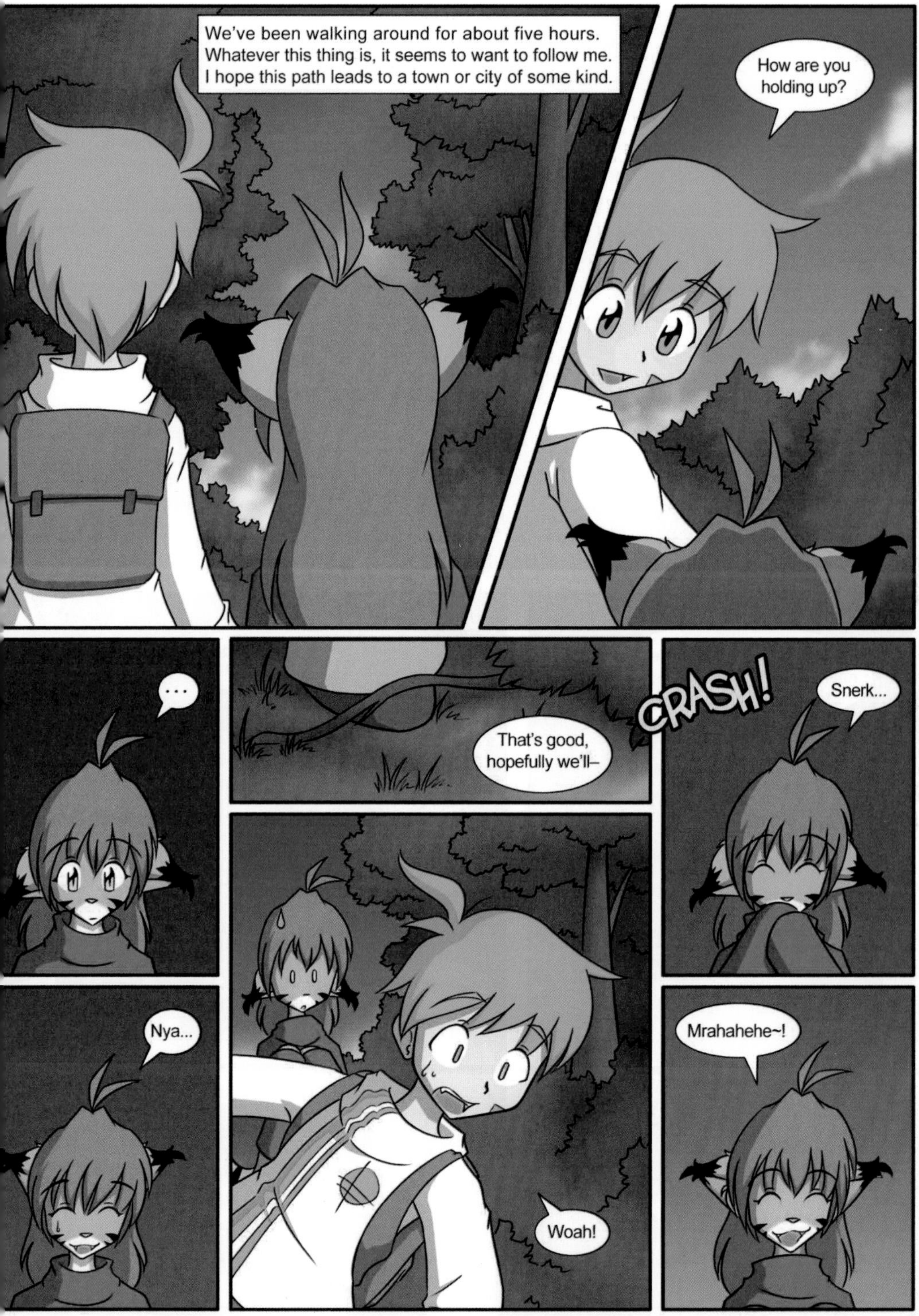
We've been walking around for about five hours. Whatever this thing is, it seems to want to follow me. I hope this path leads to a town or city of some kind.
How are you holding up?
...
That's good, hopefully we'll–
CRASH!
Snerk...
Nya...
Woah!
Mrahahehe~!

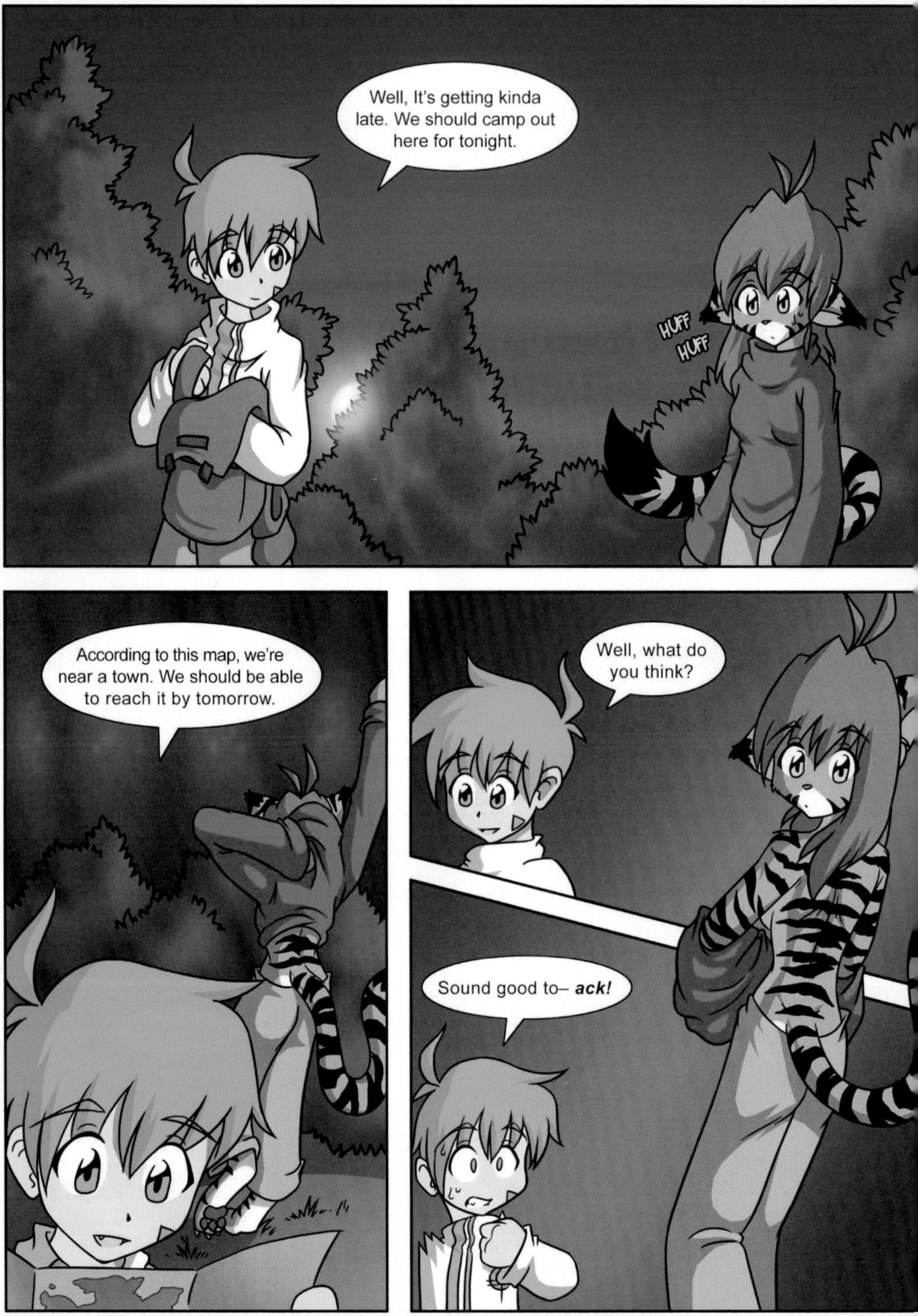
Well, It's getting kinda late. We should camp out here for tonight.
HUFF HUFF
According to this map, we're near a town. We should be able to reach it by tomorrow.
Well, what do you think?
Sound good to– ***ack!***

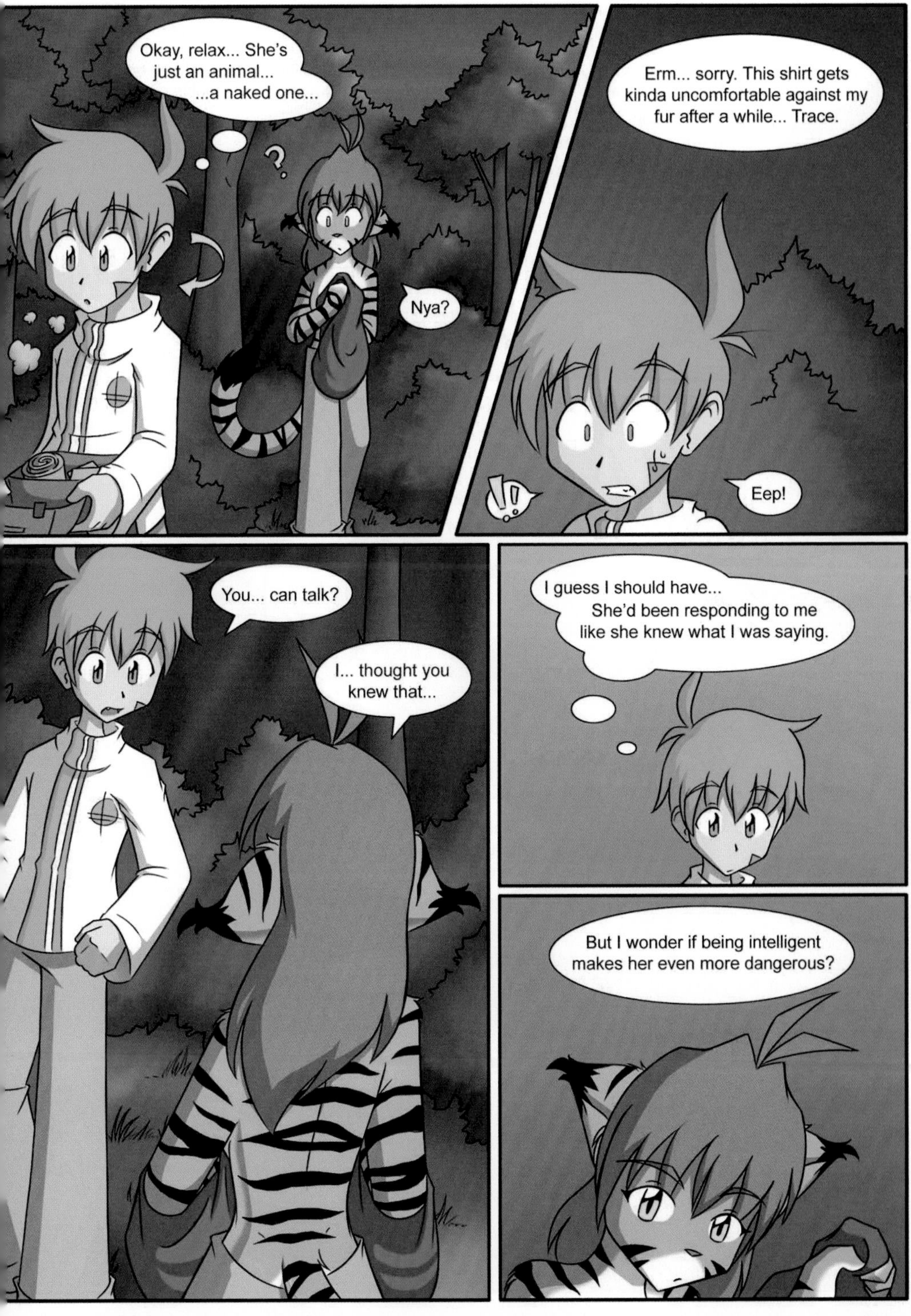
Okay, relax... She's just an animal... ...a naked one...
Nya?
Erm... sorry. This shirt gets kinda uncomfortable against my fur after a while... Trace.
Eep!
You... can talk?
I... thought you knew that...
I guess I should have... She'd been responding to me like she knew what I was saying.
But I wonder if being intelligent makes her even more dangerous?

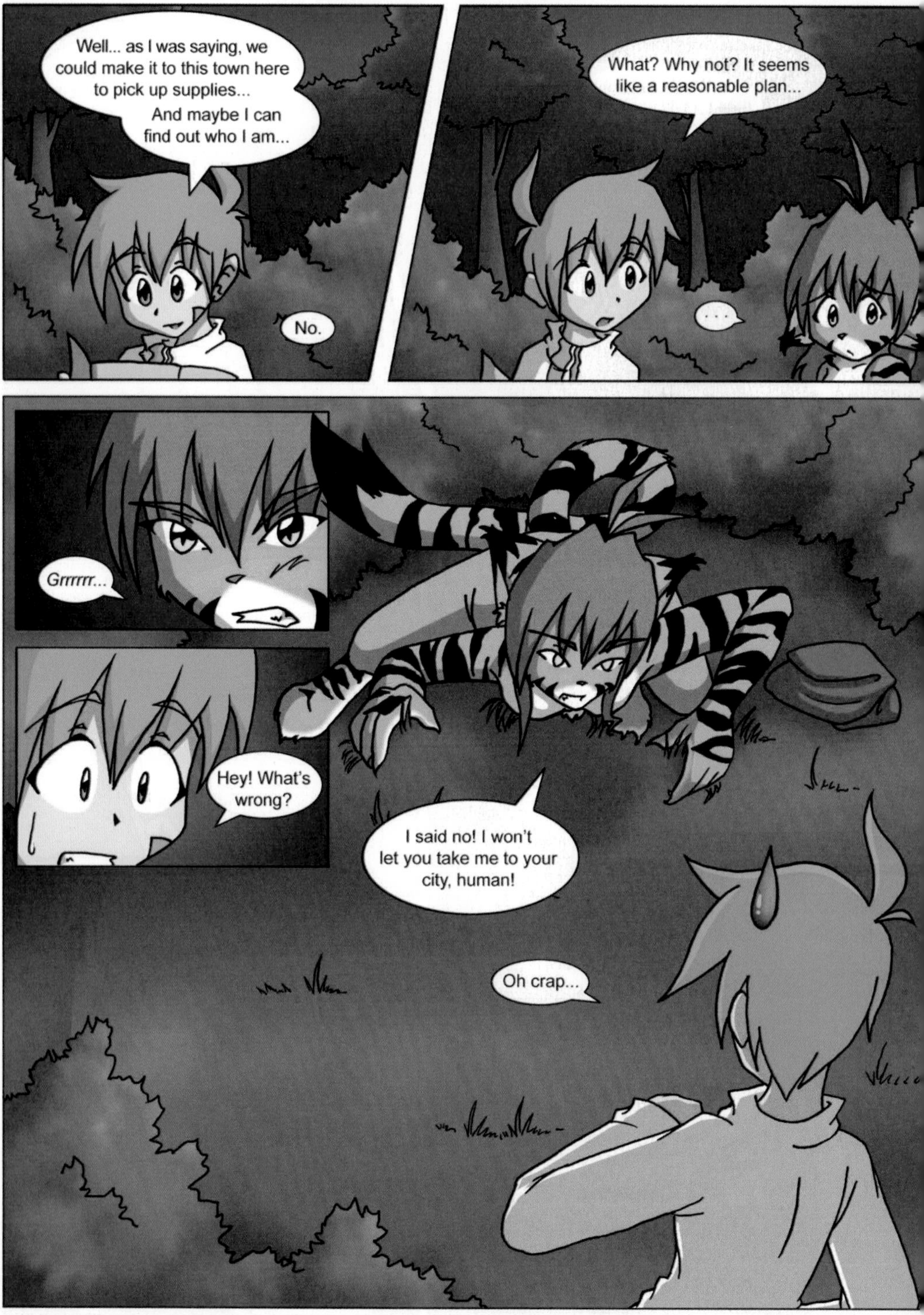
Well... as I was saying, we could make it to this town here to pick up supplies...
And maybe I can find out who I am...
No.
What? Why not? It seems like a reasonable plan...
...
Grrrrrr...
Hey! What's wrong?
I said no! I won't let you take me to your city, human!
Oh crap...

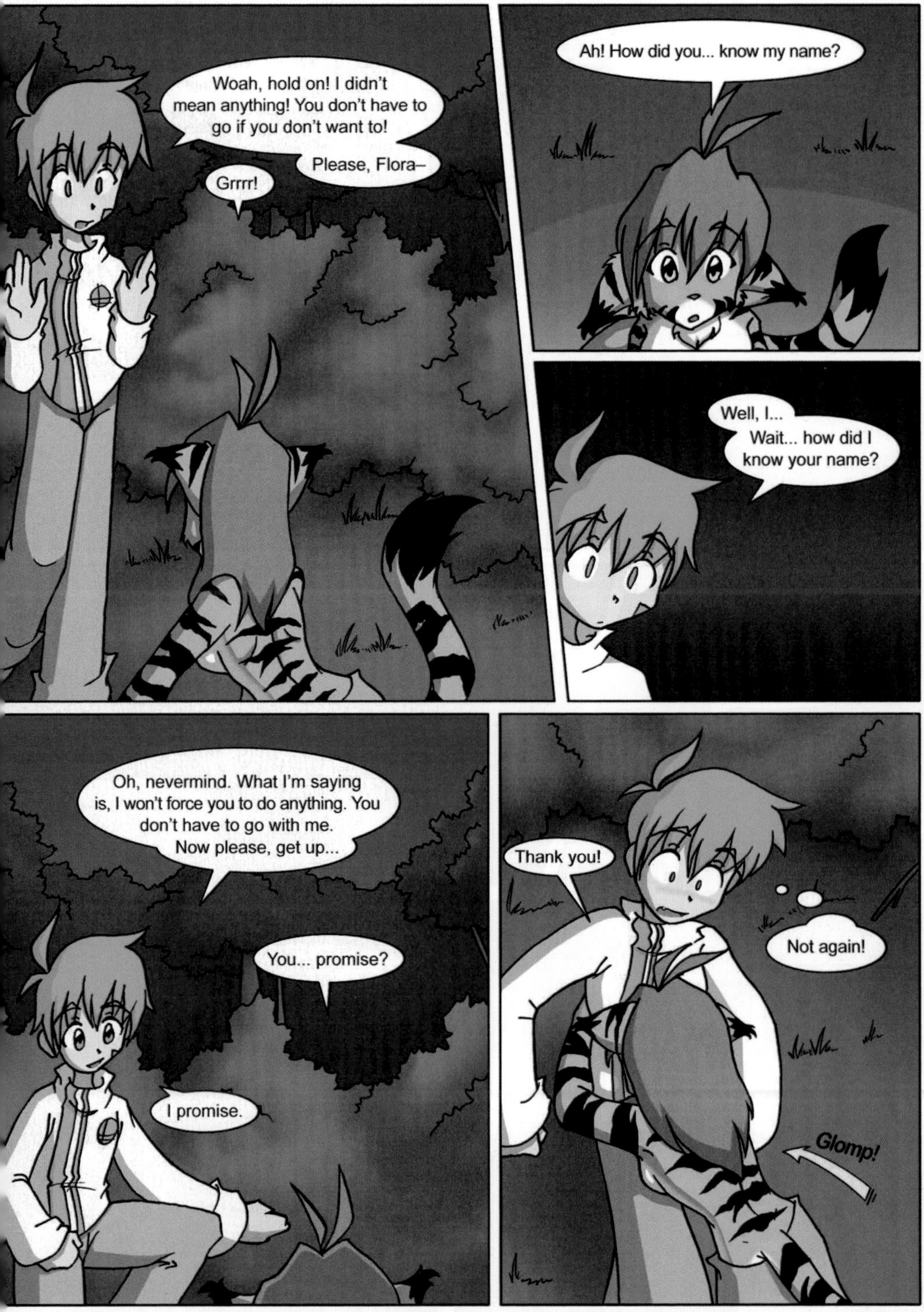
Woah, hold on! I didn't mean anything! You don't have to go if you don't want to!
Please, Flora–
Grrrr!
Ah! How did you... know my name?
Well, I...
Wait... how did I know your name?
Oh, nevermind. What I'm saying is, I won't force you to do anything. You don't have to go with me.
Now please, get up...
You... promise?
I promise.
Thank you!
Not again!
Glomp!

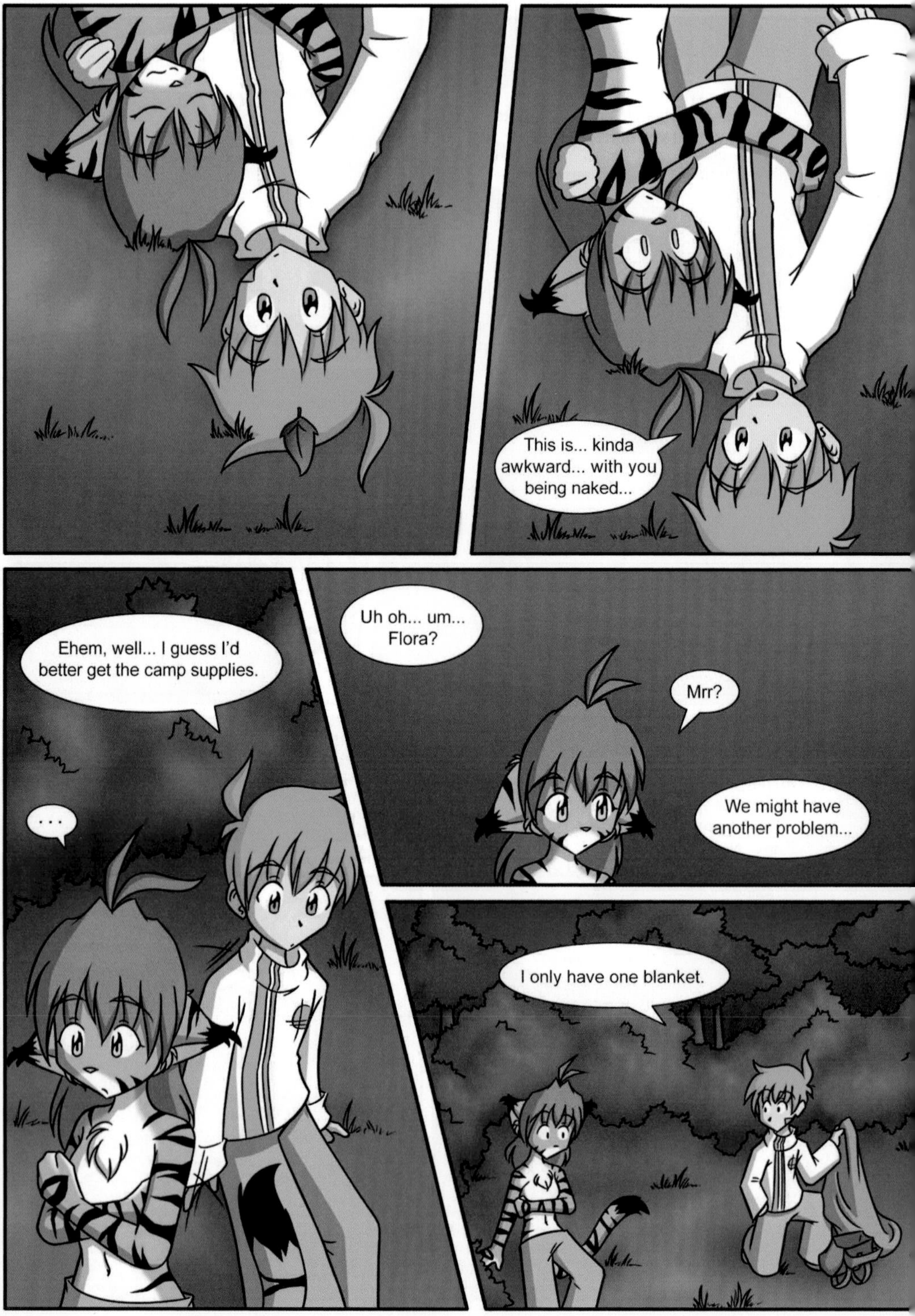
This is... kinda awkward... with you being naked...
Ehem, well... I guess I'd better get the camp supplies.
...
Uh oh... um... Flora?
Mrr?
We might have another problem...
I only have one blanket.

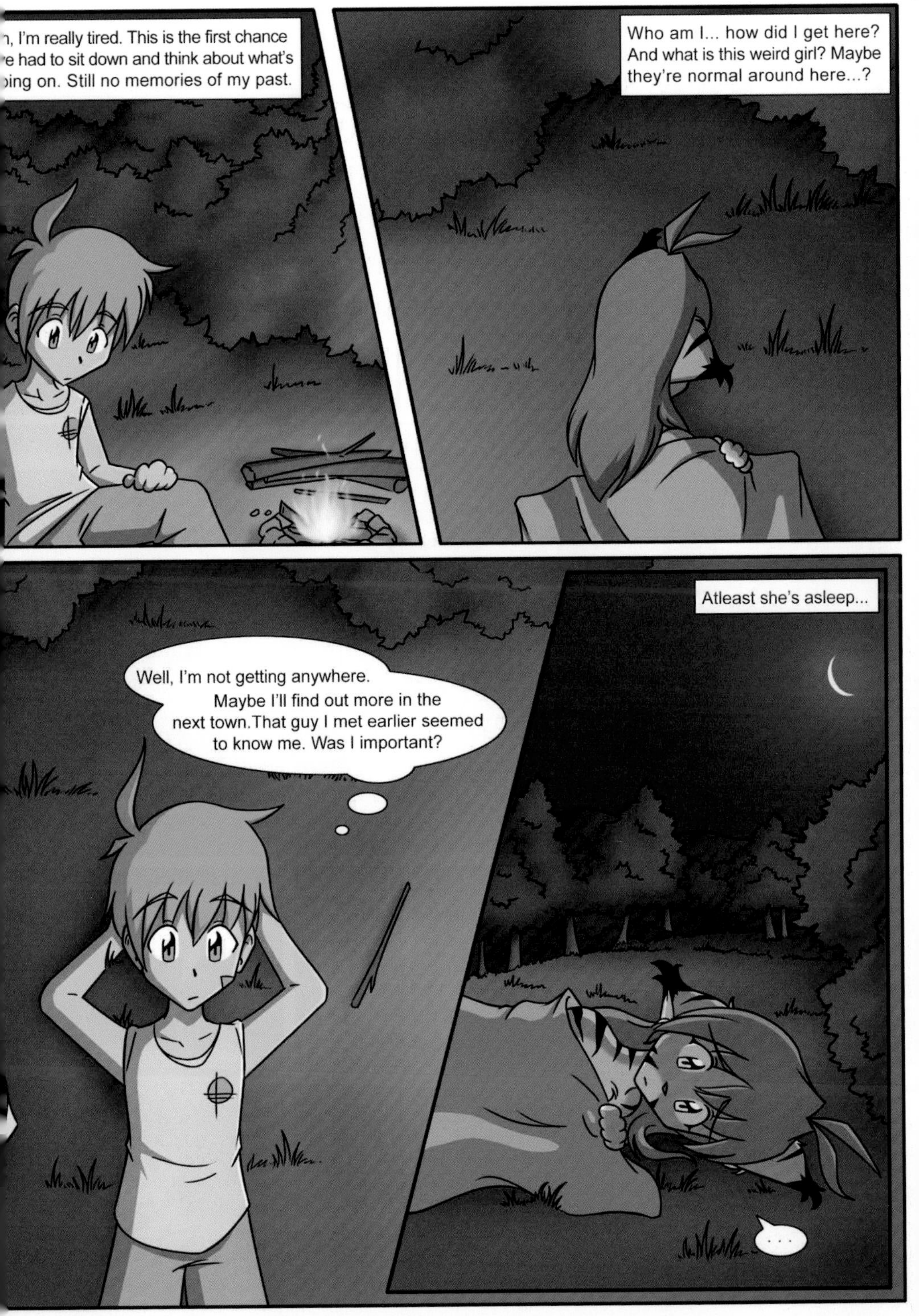

n, I'm really tired. This is the first chance 've had to sit down and think about what's oing on. Still no memories of my past.
Who am I... how did I get here? And what is this weird girl? Maybe they're normal around here...?
Well, I'm not getting anywhere. Maybe I'll find out more in the next town.That guy I met earlier seemed to know me. Was I important?
Atleast she's asleep...
...

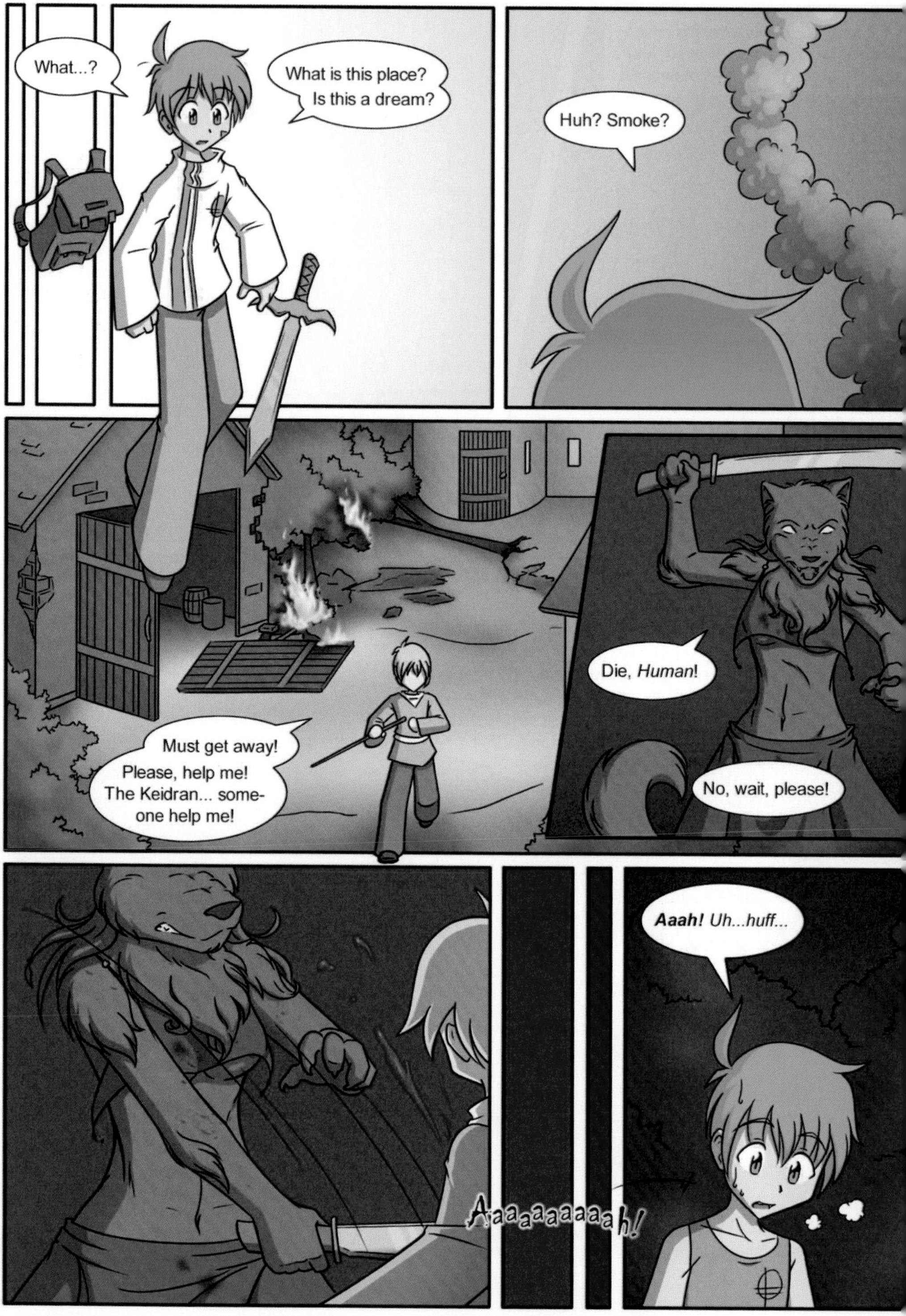
What...?
What is this place? Is this a dream?
Huh? Smoke?
Must get away! Please, help me! The Keidran... someone help me!
Die, *Human*!
No, wait, please!
Aaaaaaaaaah!
Aaah! *Uh...huff...*

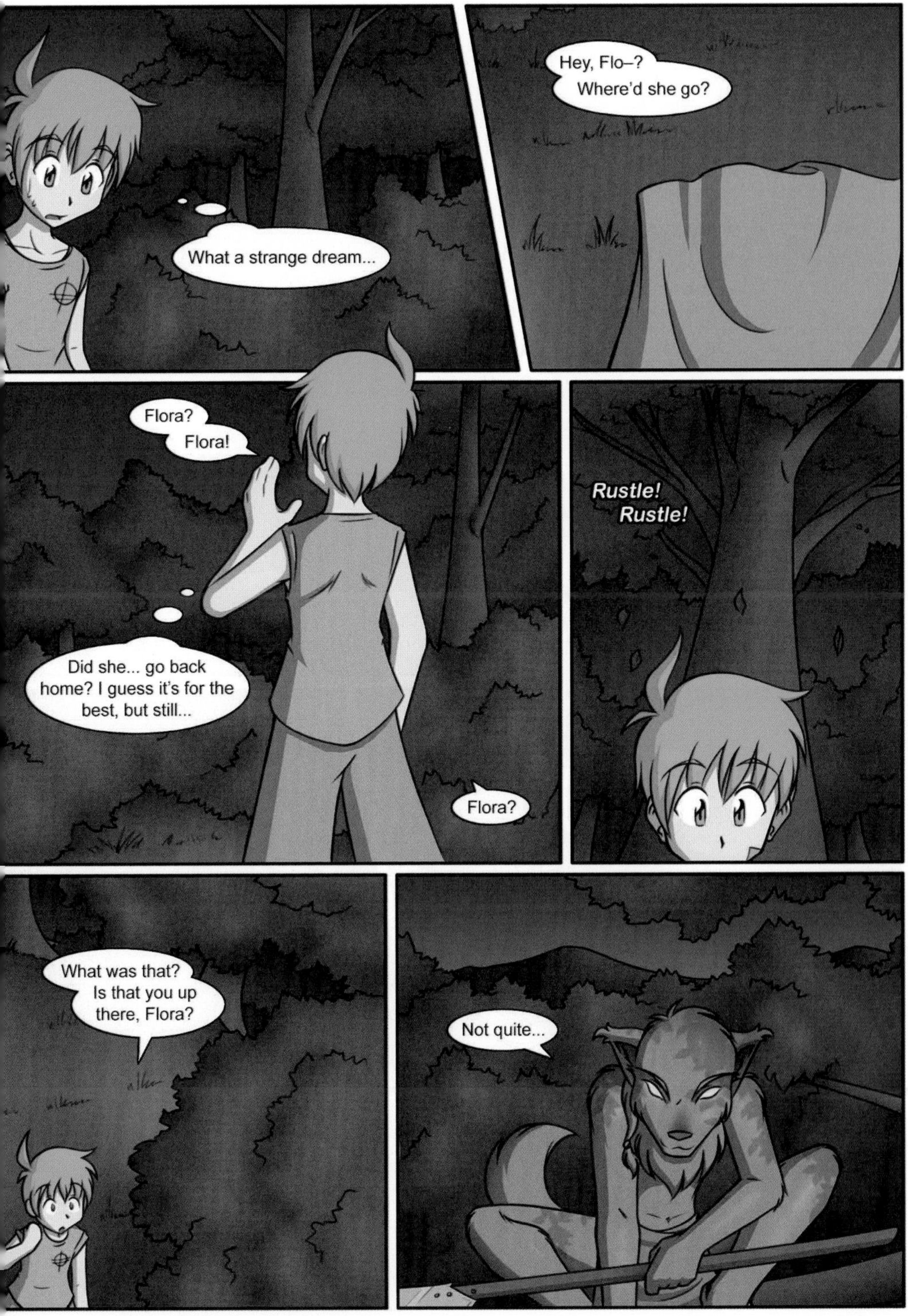
What a strange dream...
Hey, Flo–? Where'd she go?
Flora? Flora!
Did she... go back home? I guess it's for the best, but still...
Flora?
Rustle! Rustle!
What was that? Is that you up there, Flora?
Not quite...

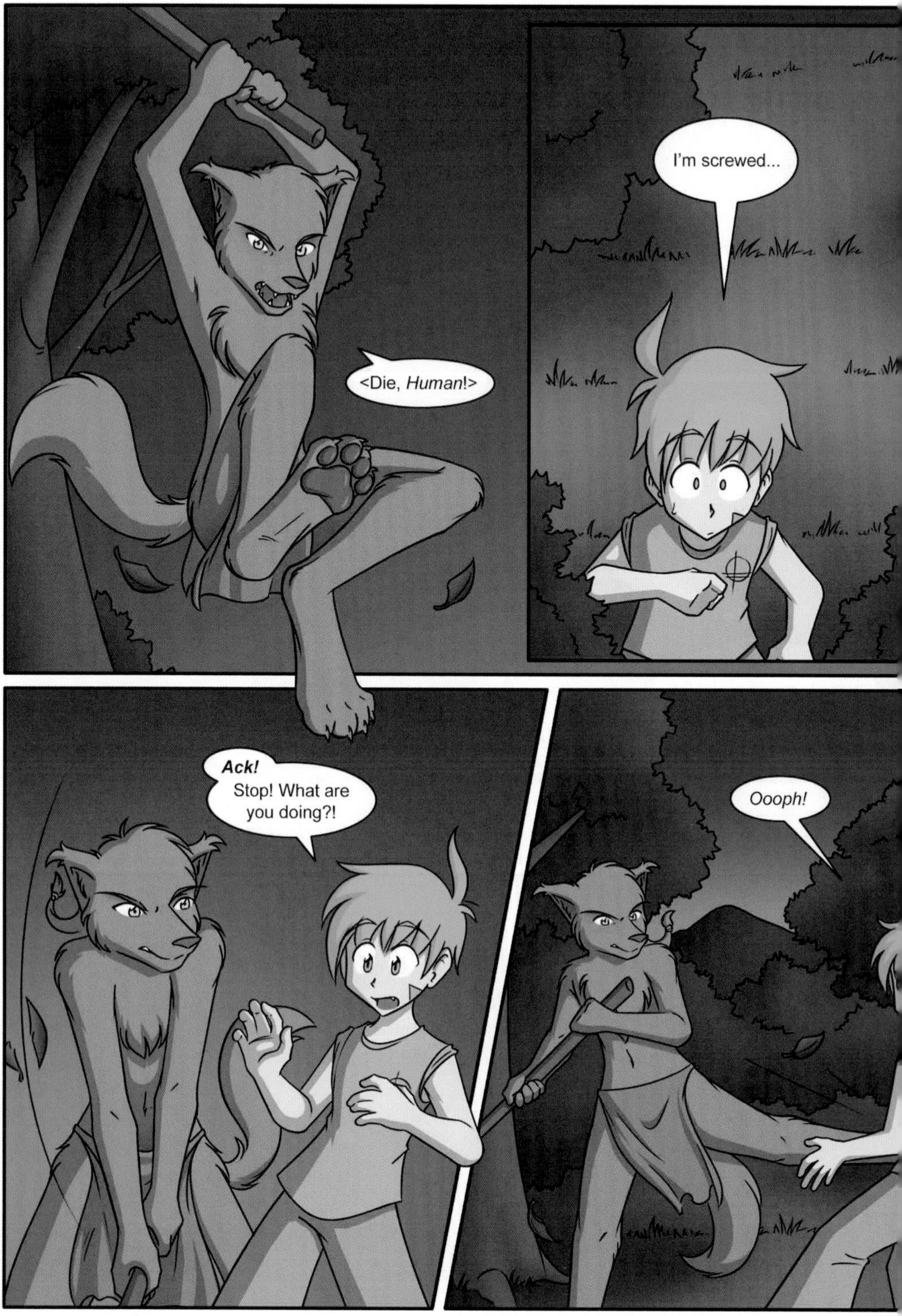
<Die, *Human*!>
I'm screwed...
Ack! Stop! What are you doing?!
Oooph!

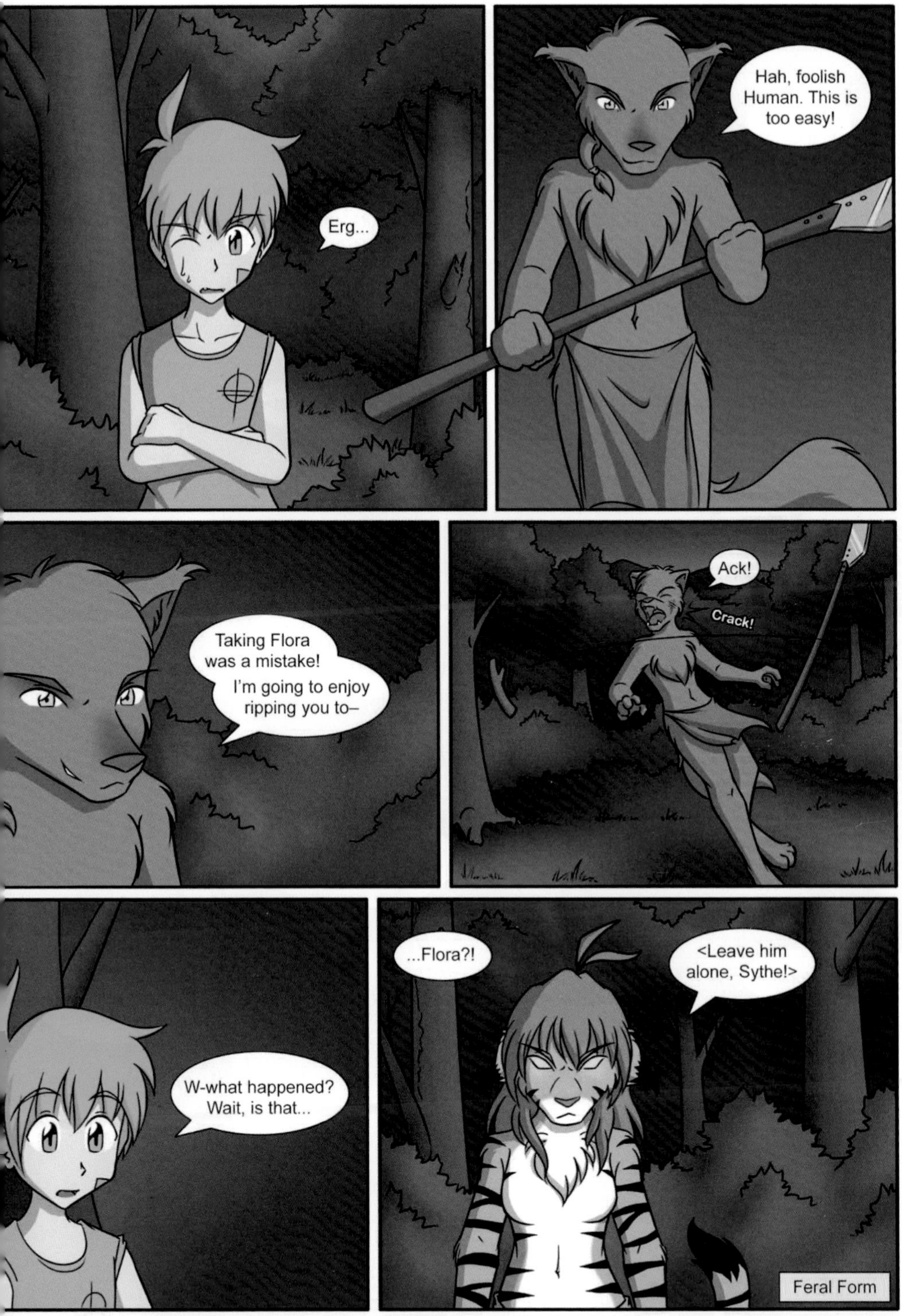
Erg...
Hah, foolish Human. This is too easy!
Taking Flora was a mistake!
I'm going to enjoy ripping you to–
Ack!
Crack!
W-what happened? Wait, is that...
...Flora?!
<Leave him alone, Sythe!>
Feral Form

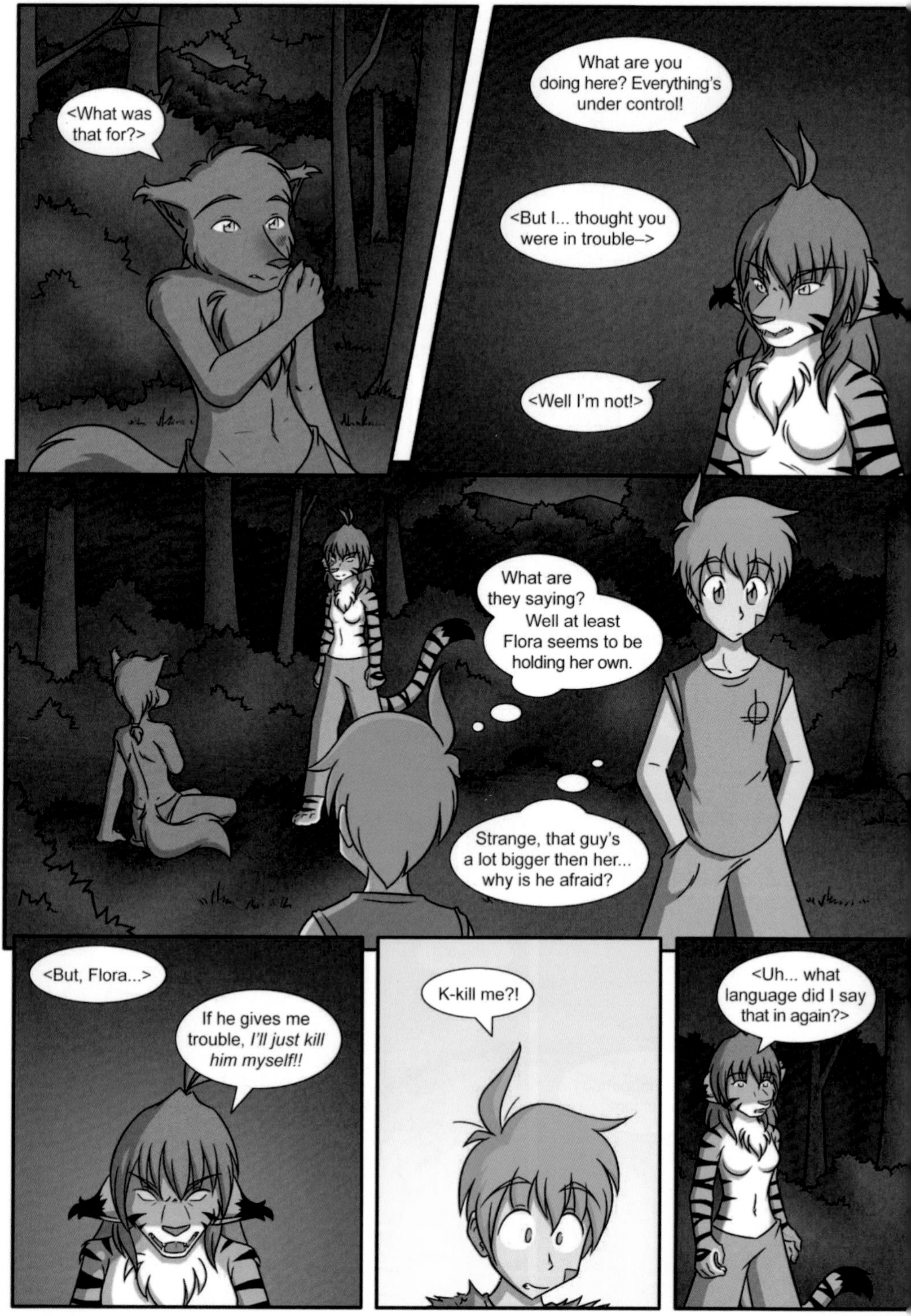
<What was that for?>
What are you doing here? Everything's under control!
<But I... thought you were in trouble–>
<Well I'm not!>
What are they saying? Well at least Flora seems to be holding her own.
Strange, that guy's a lot bigger then her... why is he afraid?
<But, Flora...>
If he gives me trouble, *I'll just kill him myself!!*
K-kill me?!
<Uh... what language did I say that in again?>

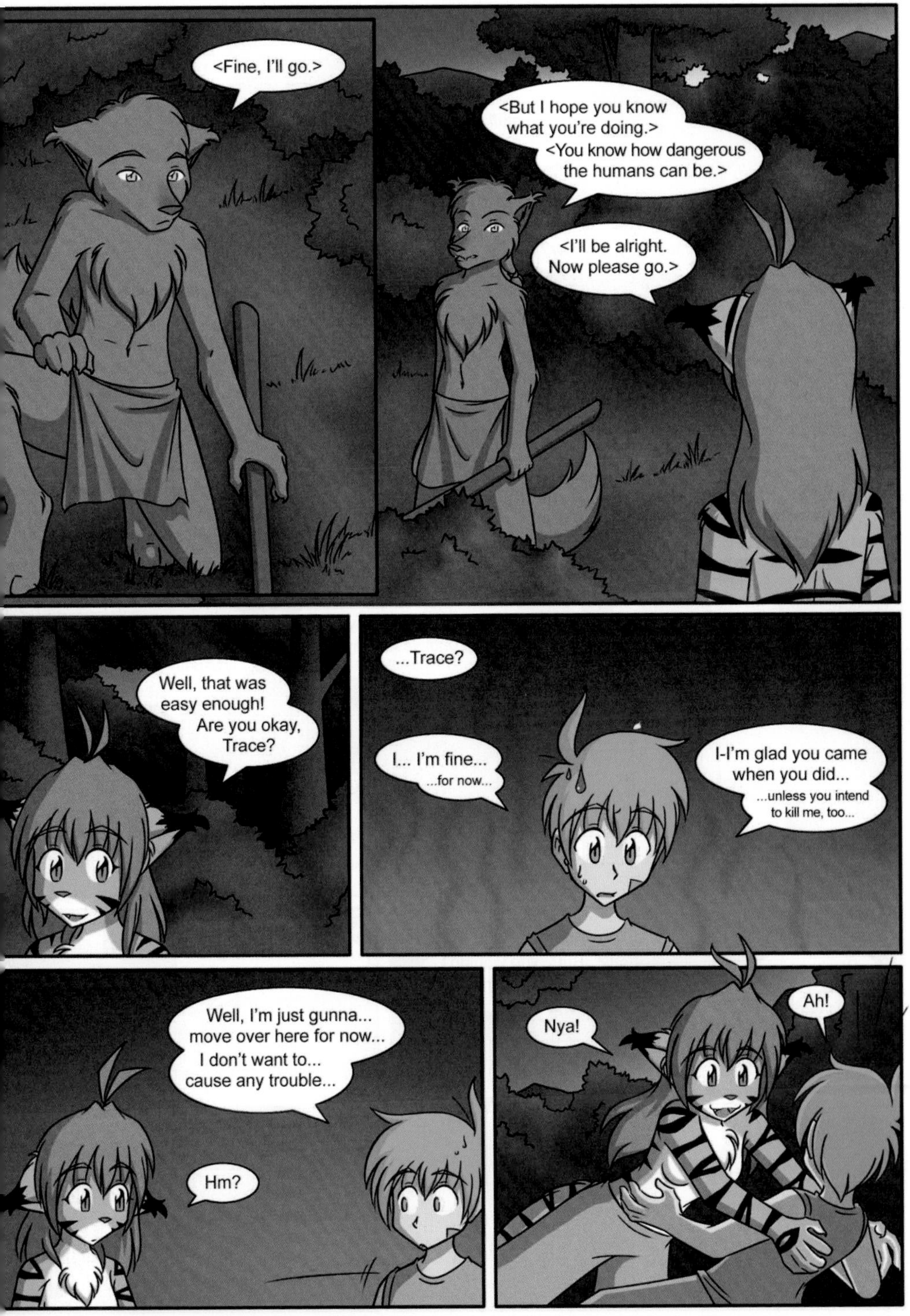

<Fine, I'll go.>
<But I hope you know what you're doing.>
<You know how dangerous the humans can be.>
<I'll be alright. Now please go.>
Well, that was easy enough!
Are you okay, Trace?
...Trace?
I... I'm fine...
...for now...
I-I'm glad you came when you did...
...unless you intend to kill me, too...
Well, I'm just gunna... move over here for now...
I don't want to... cause any trouble...
Hm?
Nya!
Ah!

Ah! What are you doing?

Trace, relax! I just said that stuff to get him to leave you alone.

Oh, I.. see... who was that guy, anyway?

Oh, that was Sythe, my bodyguard... and my fiancé.

Fiancé?

Yeah. We were in a caravan together when it was attacked.

He ran off and left me, until you saved me from the human.

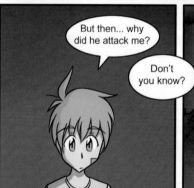

But then... why did he attack me?

Don't you know?

Know what? I don't remember anything up until yesterday.

Oh... well let's just say... our two races don't usually get along.

Oh, I see...

But... you wouldn't attack me, right?

Not unless you give me a reason to!

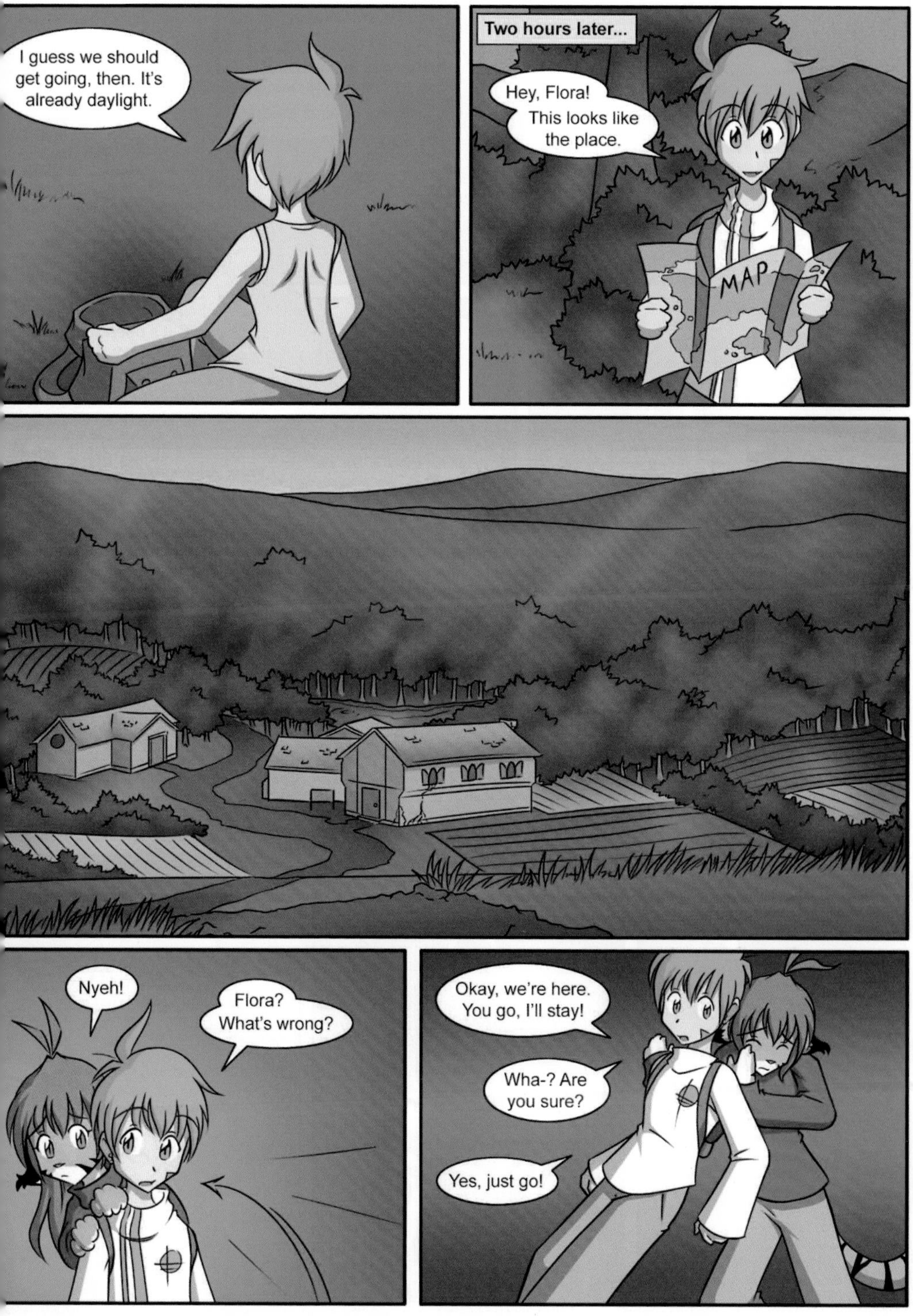

I guess we should get going, then. It's already daylight.
Two hours later...
Hey, Flora!
This looks like the place.
MAP
Nyeh!
Flora? What's wrong?
Okay, we're here. You go, I'll stay!
Wha-? Are you sure?
Yes, just go!

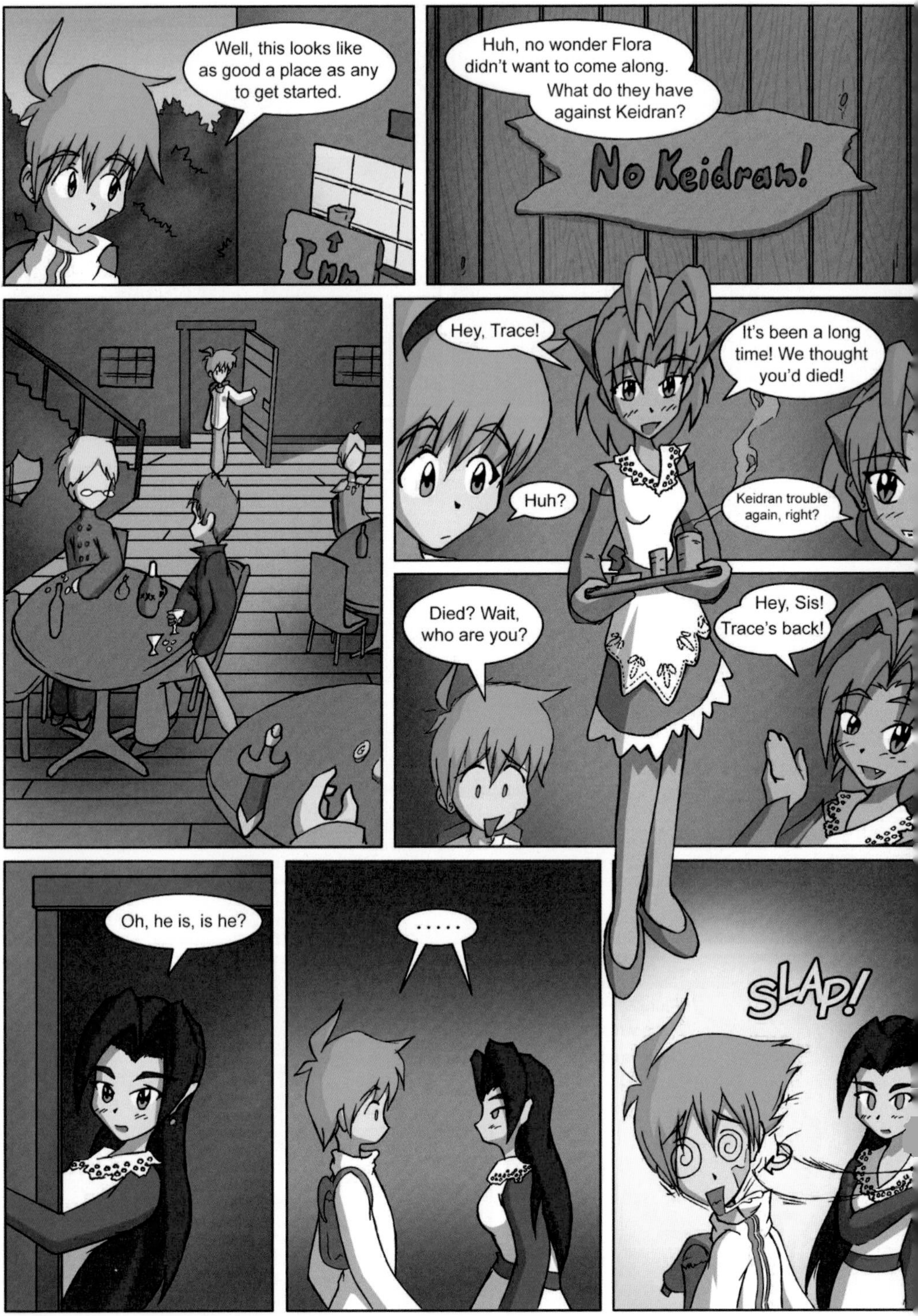
Well, this looks like as good a place as any to get started.
Inn
Huh, no wonder Flora didn't want to come along.
What do they have against Keidran?
No Keidran!
Hey, Trace!
It's been a long time! We thought you'd died!
Huh?
Keidran trouble again, right?
Died? Wait, who are you?
Hey, Sis! Trace's back!
Oh, he is, is he?
. . . . .
SLAP!

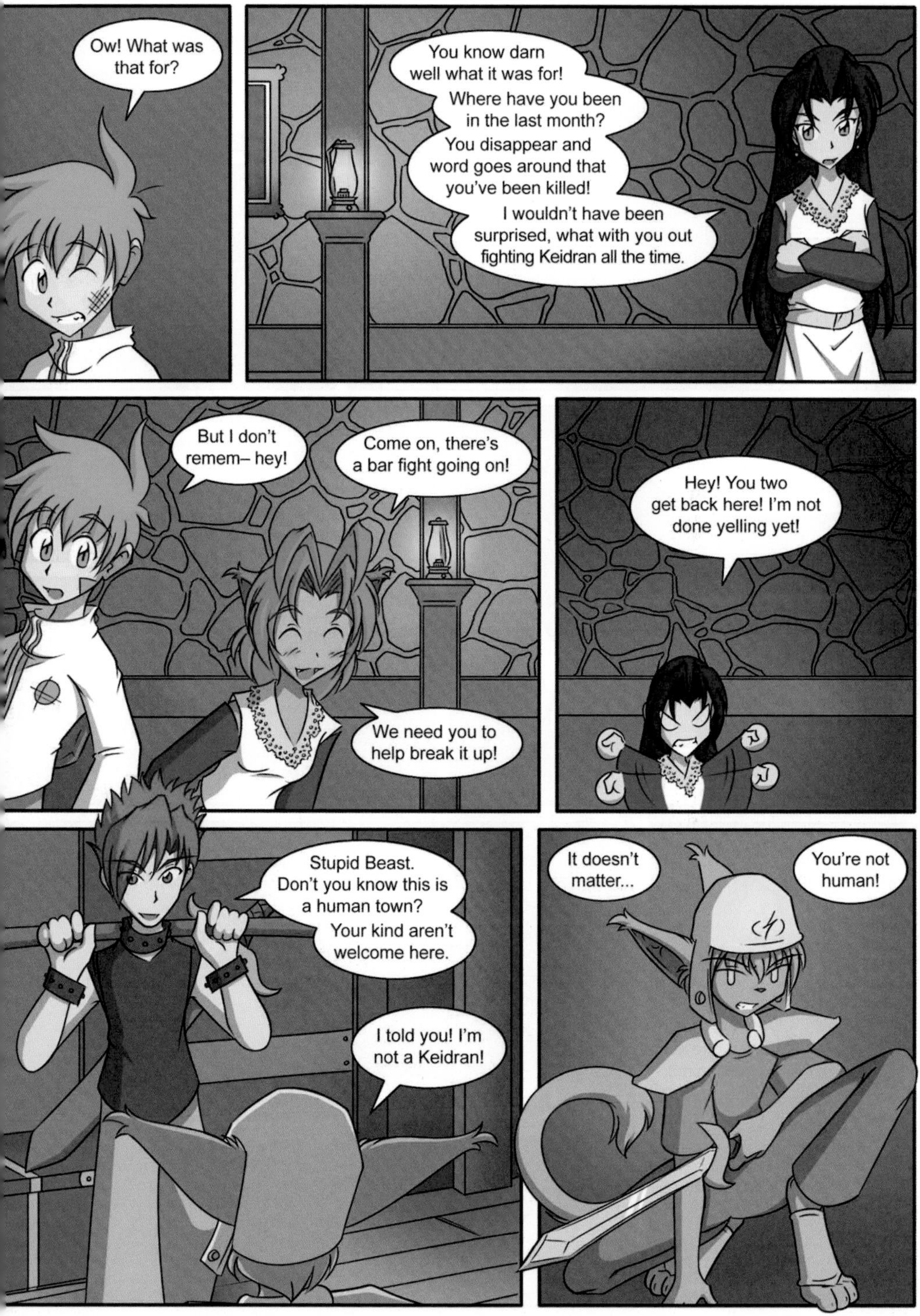
Ow! What was that for?
You know darn well what it was for!
Where have you been in the last month?
You disappear and word goes around that you've been killed!
I wouldn't have been surprised, what with you out fighting Keidran all the time.
But I don't remem– hey!
Come on, there's a bar fight going on!
We need you to help break it up!
Hey! You two get back here! I'm not done yelling yet!
Stupid Beast. Don't you know this is a human town?
Your kind aren't welcome here.
I told you! I'm not a Keidran!
It doesn't matter...
You're not human!

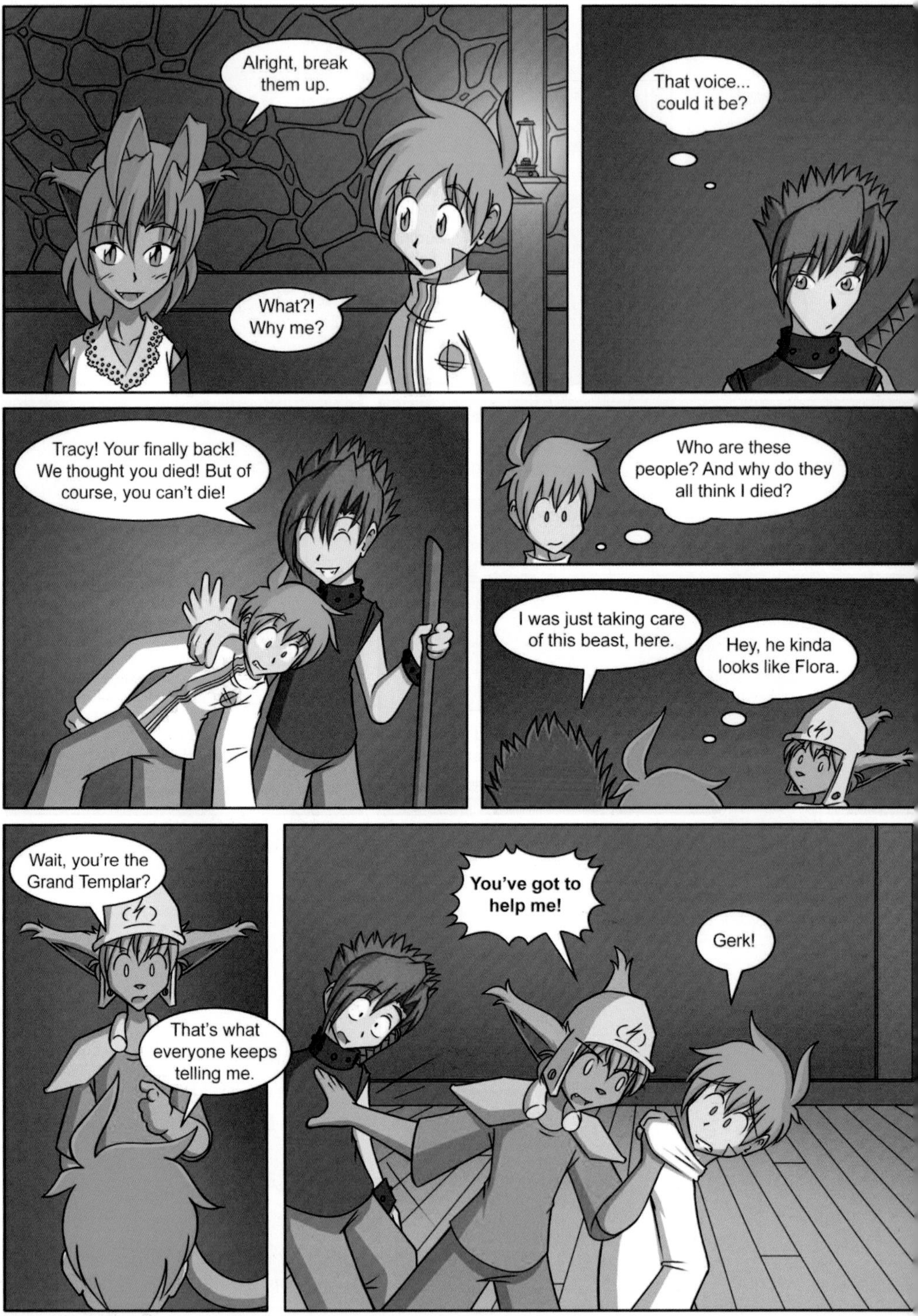
Alright, break them up.
What?! Why me?
That voice... could it be?
Tracy! Your finally back! We thought you died! But of course, you can't die!
Who are these people? And why do they all think I died?
I was just taking care of this beast, here.
Hey, he kinda looks like Flora.
Wait, you're the Grand Templar?
That's what everyone keeps telling me.
You've got to help me!
Gerk!

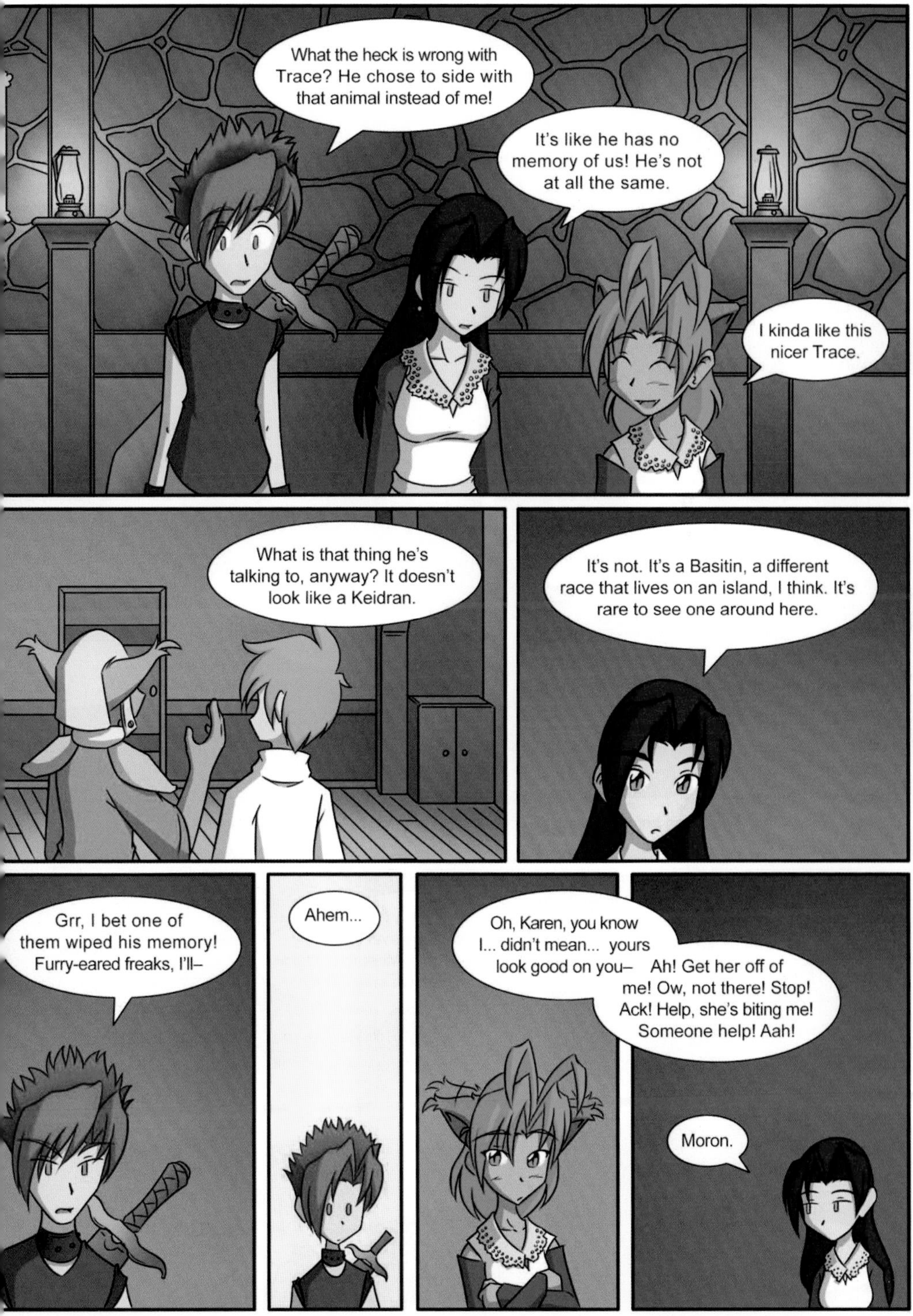
What the heck is wrong with Trace? He chose to side with that animal instead of me!
It's like he has no memory of us! He's not at all the same.
I kinda like this nicer Trace.
What is that thing he's talking to, anyway? It doesn't look like a Keidran.
It's not. It's a Basitin, a different race that lives on an island, I think. It's rare to see one around here.
Grr, I bet one of them wiped his memory! Furry-eared freaks, I'll–
Ahem...
Oh, Karen, you know I... didn't mean... yours look good on you– Ah! Get her off of me! Ow, not there! Stop! Ack! Help, she's biting me! Someone help! Aah!
Moron.

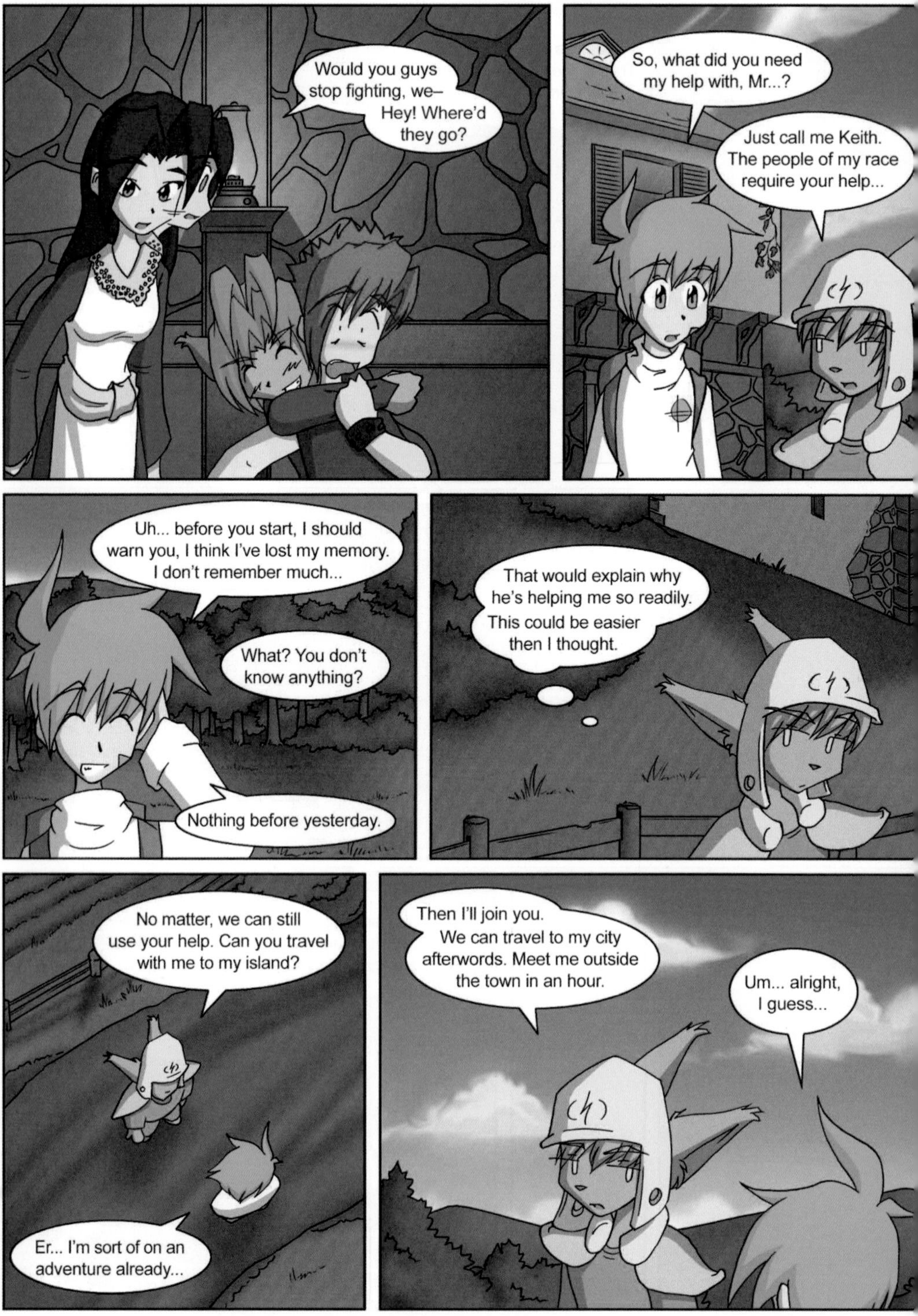

Would you guys stop fighting, we–
Hey! Where'd they go?
So, what did you need my help with, Mr...?
Just call me Keith. The people of my race require your help...
Uh... before you start, I should warn you, I think I've lost my memory. I don't remember much...
What? You don't know anything?
Nothing before yesterday.
That would explain why he's helping me so readily. This could be easier then I thought.
No matter, we can still use your help. Can you travel with me to my island?
Er... I'm sort of on an adventure already...
Then I'll join you. We can travel to my city afterwords. Meet me outside the town in an hour.
Um... alright, I guess...

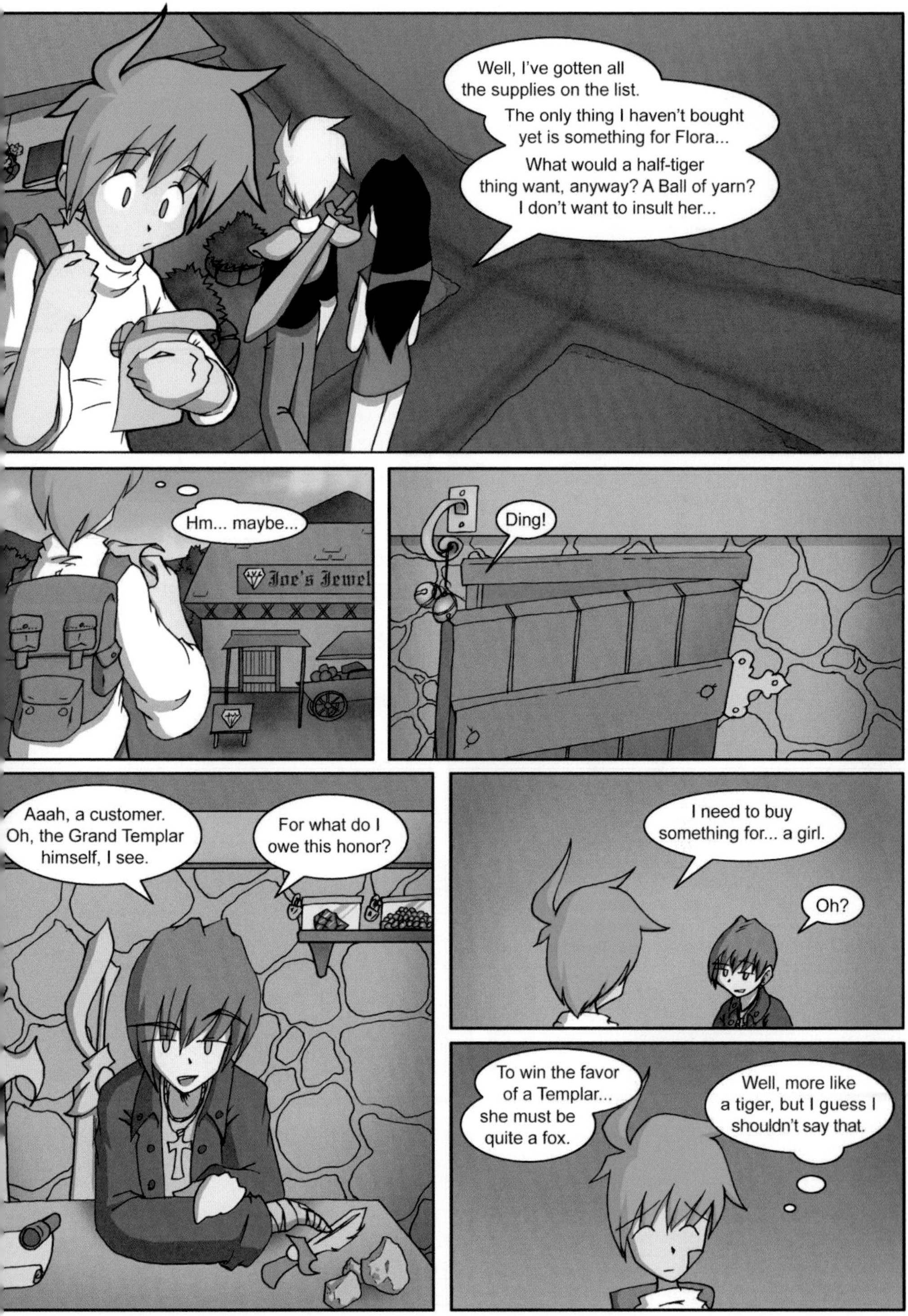
Well, I've gotten all the supplies on the list.
The only thing I haven't bought yet is something for Flora...
What would a half-tiger thing want, anyway? A Ball of yarn? I don't want to insult her...
Hm... maybe...
Joe's Jewel
Ding!
Aaah, a customer. Oh, the Grand Templar himself, I see.
For what do I owe this honor?
I need to buy something for... a girl.
Oh?
To win the favor of a Templar... she must be quite a fox.
Well, more like a tiger, but I guess I shouldn't say that.

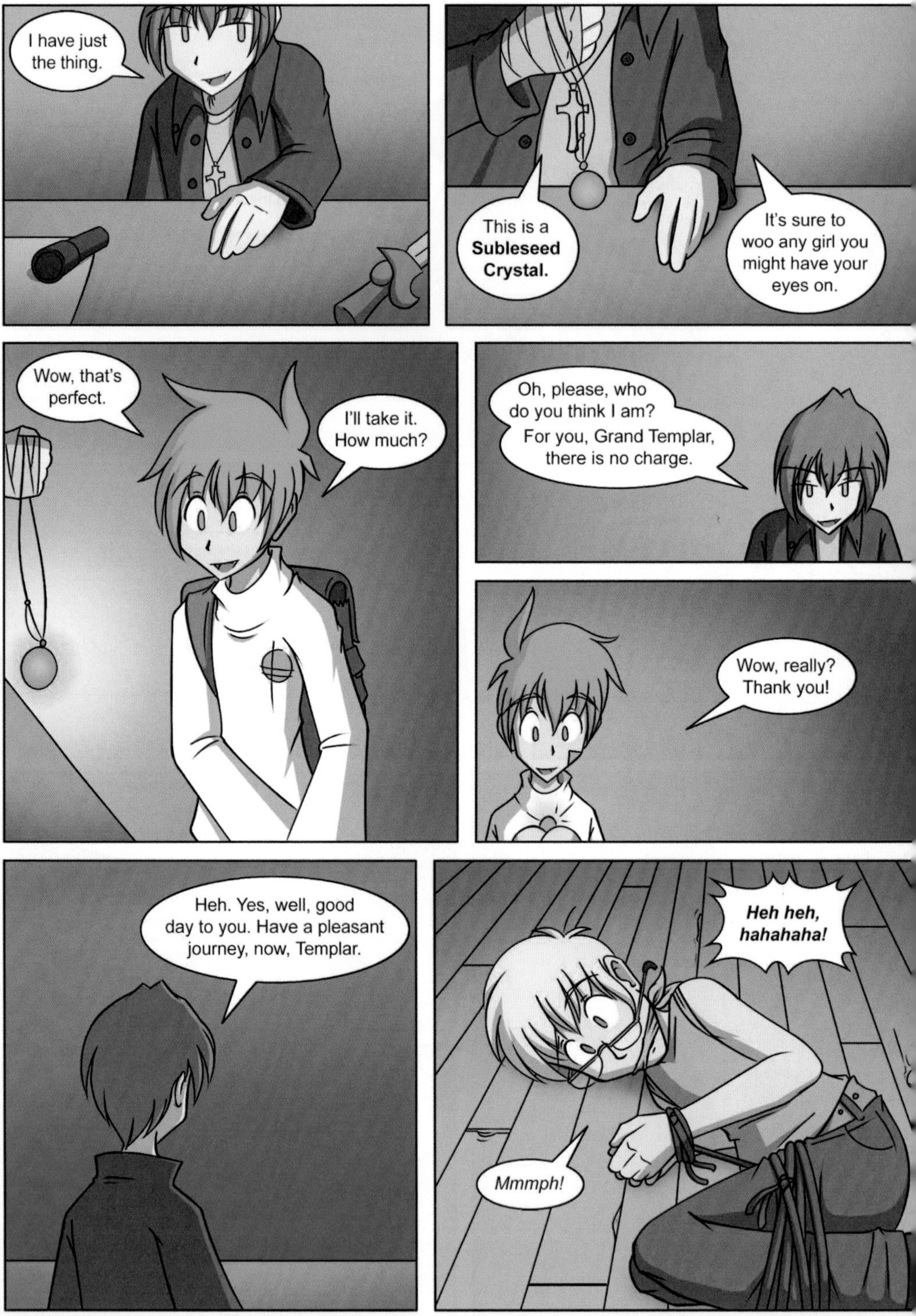
I have just the thing.
This is a **Subleseed Crystal.**
It's sure to woo any girl you might have your eyes on.
Wow, that's perfect.
I'll take it. How much?
Oh, please, who do you think I am? For you, Grand Templar, there is no charge.
Wow, really? Thank you!
Heh. Yes, well, good day to you. Have a pleasant journey, now, Templar.
Heh heh, hahahaha!
Mmmph!

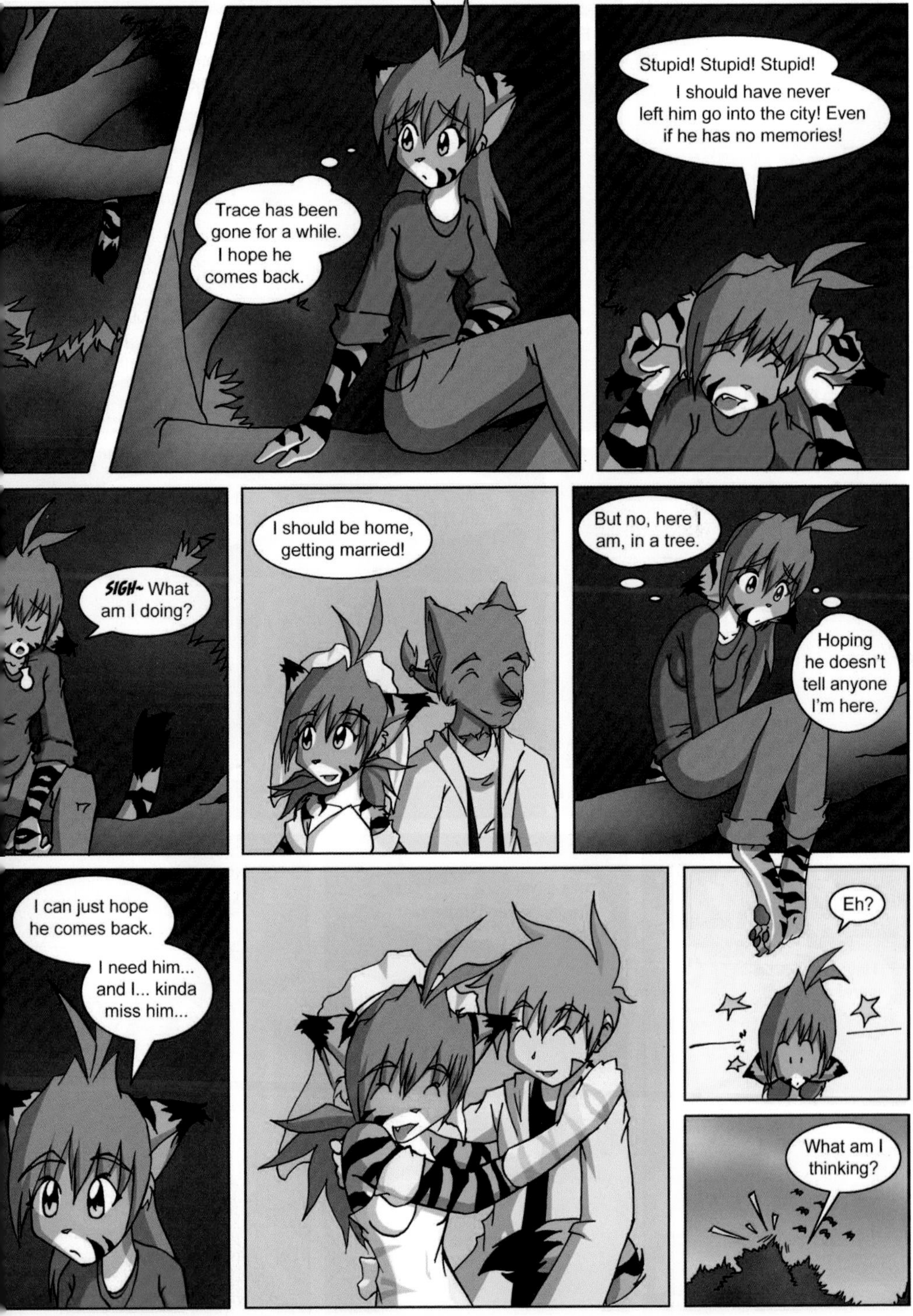
Trace has been gone for a while. I hope he comes back.
Stupid! Stupid! Stupid!
I should have never left him go into the city! Even if he has no memories!
SIGH~ What am I doing?
I should be home, getting married!
But no, here I am, in a tree.
Hoping he doesn't tell anyone I'm here.
I can just hope he comes back.
I need him... and I... kinda miss him...
Eh?
What am I thinking?

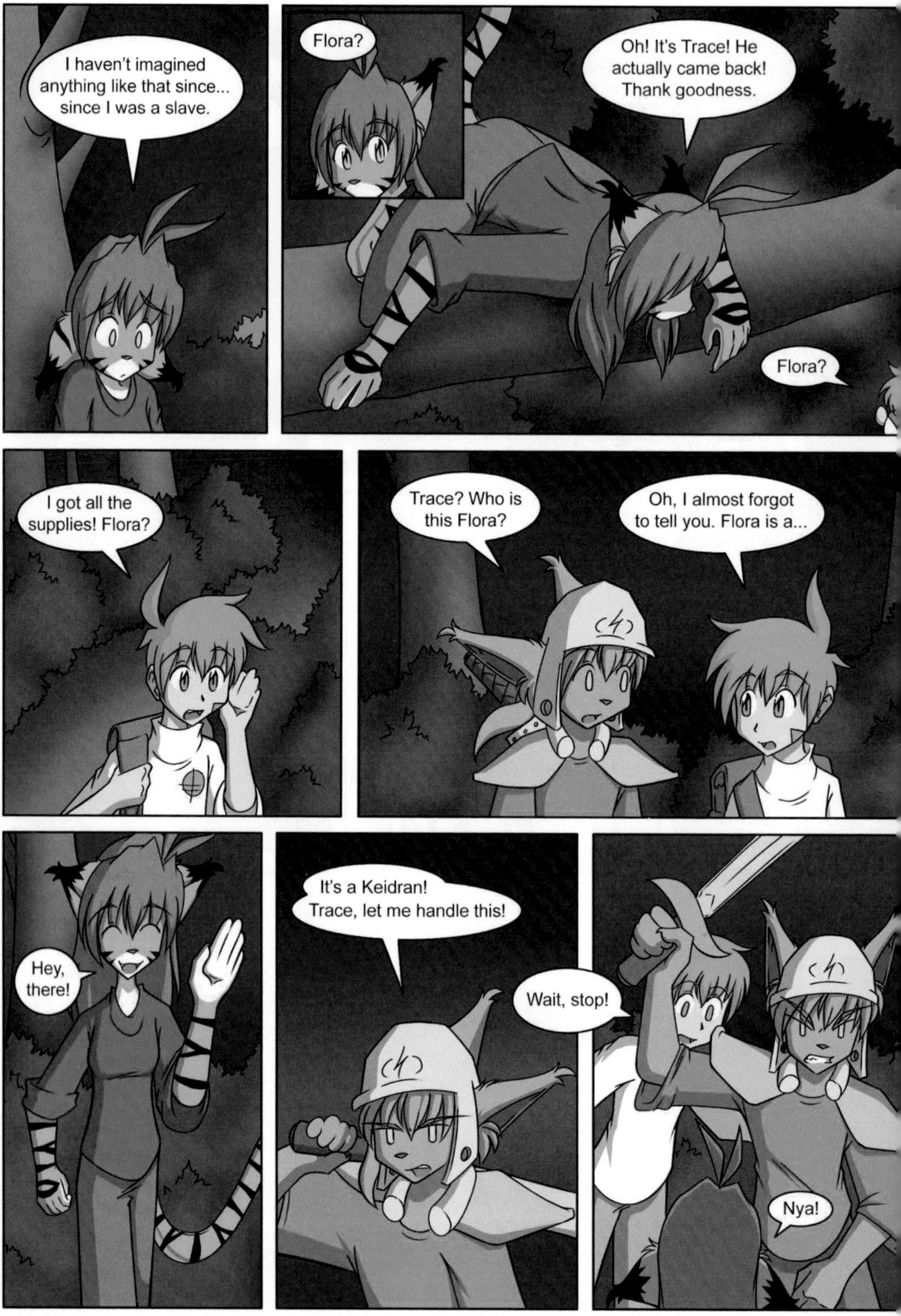
I haven't imagined anything like that since... since I was a slave.
Flora?
Oh! It's Trace! He actually came back! Thank goodness.
Flora?
I got all the supplies! Flora?
Trace? Who is this Flora?
Oh, I almost forgot to tell you. Flora is a...
Hey, there!
It's a Keidran! Trace, let me handle this!
Wait, stop!
Nya!

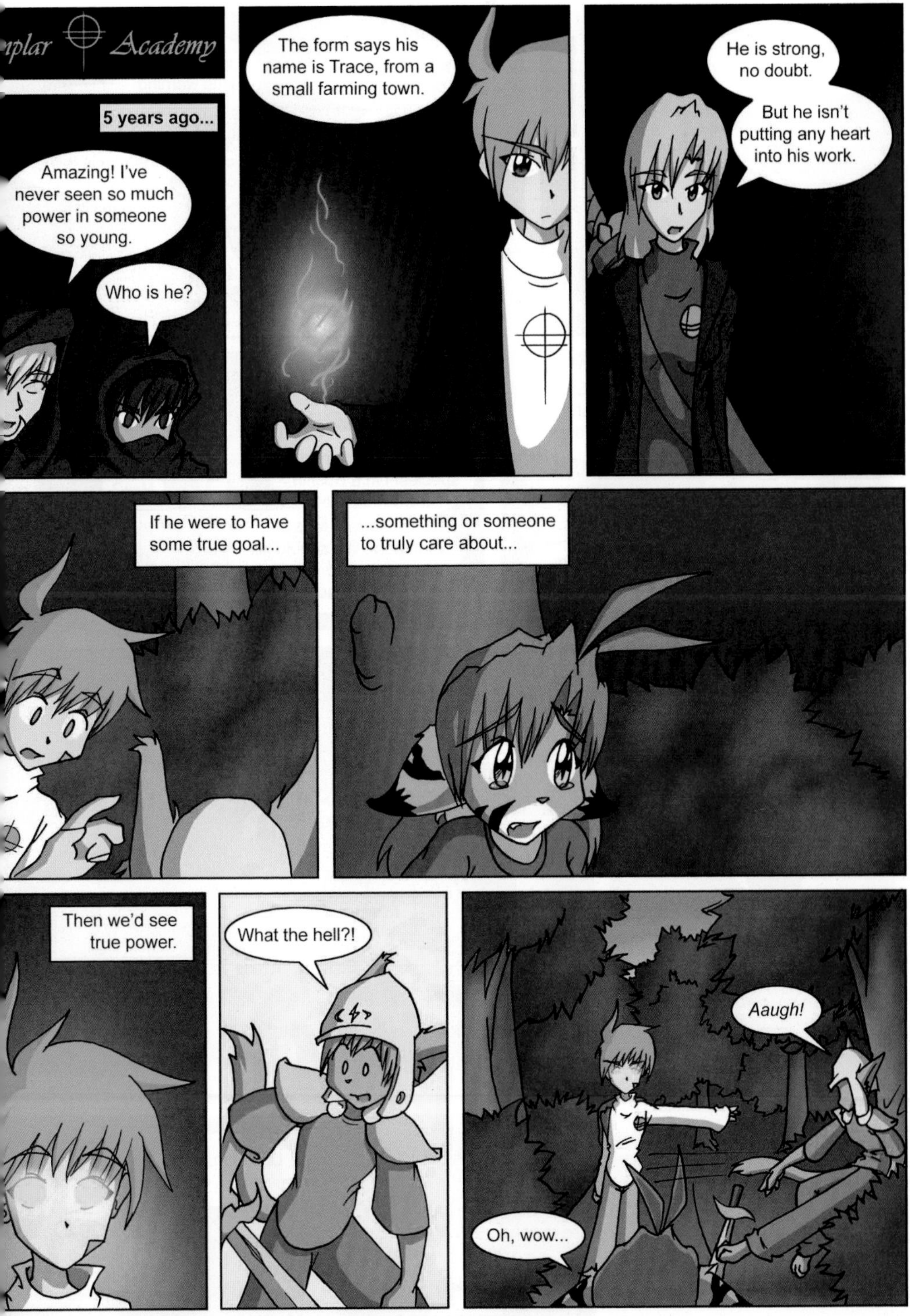

plar Academy
5 years ago...
Amazing! I've never seen so much power in someone so young.
Who is he?
The form says his name is Trace, from a small farming town.
He is strong, no doubt.
But he isn't putting any heart into his work.
If he were to have some true goal...
...something or someone to truly care about...
Then we'd see true power.
What the hell?!
Aaugh!
Oh, wow...

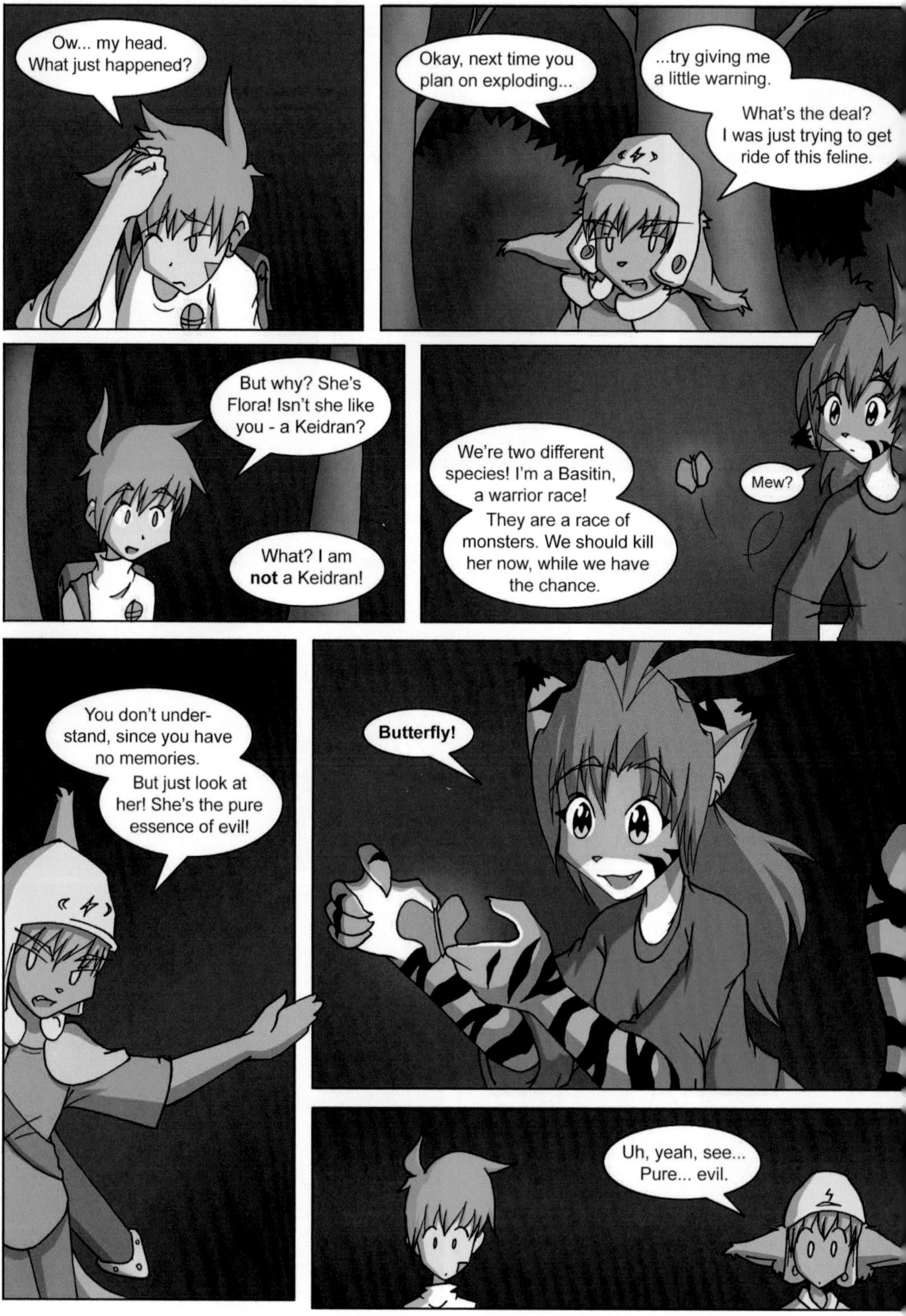
Ow... my head. What just happened?
Okay, next time you plan on exploding...
...try giving me a little warning.
What's the deal? I was just trying to get ride of this feline.
But why? She's Flora! Isn't she like you - a Keidran?
What? I am **not** a Keidran!
We're two different species! I'm a Basitin, a warrior race!
They are a race of monsters. We should kill her now, while we have the chance.
Mew?
You don't under-stand, since you have no memories.
But just look at her! She's the pure essence of evil!
Butterfly!
Uh, yeah, see... Pure... evil.

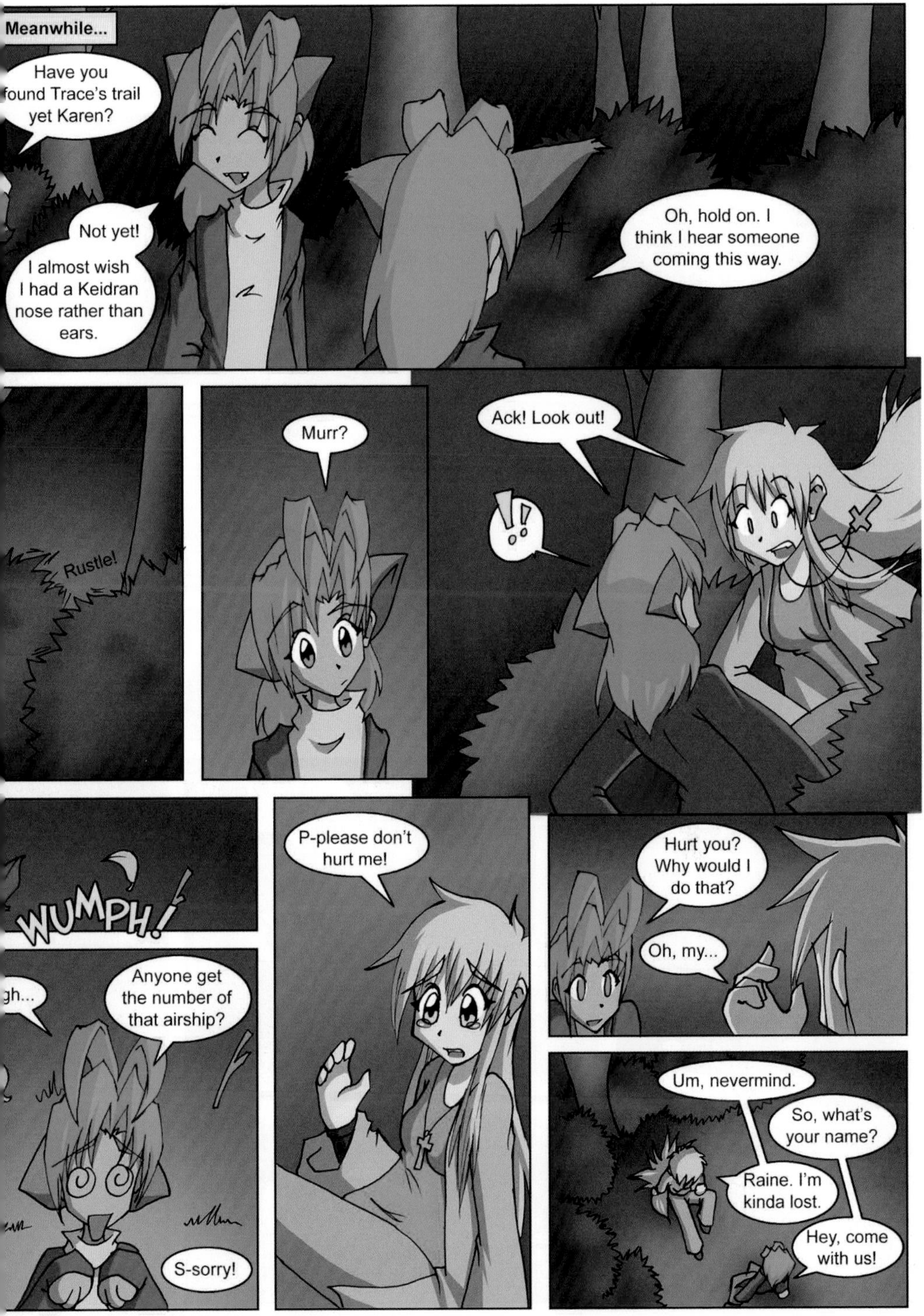

Meanwhile...
Have you found Trace's trail yet Karen?
Not yet!
I almost wish I had a Keidran nose rather than ears.
Oh, hold on. I think I hear someone coming this way.
Rustle!
Murr?
Ack! Look out!
!!
WUMPH!
P-please don't hurt me!
Hurt you? Why would I do that?
Oh, my...
Anyone get the number of that airship?
S-sorry!
Um, nevermind.
So, what's your name?
Raine. I'm kinda lost.
Hey, come with us!

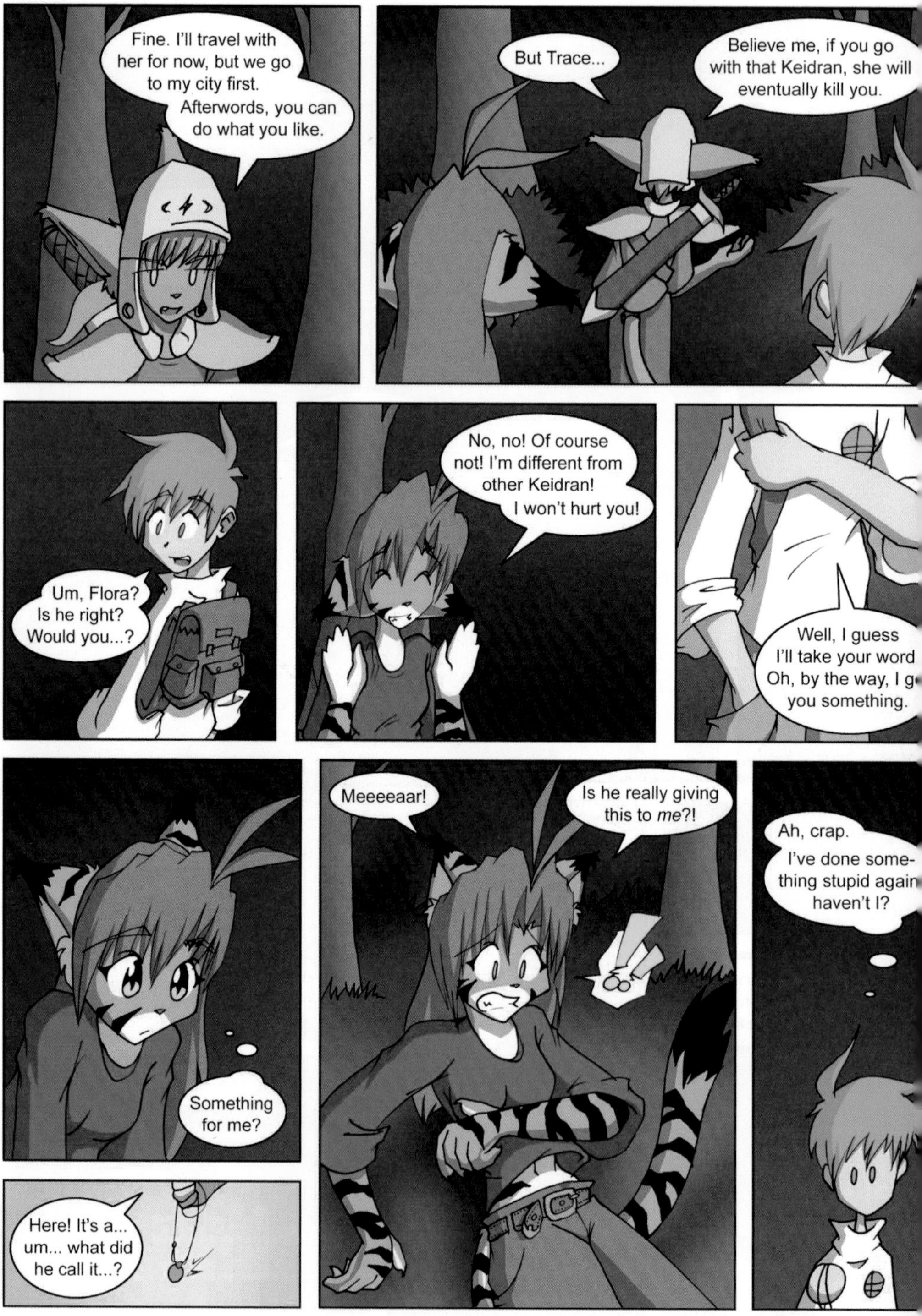
Fine. I'll travel with her for now, but we go to my city first.
Afterwords, you can do what you like.
But Trace...
Believe me, if you go with that Keidran, she will eventually kill you.
Um, Flora? Is he right? Would you...?
No, no! Of course not! I'm different from other Keidran!
I won't hurt you!
Well, I guess I'll take your word
Oh, by the way, I g
you something.
Something for me?
Here! It's a... um... what did he call it...?
Meeeeaar!
Is he really giving this to *me*?!
Ah, crap.
I've done some-thing stupid again haven't I?

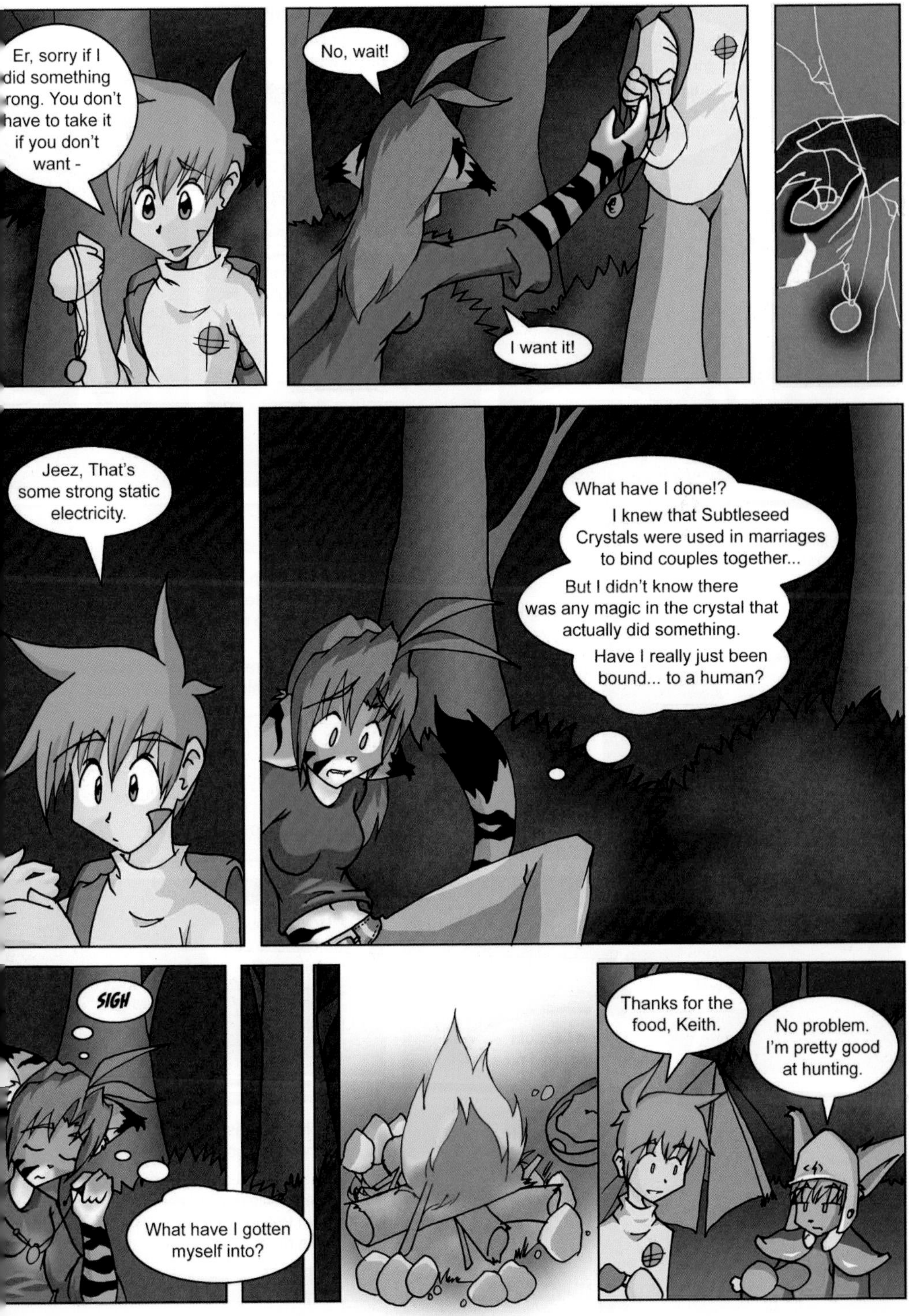
Er, sorry if I did something rong. You don't have to take it if you don't want -
No, wait!
I want it!
Jeez, That's some strong static electricity.
What have I done!?
I knew that Subtleseed Crystals were used in marriages to bind couples together...
But I didn't know there was any magic in the crystal that actually did something.
Have I really just been bound... to a human?
SIGH
What have I gotten myself into?
Thanks for the food, Keith.
No problem. I'm pretty good at hunting.

Ah! T'anks for 'ta drinks, Tracy... Isn't camphing out here fun? We shoul' do it more often, huh?

Uh, Flora, are you alright?

What did you put in that drink?

Just ale, I think...

Hah!

You mean human ale. Keidran can't handle much of that stuff.

Hah, I just notif'd how funny you huma look without fur on

She gets quite honest when she's had a few, doesn't she?

Let me try something. Hey Flora, how do you really feel about Trace and I?

Huh, Trace? I likes him. He's nice to me, not like other humans. I know humans an' Keidran aren't -hic- s'pose to get along, bu' I can't help it. ...oh, an' you? Umm... you're kinda a jerk.

Er, thanks, Flora.

You're welcome!

Maybe I should help you to bed now.

Okay!

How's 'bout you come to bed wits me?

I don think tha good id

Hmph, that wasn't what I was expecting. Either she's a good actress, or as impossible as it seems, this Keidran truly does have feelings for a human. Interesting...

TwoKinds

Chapter Two

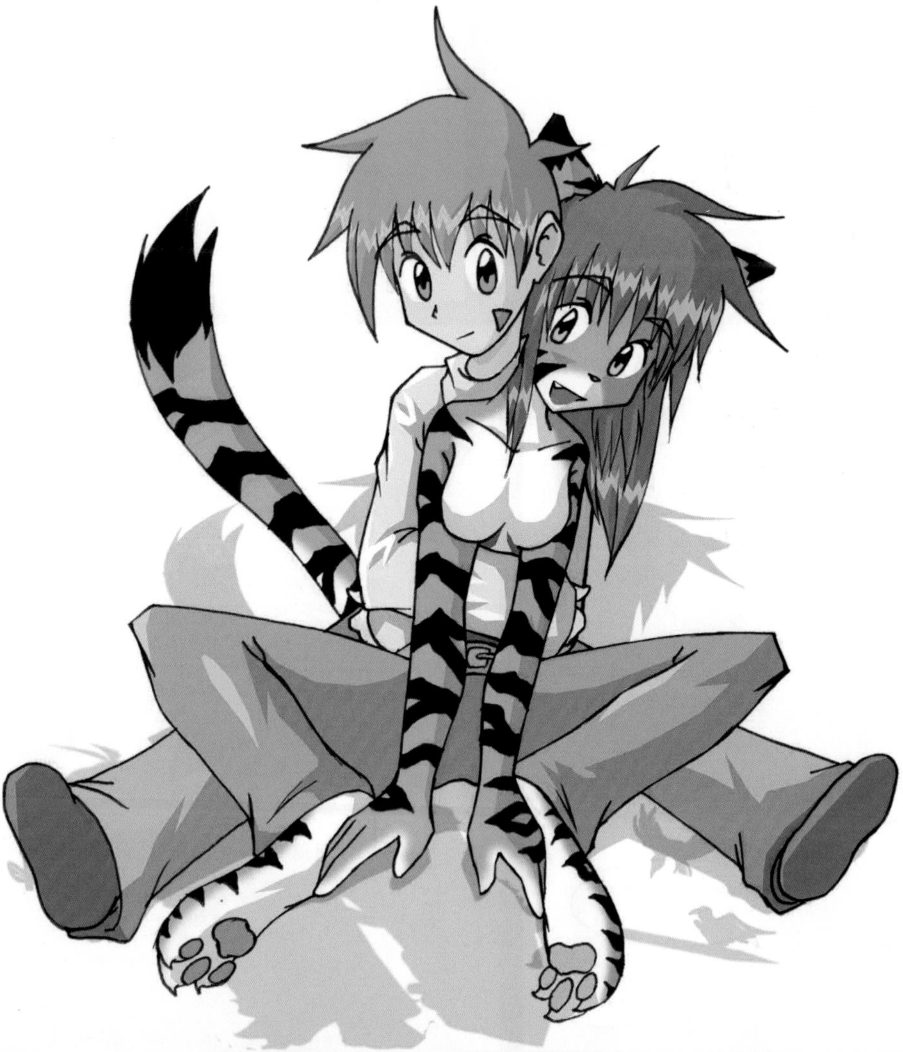

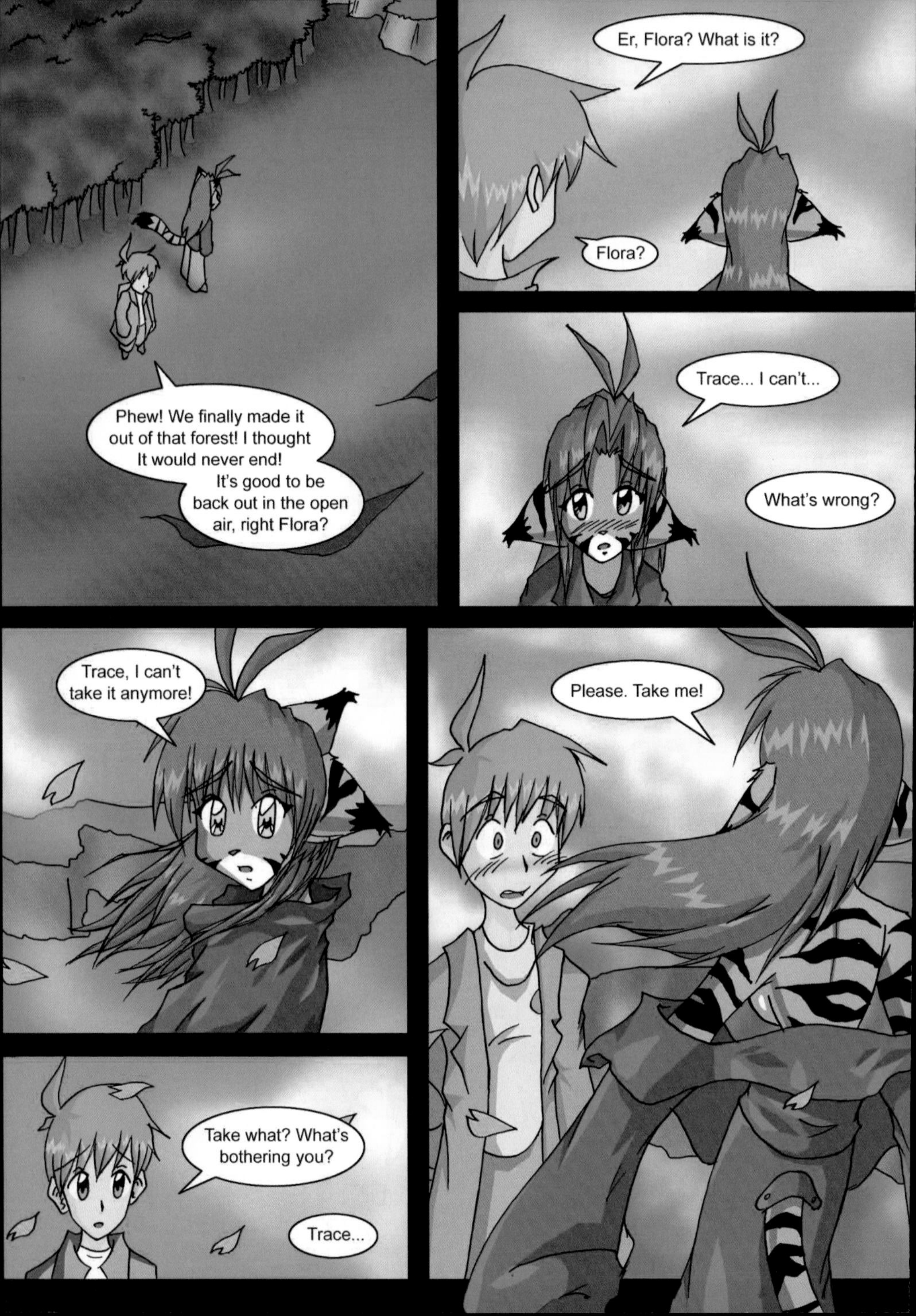

Phew! We finally made it out of that forest! I thought It would never end!
It's good to be back out in the open air, right Flora?
Er, Flora? What is it?
Flora?
Trace... I can't...
What's wrong?
Trace, I can't take it anymore!
Take what? What's bothering you?
Trace...
Please. Take me!

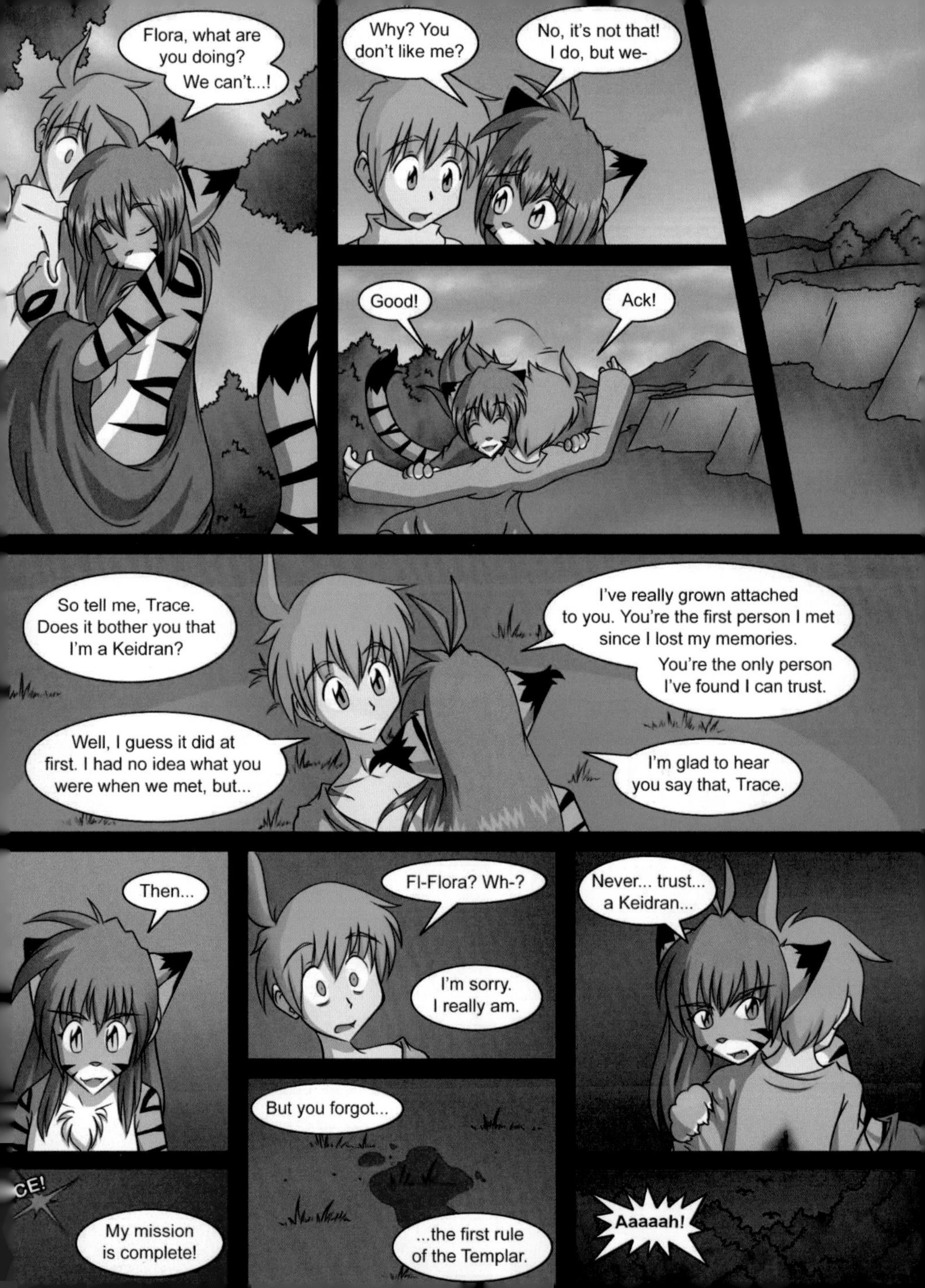
Flora, what are you doing? We can't...!
Why? You don't like me?
No, it's not that! I do, but we-
Good!
Ack!
So tell me, Trace. Does it bother you that I'm a Keidran?
Well, I guess it did at first. I had no idea what you were when we met, but...
I've really grown attached to you. You're the first person I met since I lost my memories.
You're the only person I've found I can trust.
I'm glad to hear you say that, Trace.
Then...
Fl-Flora? Wh-?
I'm sorry. I really am.
Never... trust... a Keidran...
But you forgot...
...the first rule of the Templar.
Aaaaah!
CE!
My mission is complete!

Merr?

Wha... how did I get in a tent? I don't remember anything from last night.

Oh, that noise... Trace is screaming in his sleep again.

...I'm worried about him...

Psst! Flora!

Ow, my head... Who's yelling?

What? Sythe? Why are you here?

Don't you know there's a Basitin nearby?

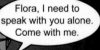

Flora, I need to speak with you alone. Come with me.

Uh, okay...

. . . . .

Alright, this is far enough. What is it?

Flora, we must kill Trace, now!

What?!

Why?!

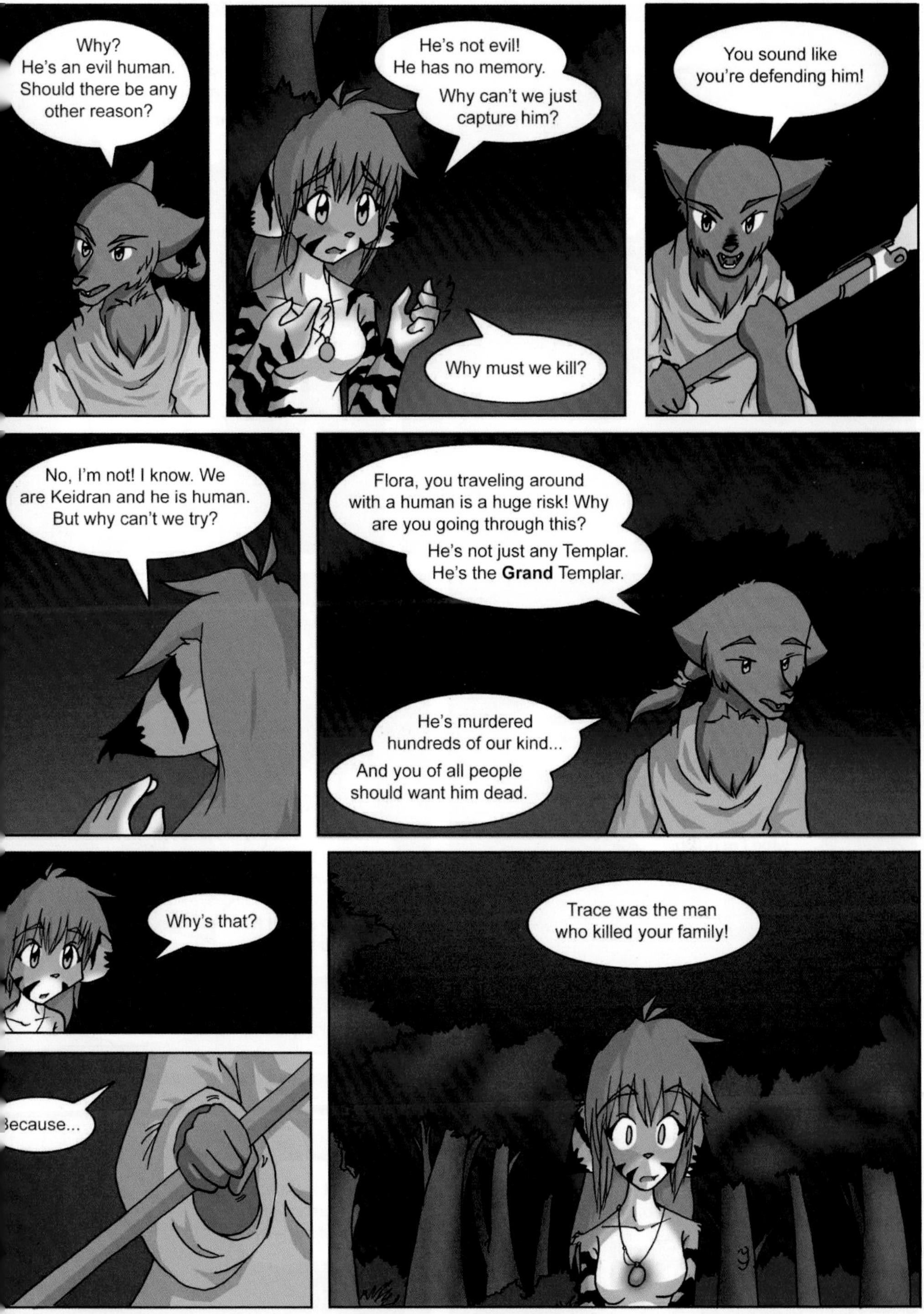
Why? He's an evil human. Should there be any other reason?
He's not evil! He has no memory.
Why can't we just capture him?
Why must we kill?
You sound like you're defending him!
No, I'm not! I know. We are Keidran and he is human. But why can't we try?
Flora, you traveling around with a human is a huge risk! Why are you going through this?
He's not just any Templar. He's the **Grand** Templar.
He's murdered hundreds of our kind...
And you of all people should want him dead.
Why's that?
Because...
Trace was the man who killed your family!

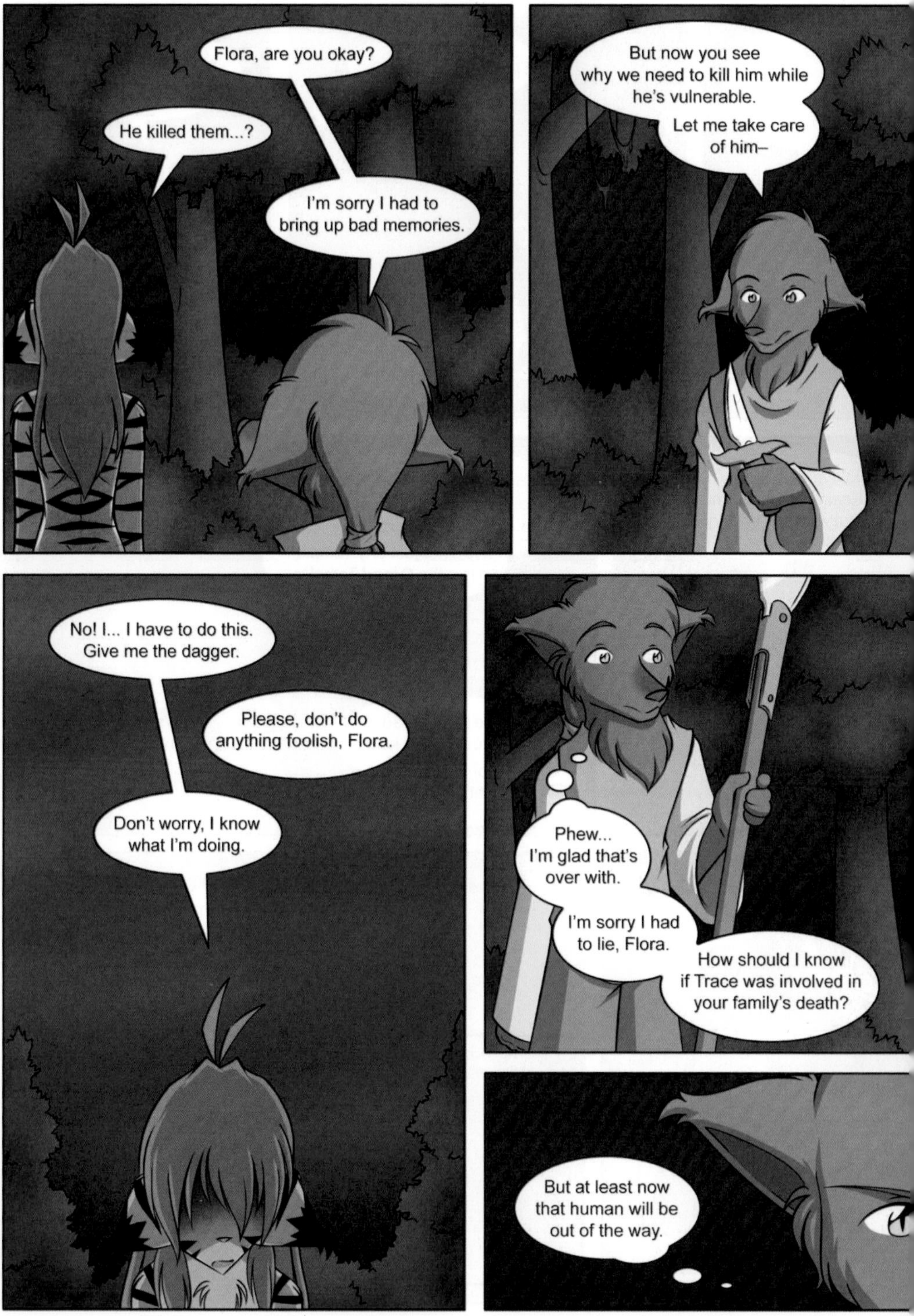

Flora, are you okay?
He killed them...?
I'm sorry I had to bring up bad memories.
But now you see why we need to kill him while he's vulnerable.
Let me take care of him–
No! I... I have to do this. Give me the dagger.
Please, don't do anything foolish, Flora.
Don't worry, I know what I'm doing.
Phew... I'm glad that's over with.
I'm sorry I had to lie, Flora.
How should I know if Trace was involved in your family's death?
But at least now that human will be out of the way.

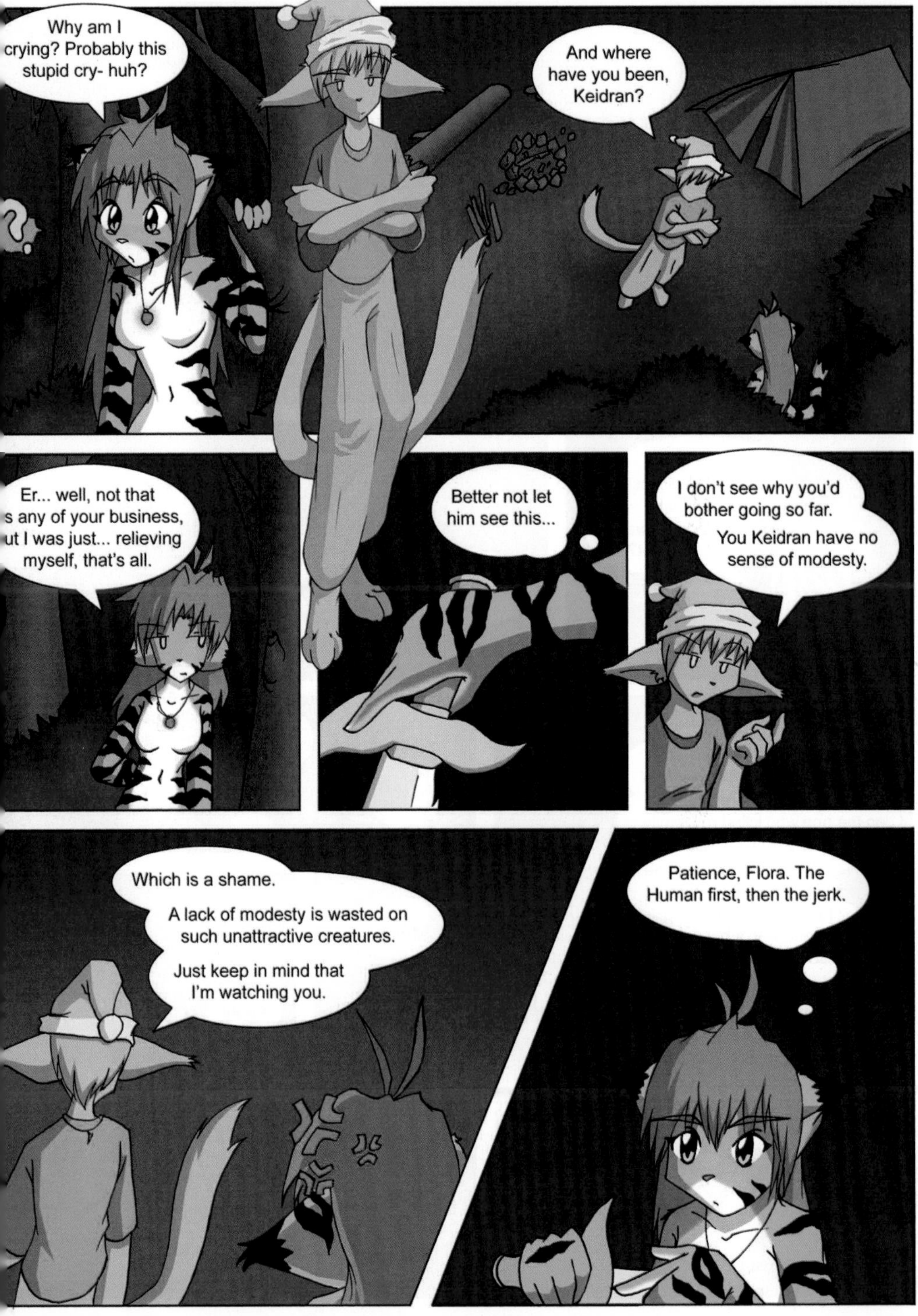
Why am I crying? Probably this stupid cry- huh?
And where have you been, Keidran?
Er... well, not that s any of your business, ut I was just... relieving myself, that's all.
Better not let him see this...
I don't see why you'd bother going so far.
You Keidran have no sense of modesty.
Which is a shame.
A lack of modesty is wasted on such unattractive creatures.
Just keep in mind that I'm watching you.
Patience, Flora. The Human first, then the jerk.

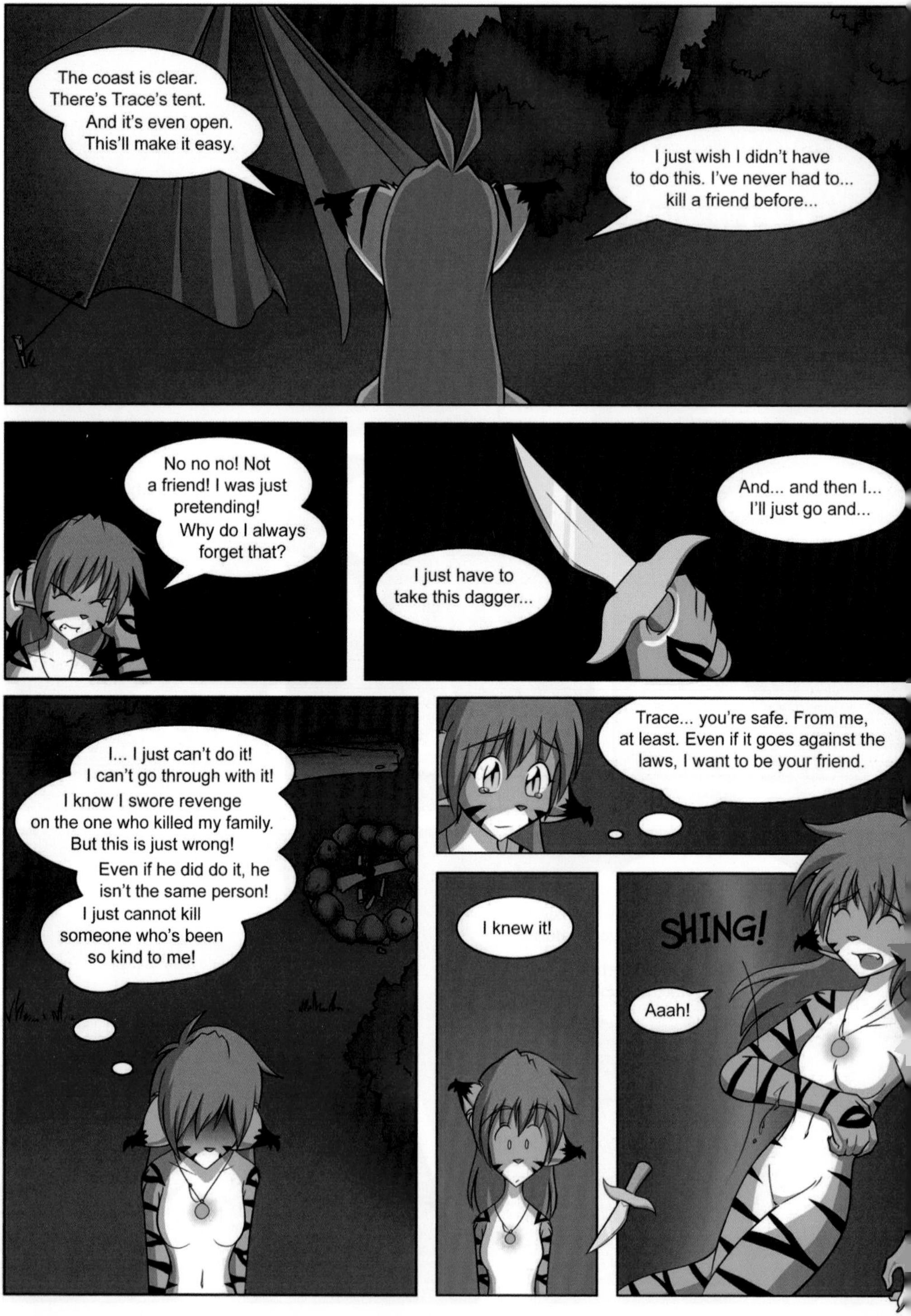
The coast is clear. There's Trace's tent. And it's even open. This'll make it easy.
I just wish I didn't have to do this. I've never had to... kill a friend before...
No no no! Not a friend! I was just pretending! Why do I always forget that?
I just have to take this dagger...
And... and then I... I'll just go and...
I... I just can't do it! I can't go through with it! I know I swore revenge on the one who killed my family. But this is just wrong! Even if he did do it, he isn't the same person! I just cannot kill someone who's been so kind to me!
Trace... you're safe. From me, at least. Even if it goes against the laws, I want to be your friend.
I knew it!
SHING!
Aaah!

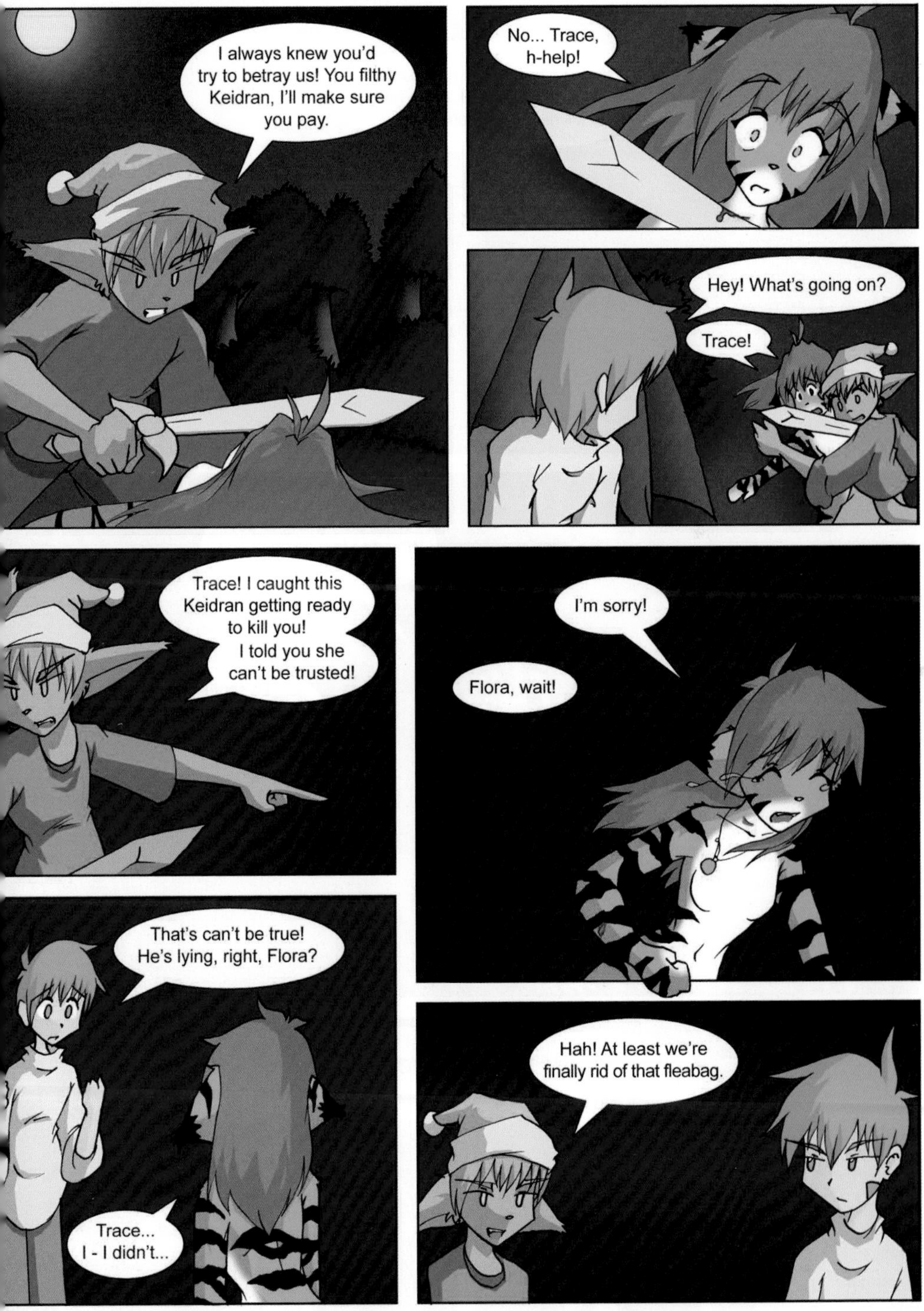
I always knew you'd try to betray us! You filthy Keidran, I'll make sure you pay.
No... Trace, h-help!
Hey! What's going on?
Trace!
Trace! I caught this Keidran getting ready to kill you!
I told you she can't be trusted!
That's can't be true! He's lying, right, Flora?
Trace... I - I didn't...
I'm sorry!
Flora, wait!
Hah! At least we're finally rid of that fleabag.

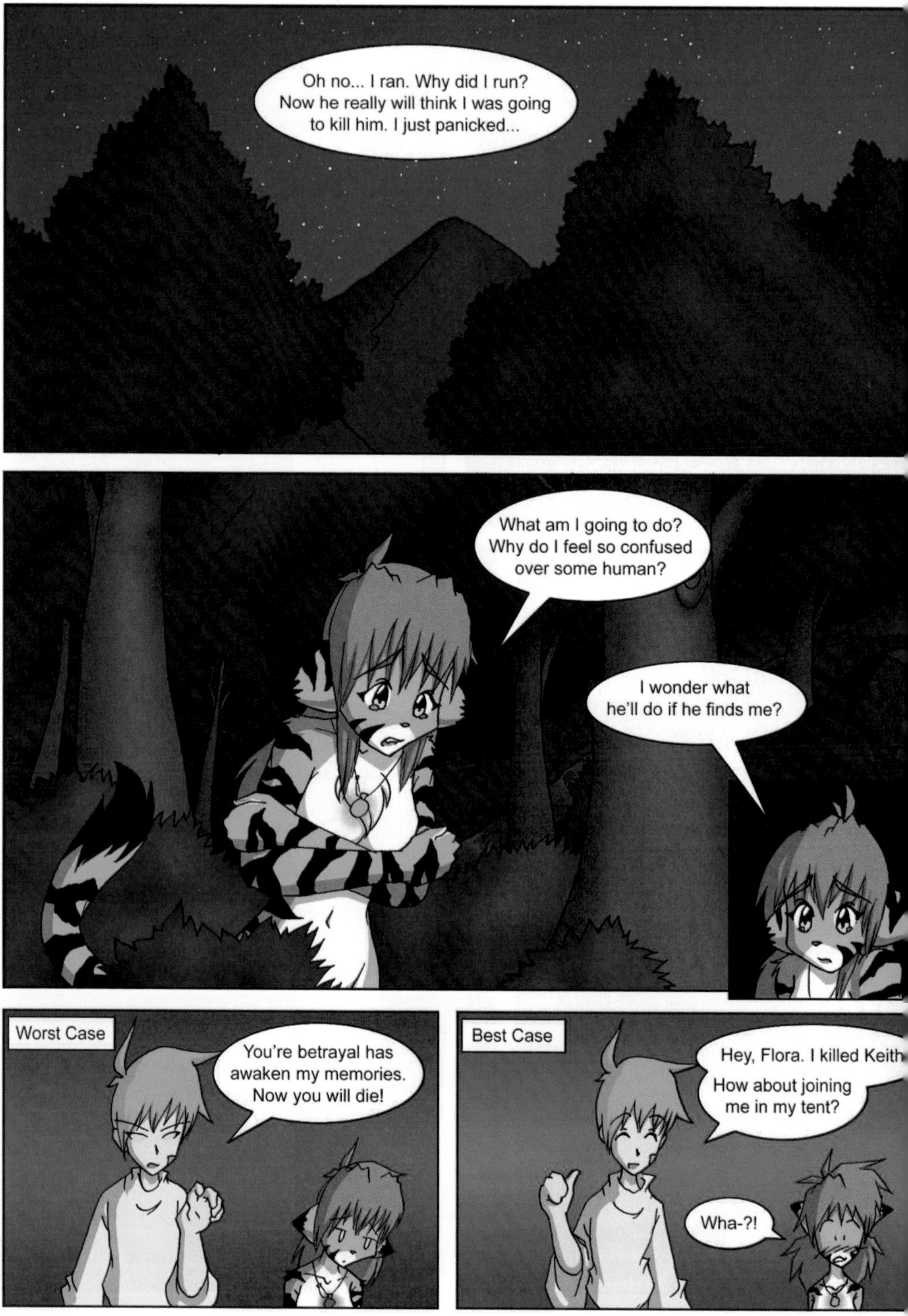
Oh no... I ran. Why did I run? Now he really will think I was going to kill him. I just panicked...
What am I going to do? Why do I feel so confused over some human?
I wonder what he'll do if he finds me?
Worst Case
You're betrayal has awaken my memories. Now you will die!
Best Case
Hey, Flora. I killed Keith
How about joining me in my tent?
Wha-?!

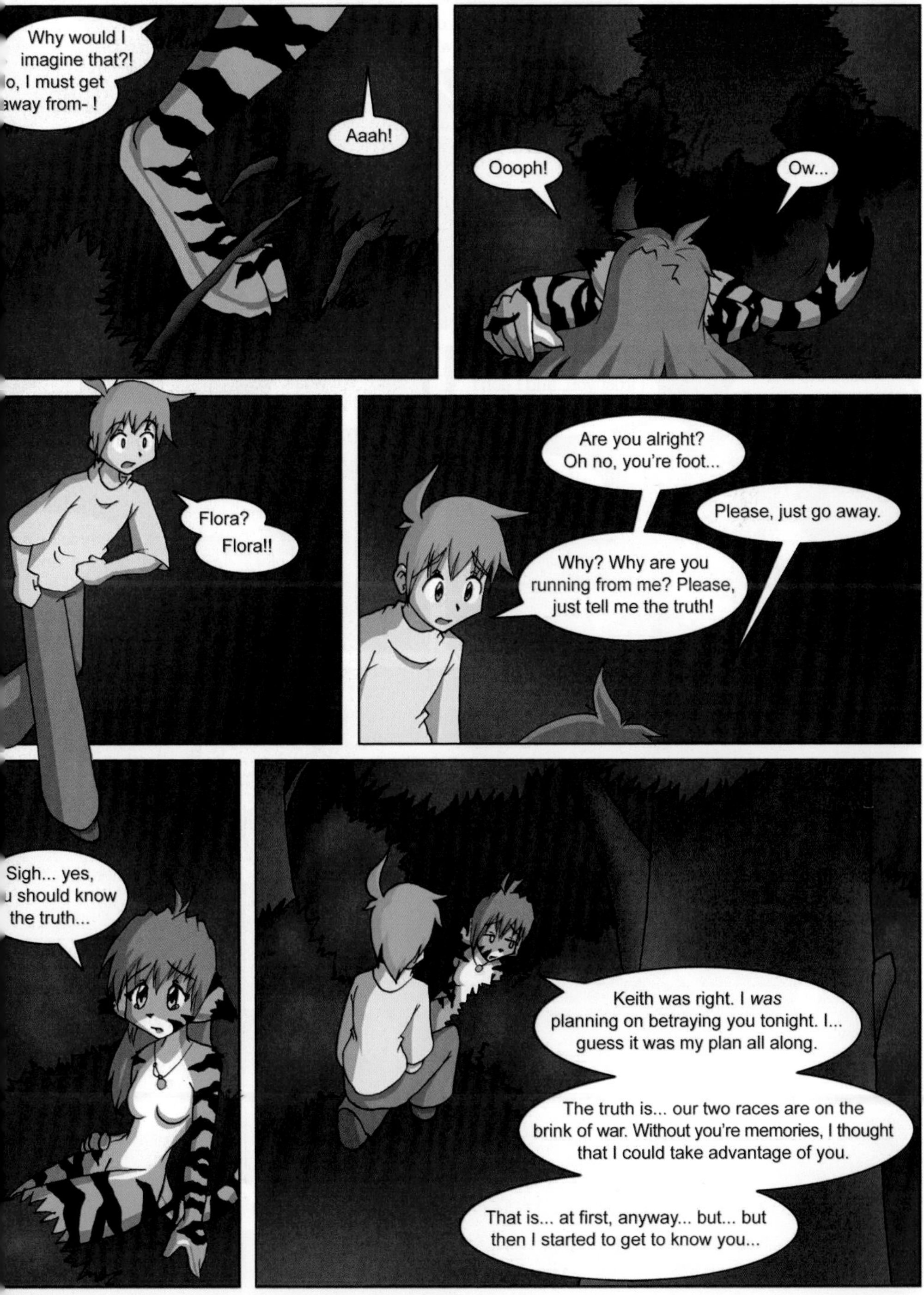

Why would I imagine that?! o, I must get away from- !
Aaah!
Oooph!
Ow...
Flora? Flora!!
Are you alright? Oh no, you're foot...
Please, just go away.
Why? Why are you running from me? Please, just tell me the truth!
Sigh... yes, u should know the truth...
Keith was right. I *was* planning on betraying you tonight. I... guess it was my plan all along.
The truth is... our two races are on the brink of war. Without you're memories, I thought that I could take advantage of you.
That is... at first, anyway... but... but then I started to get to know you...

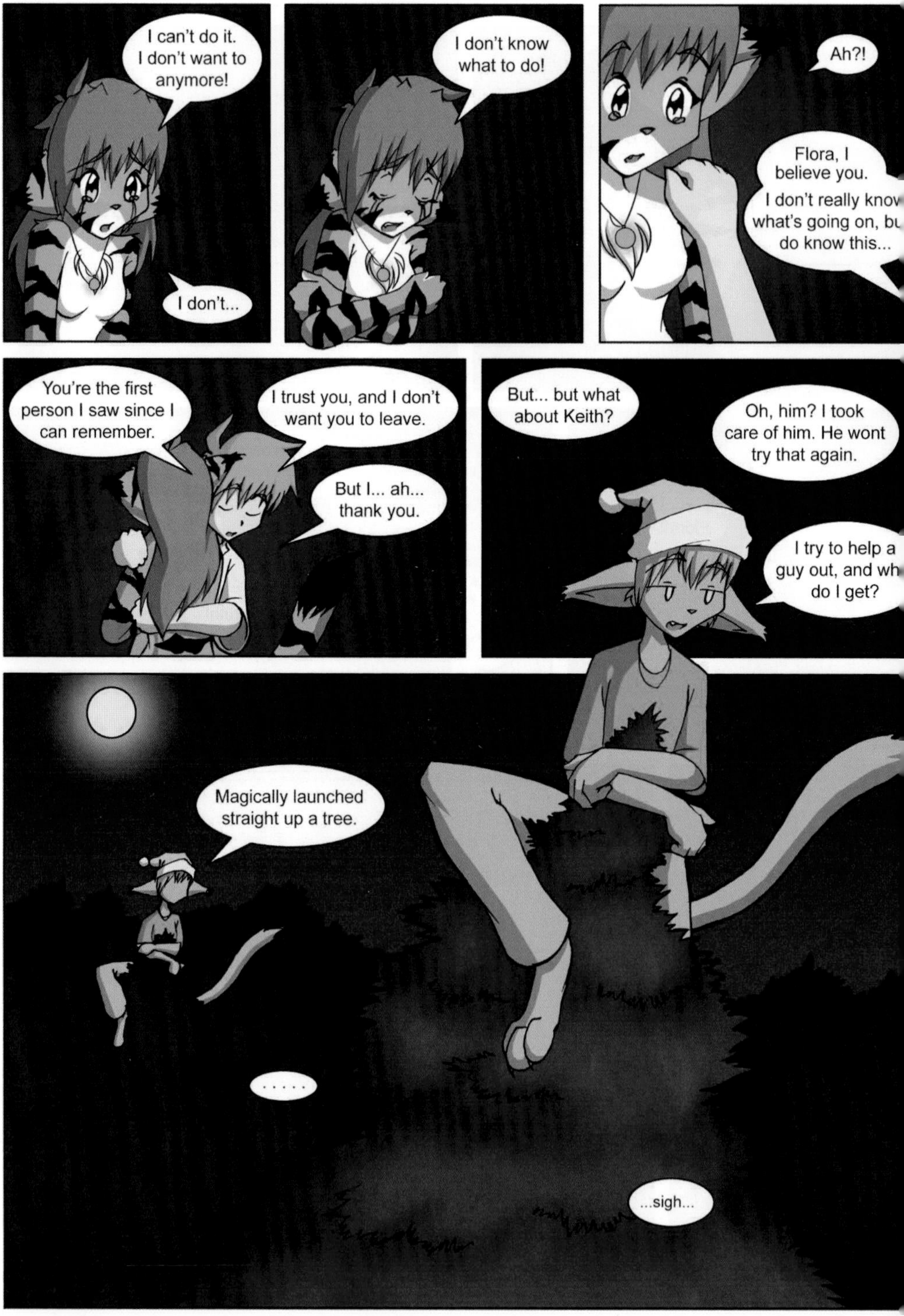
I can't do it. I don't want to anymore!
I don't...
I don't know what to do!
Ah?!
Flora, I believe you. I don't really
what's going on,
do know this...
You're the first person I saw since I can remember.
I trust you, and I don't want you to leave.
But I... ah... thank you.
But... but what about Keith?
Oh, him? I took care of him. He wont try that again.
I try to help a guy out, and
do I get?
Magically launched straight up a tree.
.....
...sigh...

TwoKinds

Chapter Three

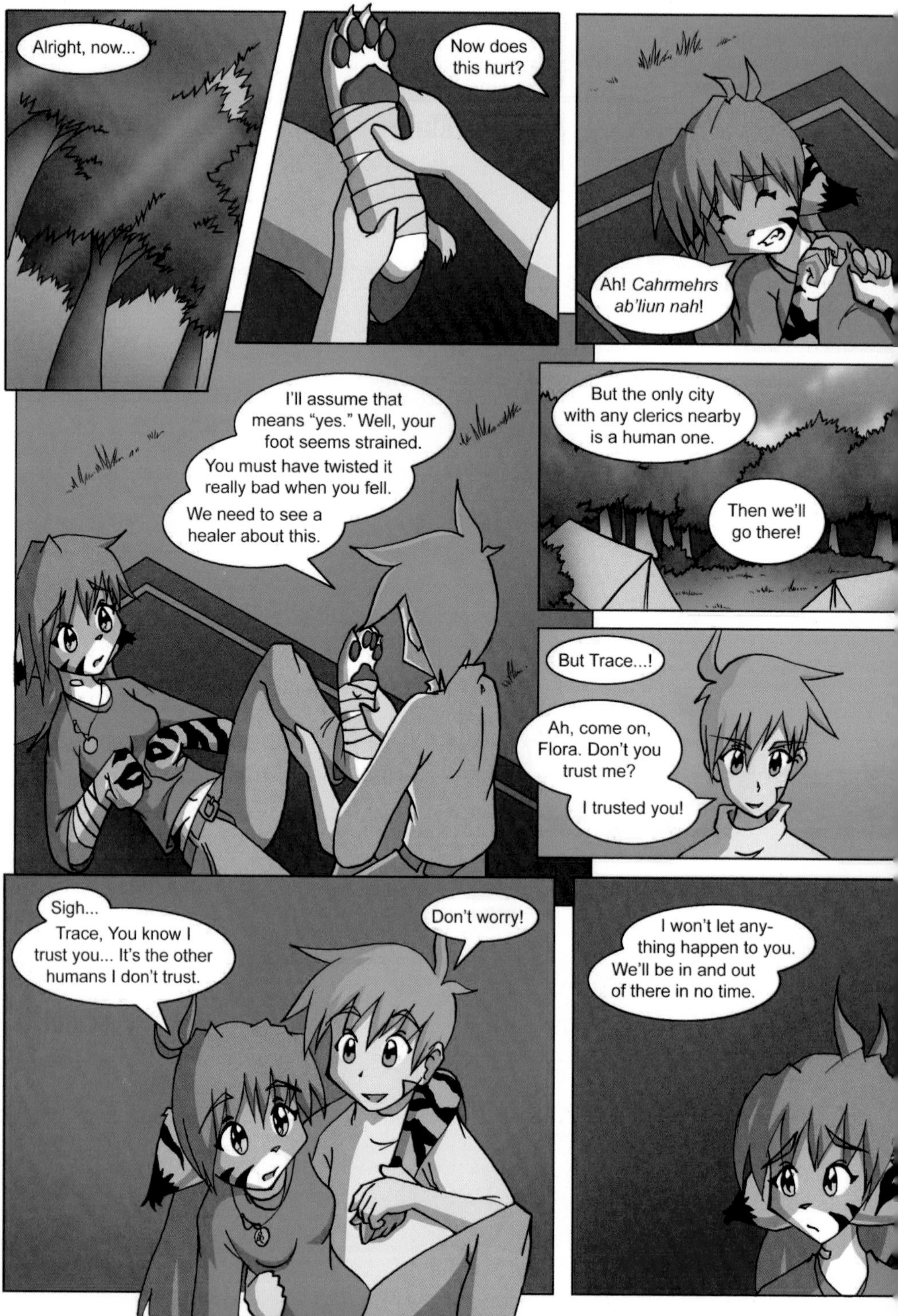
Alright, now...
Now does this hurt?
Ah! *Cahrmehrs ab'liun nah*!
I'll assume that means "yes." Well, your foot seems strained.
You must have twisted it really bad when you fell.
We need to see a healer about this.
But the only city with any clerics nearby is a human one.
Then we'll go there!
But Trace...!
Ah, come on, Flora. Don't you trust me?
I trusted you!
Sigh...
Trace, You know I trust you... It's the other humans I don't trust.
Don't worry!
I won't let any-thing happen to you. We'll be in and out of there in no time.

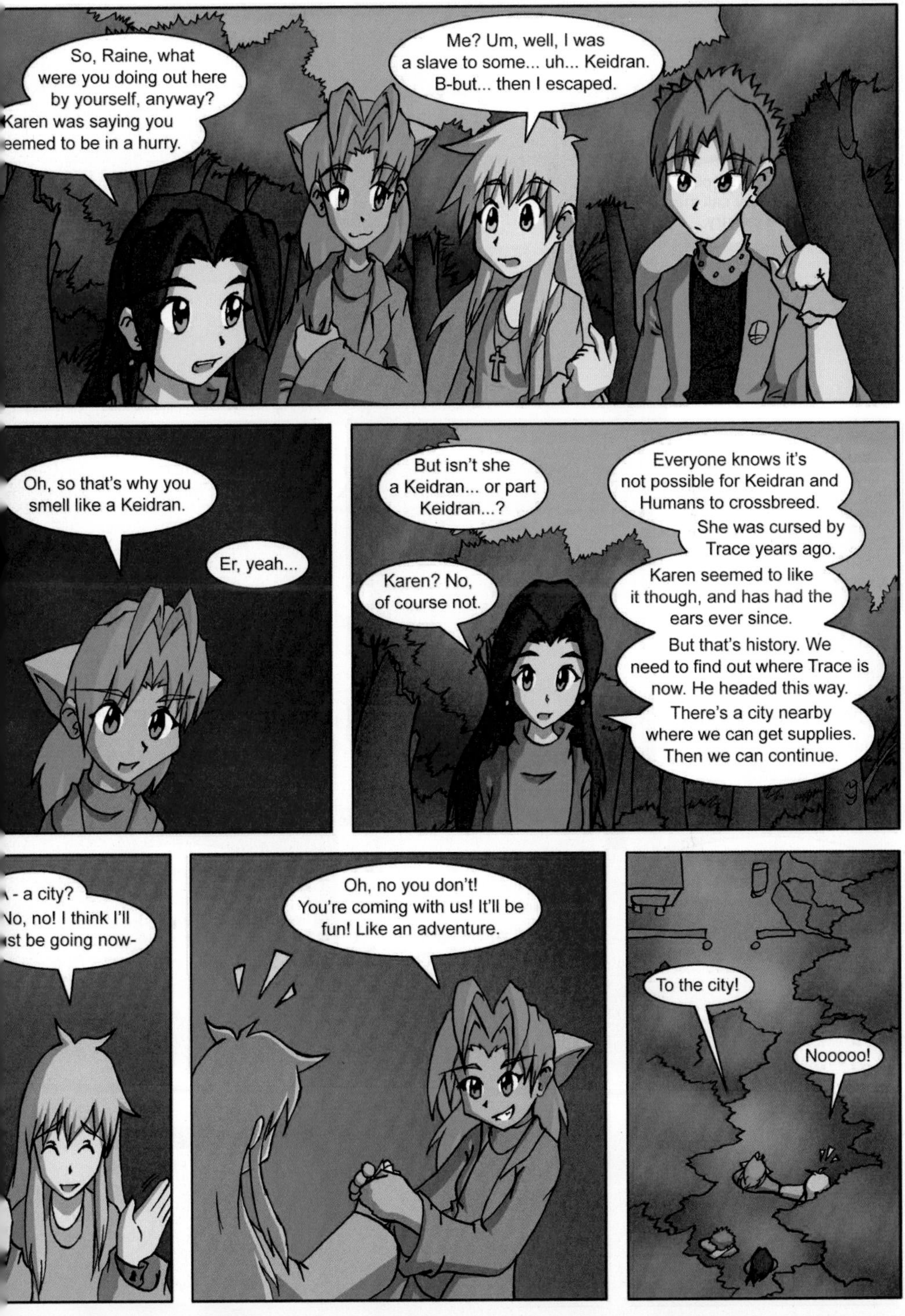
So, Raine, what were you doing out here by yourself, anyway? Karen was saying you eemed to be in a hurry.
Me? Um, well, I was a slave to some... uh... Keidran. B-but... then I escaped.
Oh, so that's why you smell like a Keidran.
Er, yeah...
But isn't she a Keidran... or part Keidran...?
Karen? No, of course not.
Everyone knows it's not possible for Keidran and Humans to crossbreed.
She was cursed by Trace years ago.
Karen seemed to like it though, and has had the ears ever since.
But that's history. We need to find out where Trace is now. He headed this way.
There's a city nearby where we can get supplies. Then we can continue.
- a city? o, no! I think I'll st be going now-
Oh, no you don't! You're coming with us! It'll be fun! Like an adventure.
To the city!
Nooooo!

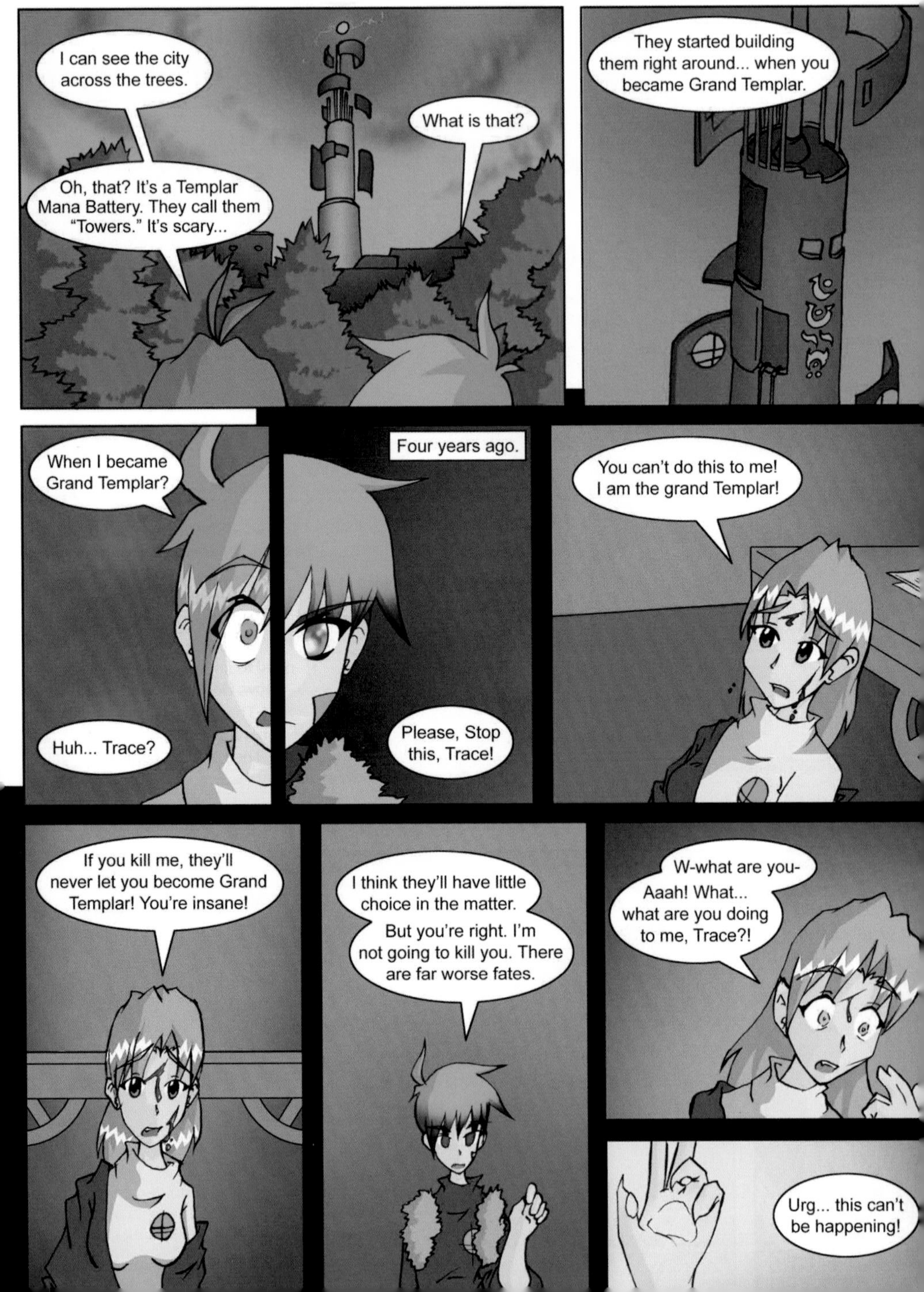

I can see the city across the trees.
What is that?
Oh, that? It's a Templar Mana Battery. They call them "Towers." It's scary...
They started building them right around... when you became Grand Templar.
When I became Grand Templar?
Huh... Trace?
Four years ago.
Please, Stop this, Trace!
You can't do this to me! I am the grand Templar!
If you kill me, they'll never let you become Grand Templar! You're insane!
I think they'll have little choice in the matter.
But you're right. I'm not going to kill you. There are far worse fates.
W-what are you-
Aaah! What... what are you doing to me, Trace?!
Urg... this can't be happening!

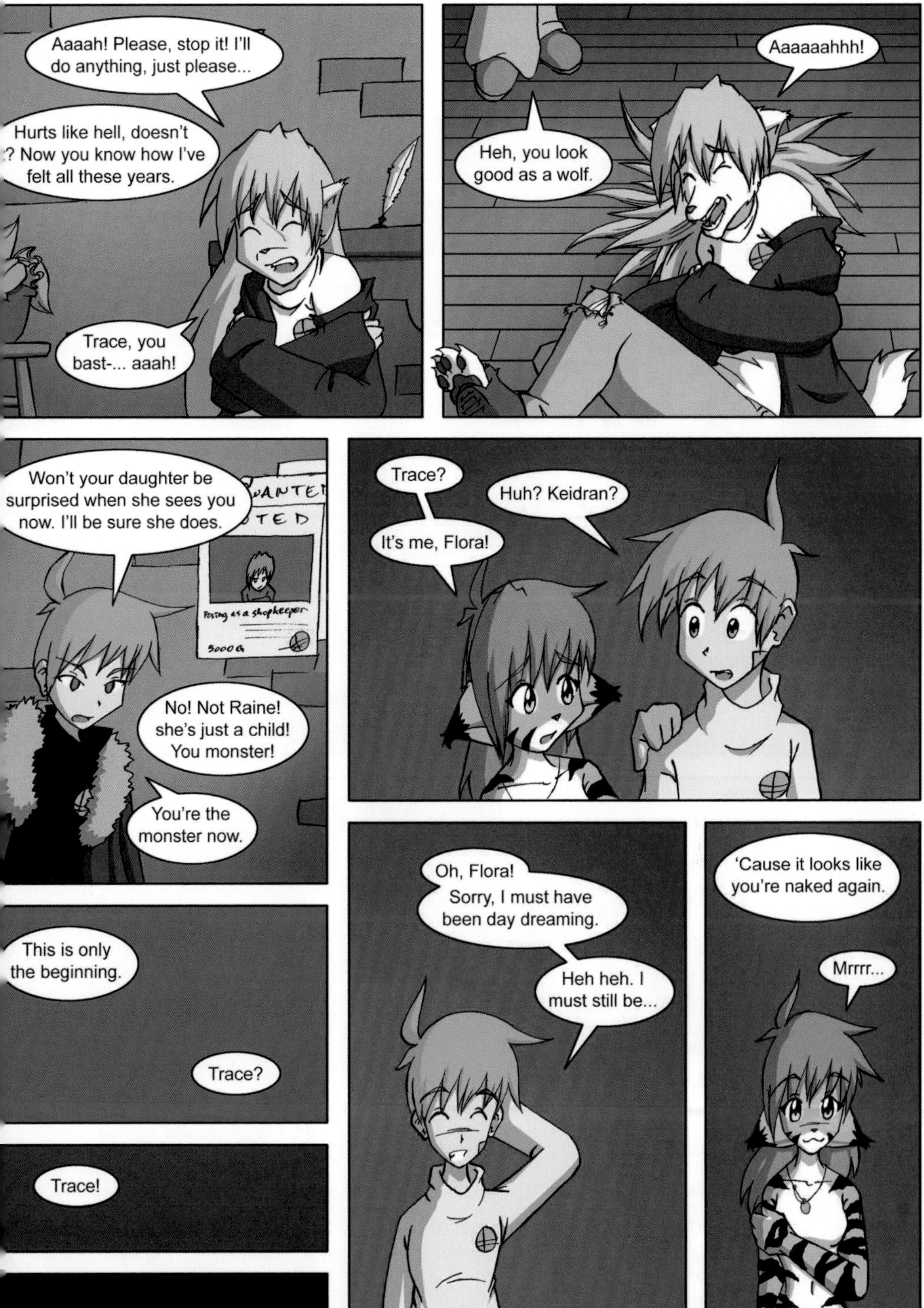
Aaaah! Please, stop it! I'll do anything, just please...
Hurts like hell, doesn't
? Now you know how I've
felt all these years.
Trace, you bast-... aaah!
Aaaaaahhh!
Heh, you look good as a wolf.
Won't your daughter be surprised when she sees you now. I'll be sure she does.
Posing as a shopkeeper
No! Not Raine! she's just a child! You monster!
You're the monster now.
Trace?
It's me, Flora!
Huh? Keidran?
This is only the beginning.
Trace?
Trace!
Oh, Flora! Sorry, I must have been day dreaming.
Heh heh. I must still be...
'Cause it looks like you're naked again.
Mrrrr...

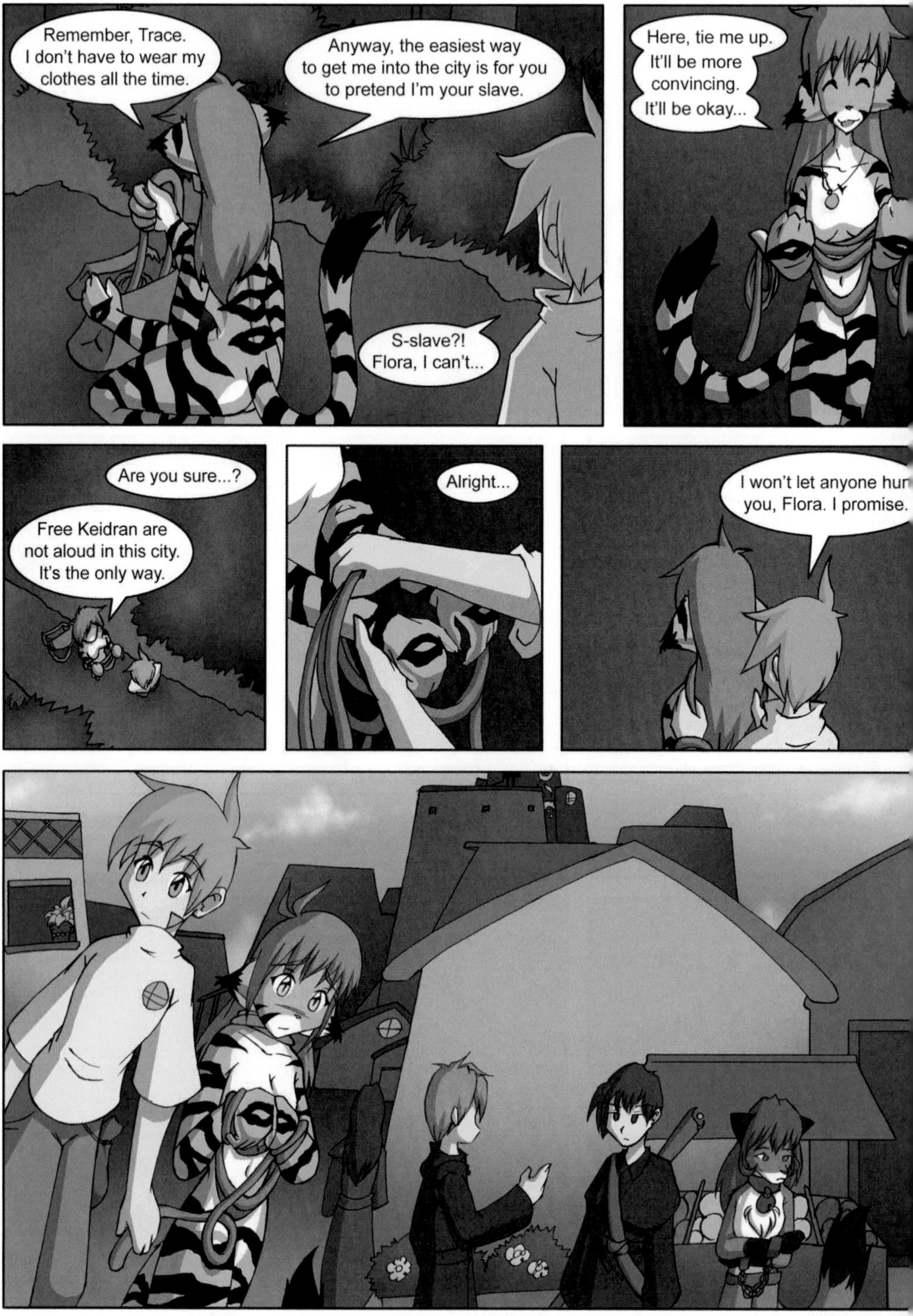
Remember, Trace.
I don't have to wear my clothes all the time.
Anyway, the easiest way to get me into the city is for you to pretend I'm your slave.
S-slave?! Flora, I can't...
Here, tie me up.
It'll be more convincing.
It'll be okay...
Are you sure...?
Free Keidran are not aloud in this city. It's the only way.
Alright...
I won't let anyone hur
you, Flora. I promise.

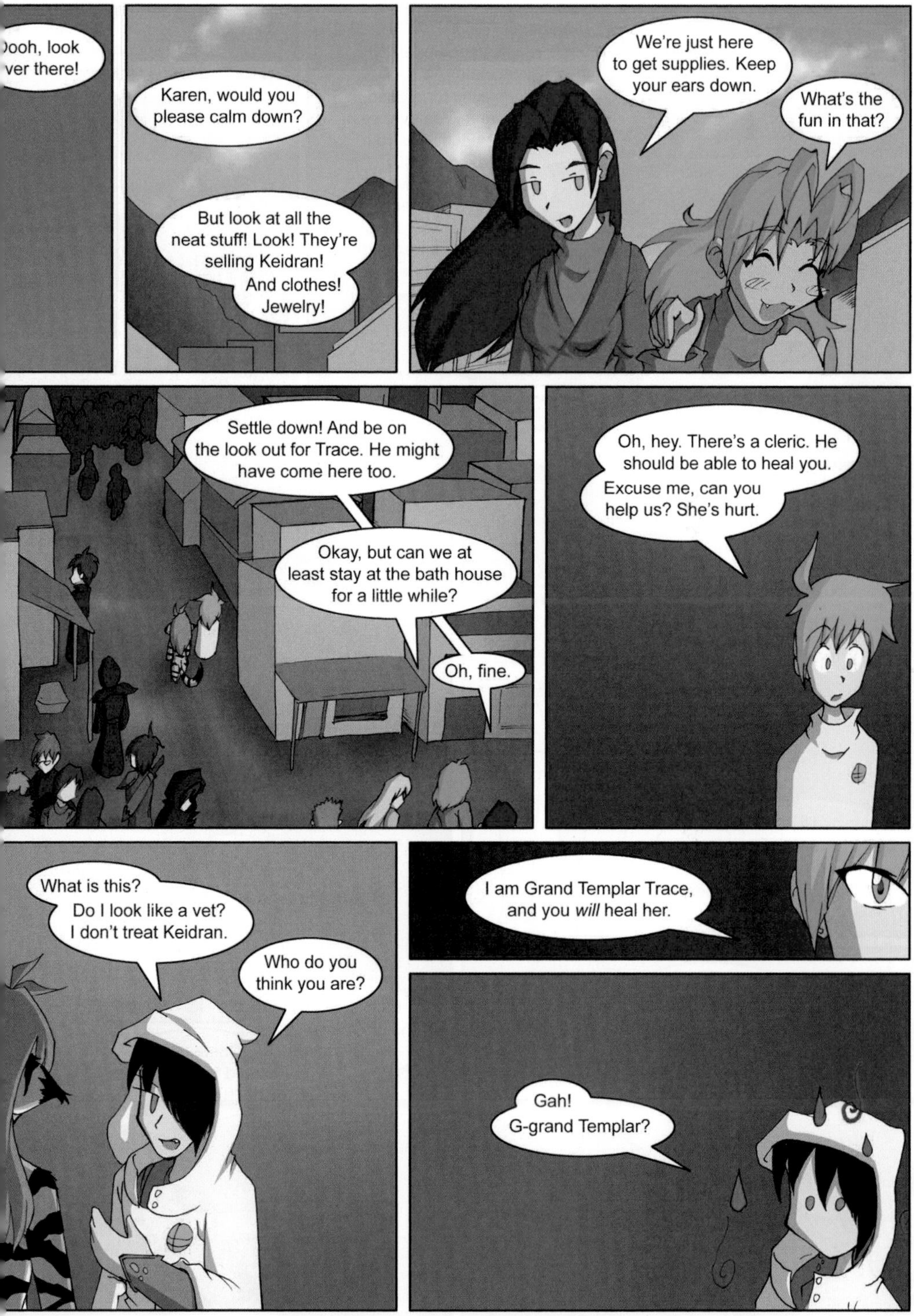

)ooh, look ver there!
Karen, would you please calm down?
But look at all the neat stuff! Look! They're selling Keidran!
And clothes! Jewelry!
We're just here to get supplies. Keep your ears down.
What's the fun in that?
Settle down! And be on the look out for Trace. He might have come here too.
Okay, but can we at least stay at the bath house for a little while?
Oh, fine.
Oh, hey. There's a cleric. He should be able to heal you.
Excuse me, can you help us? She's hurt.
What is this? Do I look like a vet? I don't treat Keidran.
Who do you think you are?
I am Grand Templar Trace, and you *will* heal her.
Gah! G-grand Templar?

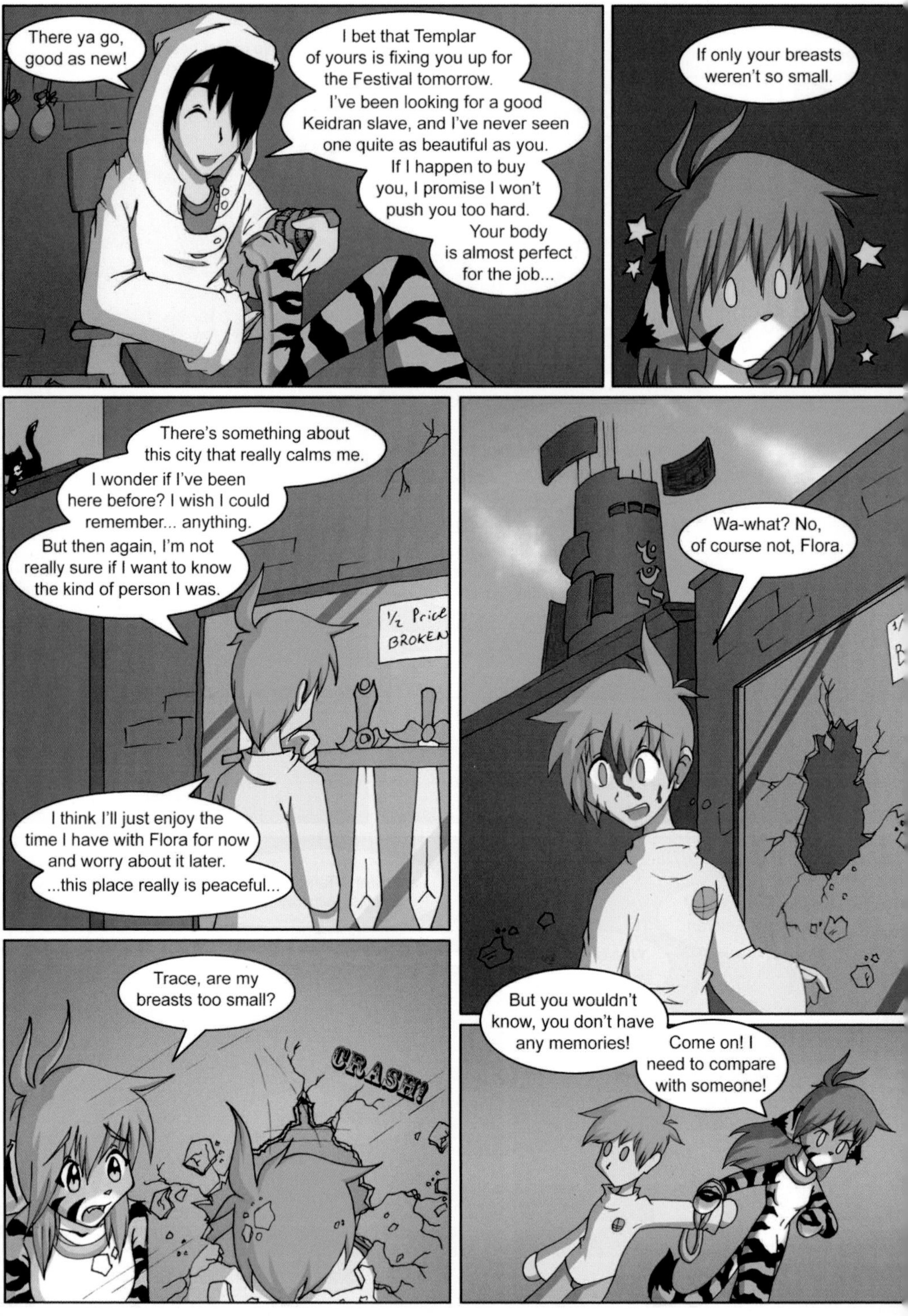

There ya go, good as new!
I bet that Templar of yours is fixing you up for the Festival tomorrow. I've been looking for a good Keidran slave, and I've never seen one quite as beautiful as you. If I happen to buy you, I promise I won't push you too hard. Your body is almost perfect for the job...
If only your breasts weren't so small.
There's something about this city that really calms me. I wonder if I've been here before? I wish I could remember... anything. But then again, I'm not really sure if I want to know the kind of person I was.
1/2 Price BROKEN
I think I'll just enjoy the time I have with Flora for now and worry about it later. ...this place really is peaceful...
Wa-what? No, of course not, Flora.
Trace, are my breasts too small?
CRASH!
But you wouldn't know, you don't have any memories!
Come on! I need to compare with someone!

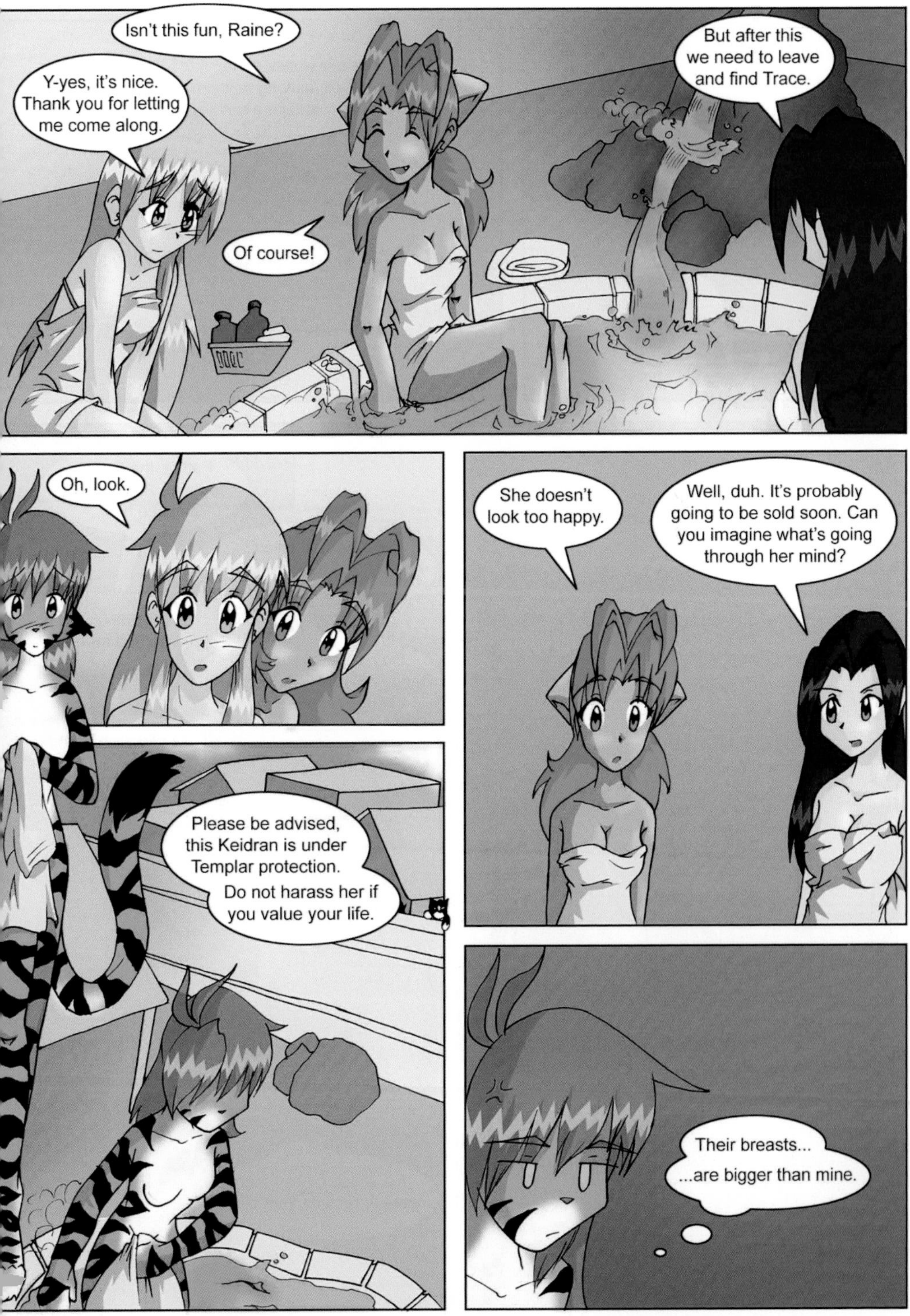
Isn't this fun, Raine?
Y-yes, it's nice. Thank you for letting me come along.
Of course!
But after this we need to leave and find Trace.
Oh, look.
She doesn't look too happy.
Well, duh. It's probably going to be sold soon. Can you imagine what's going through her mind?
Please be advised, this Keidran is under Templar protection.
Do not harass her if you value your life.
Their breasts...
...are bigger than mine.

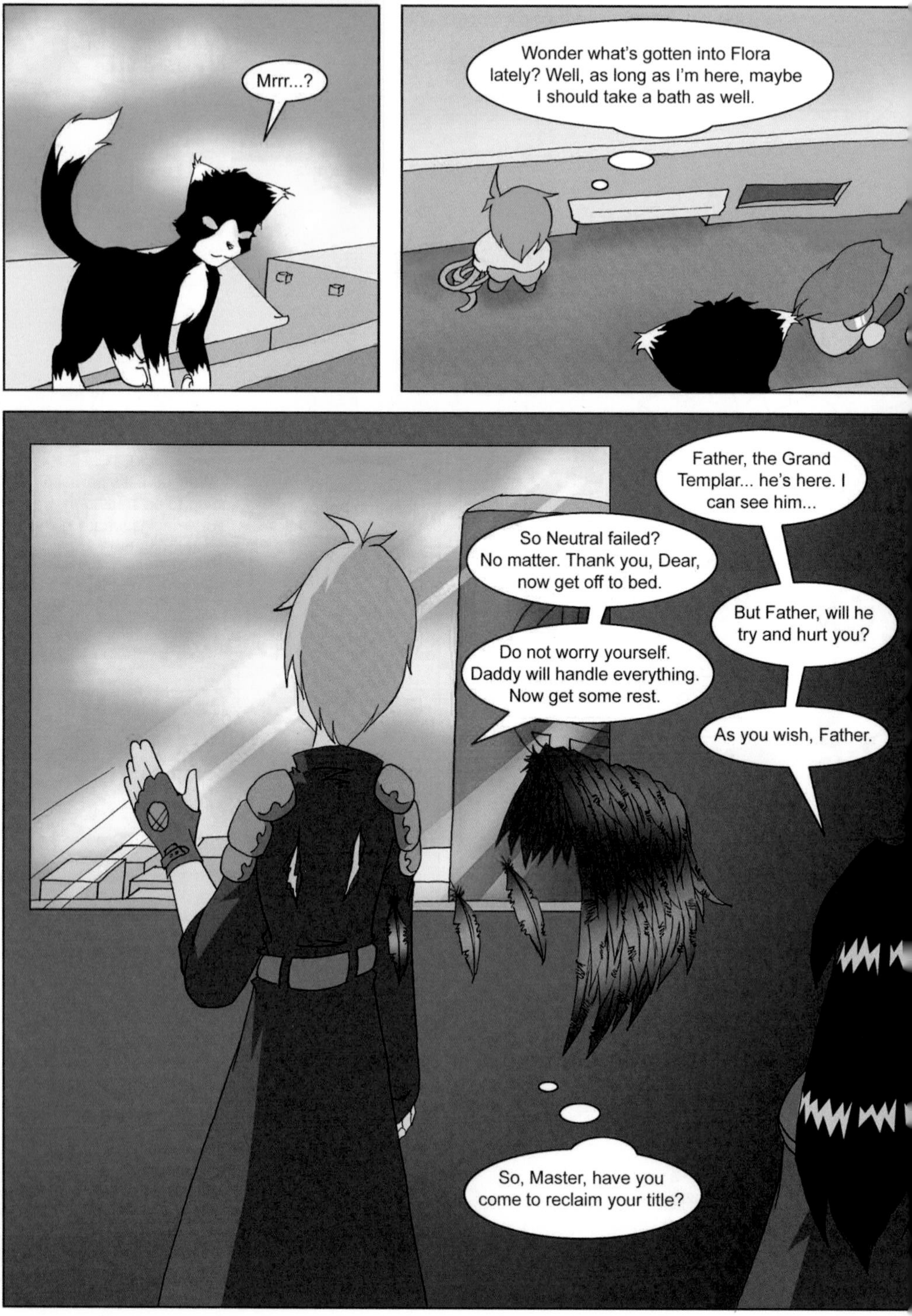
Mrrr...?
Wonder what's gotten into Flora lately? Well, as long as I'm here, maybe I should take a bath as well.
Father, the Grand Templar... he's here. I can see him...
So Neutral failed? No matter. Thank you, Dear, now get off to bed.
But Father, will he try and hurt you?
Do not worry yourself. Daddy will handle everything. Now get some rest.
As you wish, Father.
So, Master, have you come to reclaim your title?

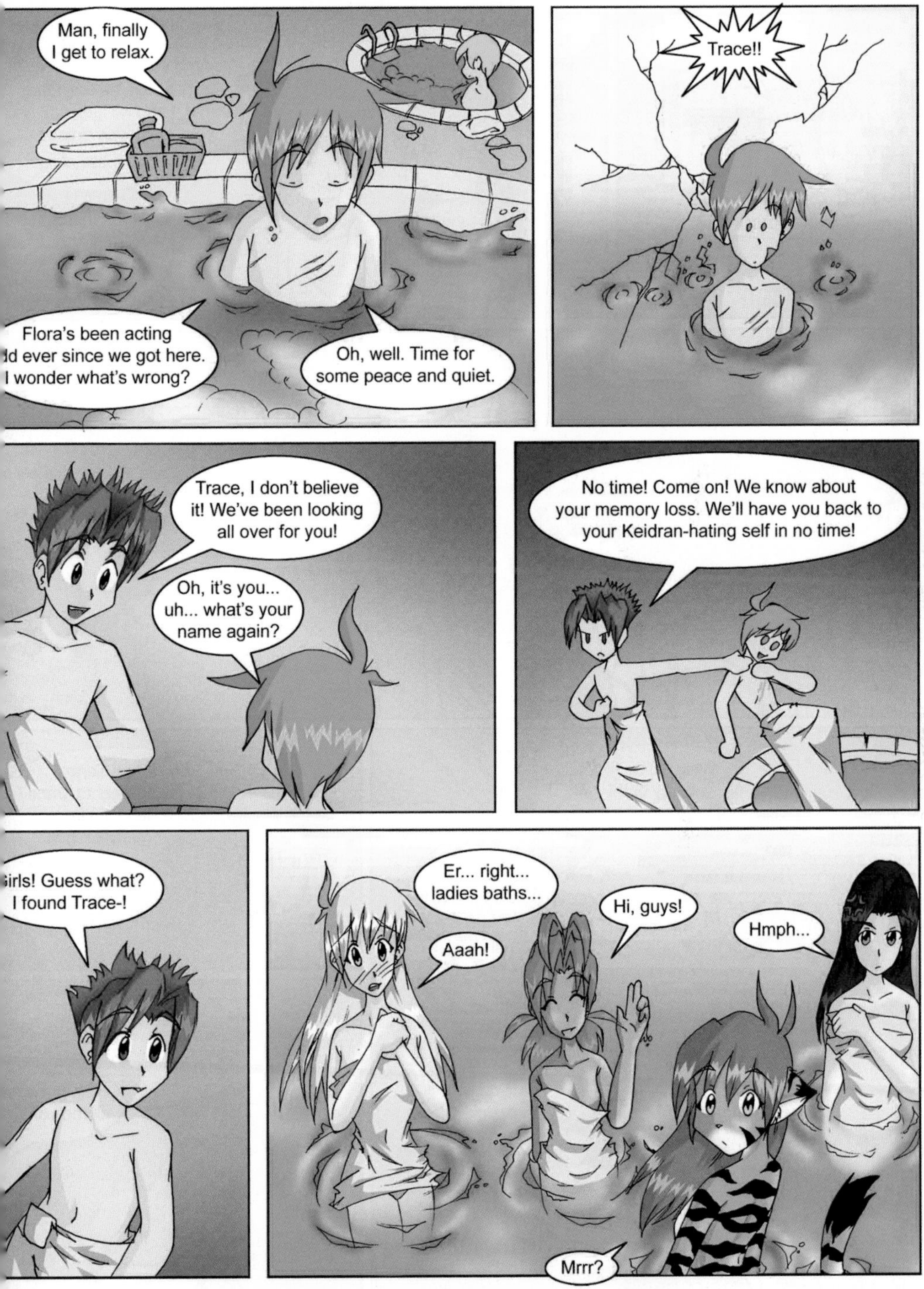
Man, finally
I get to relax.
Flora's been acting
ld ever since we got here.
I wonder what's wrong?
Oh, well. Time for
some peace and quiet.
Trace!!
Trace, I don't believe
it! We've been looking
all over for you!
Oh, it's you...
uh... what's your
name again?
No time! Come on! We know about
your memory loss. We'll have you back to
your Keidran-hating self in no time!
irls! Guess what?
I found Trace-!
Er... right...
ladies baths...
Aaah!
Hi, guys!
Hmph...
Mrrr?

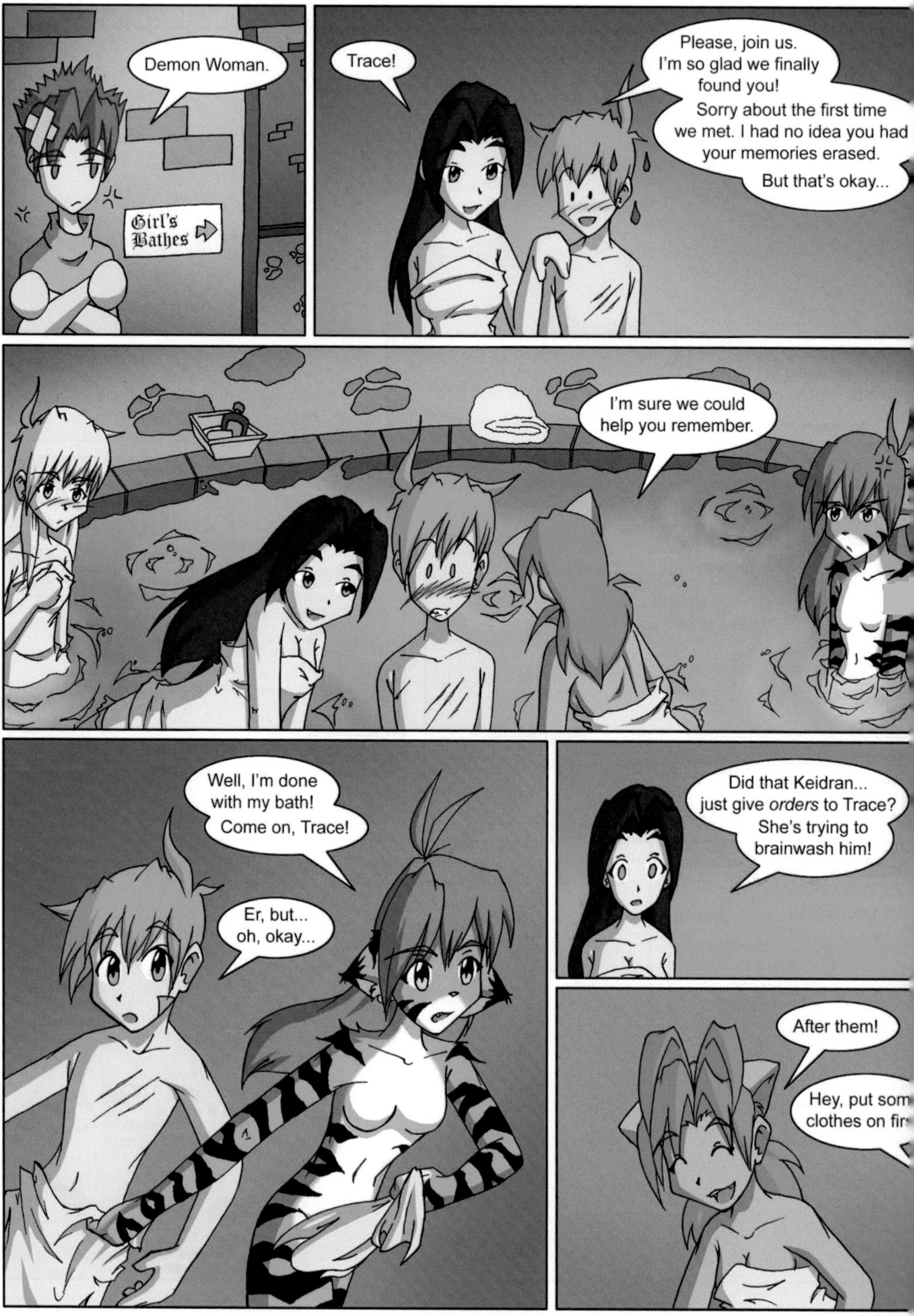

Demon Woman.
Girl's Bathes
Trace!
Please, join us. I'm so glad we finally found you!
Sorry about the first time we met. I had no idea you had your memories erased.
But that's okay...
I'm sure we could help you remember.
Well, I'm done with my bath! Come on, Trace!
Er, but... oh, okay...
Did that Keidran... just give *orders* to Trace? She's trying to brainwash him!
After them!

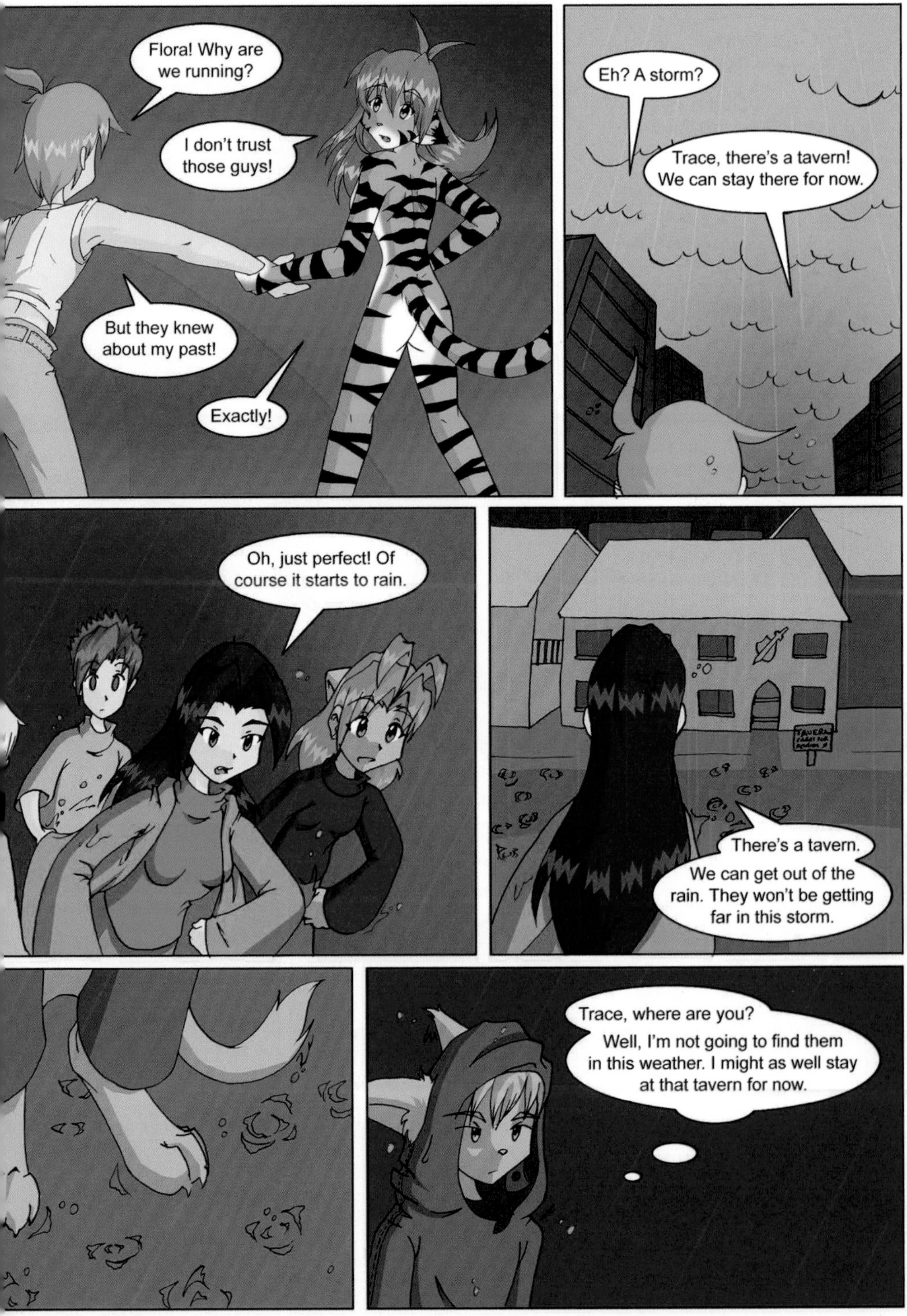
Flora! Why are we running?
I don't trust those guys!
But they knew about my past!
Exactly!
Eh? A storm?
Trace, there's a tavern! We can stay there for now.
Oh, just perfect! Of course it starts to rain.
There's a tavern.
We can get out of the rain. They won't be getting far in this storm.
Trace, where are you?
Well, I'm not going to find them in this weather. I might as well stay at that tavern for now.

Ah, greetings, Grand Templar! Welcome to my humble tavern! What may I get you?

Um, we just need a room.

Certainly. I have a suite prepared for you.

And a nice, strong steel cage in the basement for your Keidran. We guarantee she won't be able to escape, and we've taken the liberty of clearing out the rats about three months ago.

What?! I don't want her alone in a cage!

Huh? Alone? Oh, I get it.

So she's a breeder, eh?

In that case, we have plenty of virile male Keidrans.

One night and you can expect her to have kittens in no time.

No, NO!

Nyaaaaa!

I- I think I'll just have her stay in my room for tonight!

Ooooh, this will be interesting.

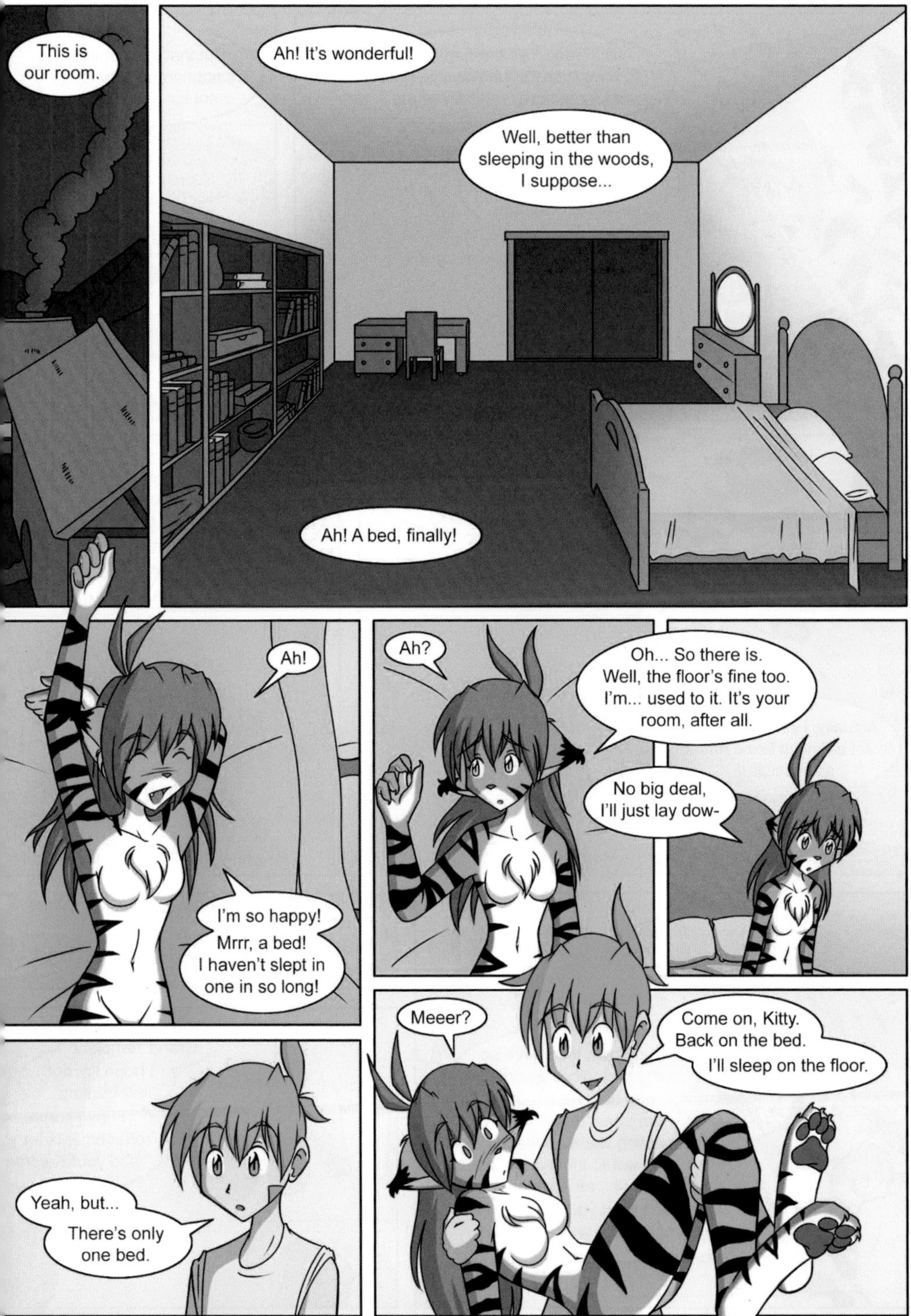
This is our room.
Ah! It's wonderful!
Well, better than sleeping in the woods, I suppose...
Ah! A bed, finally!
Ah!
I'm so happy! Mrrr, a bed! I haven't slept in one in so long!
Ah?
Oh... So there is. Well, the floor's fine too. I'm... used to it. It's your room, after all.
No big deal, I'll just lay dow-
Yeah, but... There's only one bed.
Meeer?
Come on, Kitty. Back on the bed. I'll sleep on the floor.

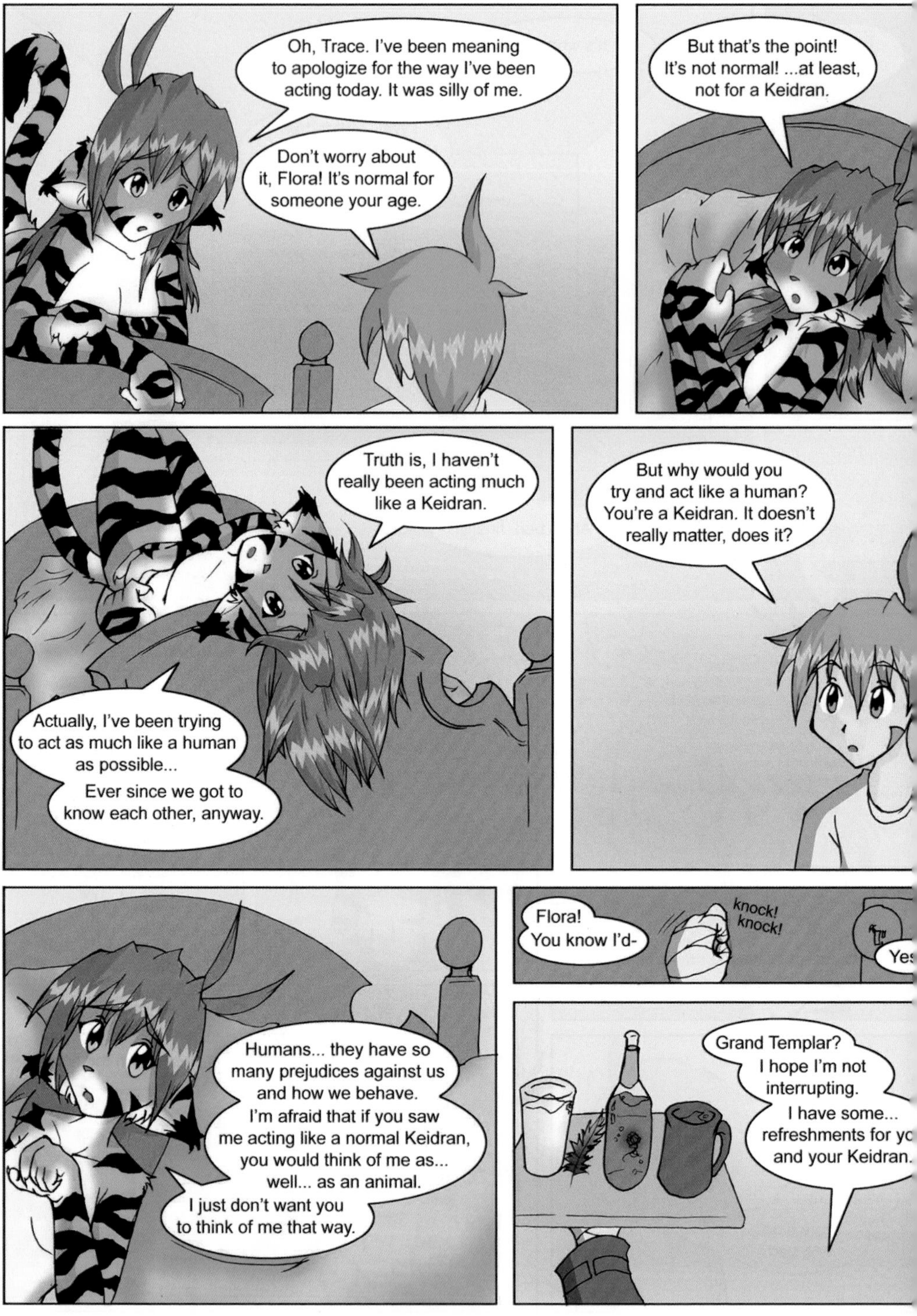

Oh, Trace. I've been meaning to apologize for the way I've been acting today. It was silly of me.
Don't worry about it, Flora! It's normal for someone your age.
But that's the point! It's not normal! ...at least, not for a Keidran.
Truth is, I haven't really been acting much like a Keidran.
Actually, I've been trying to act as much like a human as possible...
Ever since we got to know each other, anyway.
But why would you try and act like a human? You're a Keidran. It doesn't really matter, does it?
Humans... they have so many prejudices against us and how we behave.
I'm afraid that if you saw me acting like a normal Keidran, you would think of me as... well... as an animal.
I just don't want you to think of me that way.
Flora! You know I'd-
knock! knock!
Grand Templar? I hope I'm not interrupting.
I have some... refreshments for yo and your Keidran.

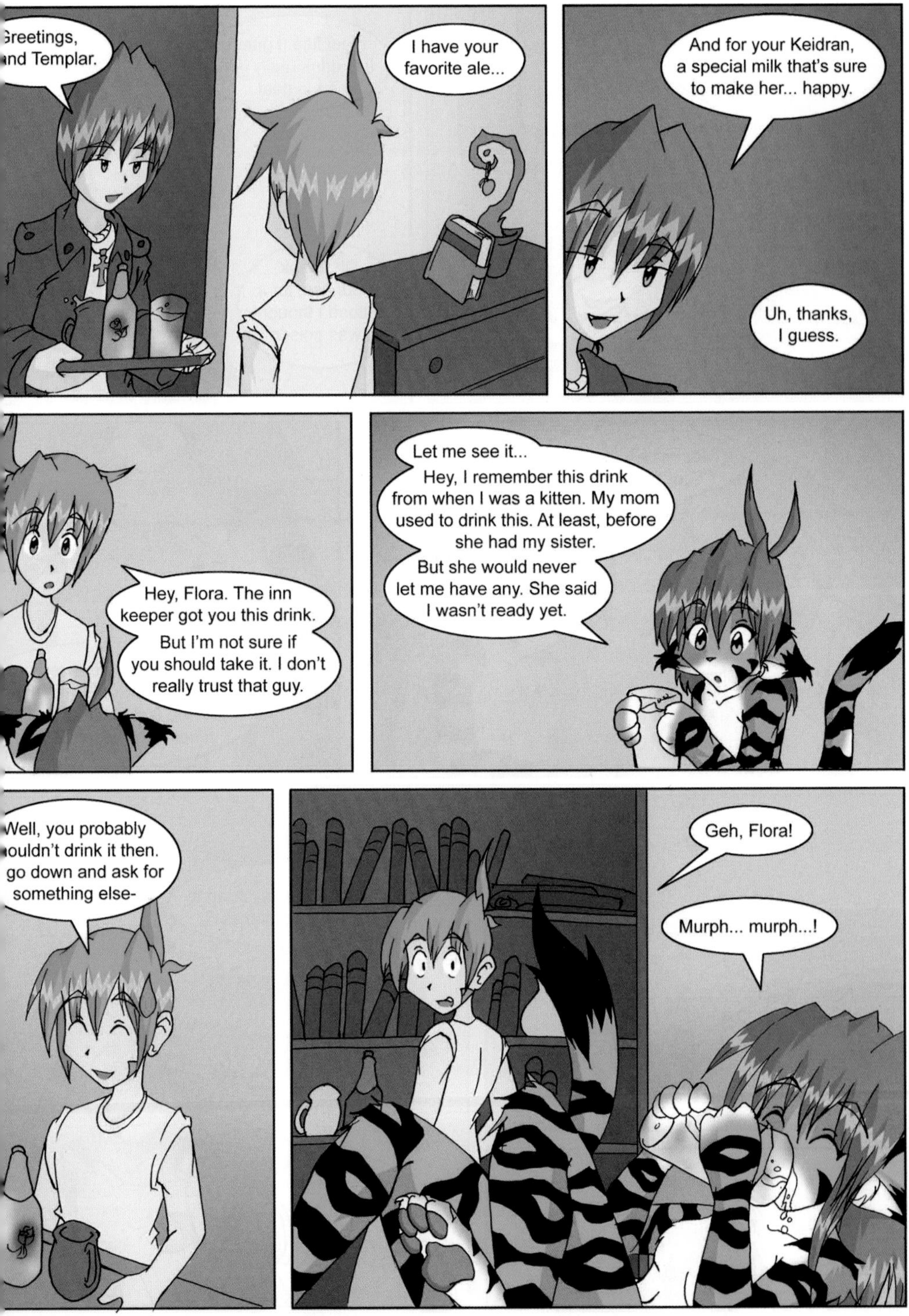
reetings,
nd Templar.
I have your favorite ale...
And for your Keidran, a special milk that's sure to make her... happy.
Uh, thanks, I guess.
Hey, Flora. The inn keeper got you this drink.
But I'm not sure if you should take it. I don't really trust that guy.
Let me see it...
Hey, I remember this drink from when I was a kitten. My mom used to drink this. At least, before she had my sister.
But she would never let me have any. She said I wasn't ready yet.
Well, you probably
ouldn't drink it then.
go down and ask for
something else-
Geh, Flora!
Murph... murph...!

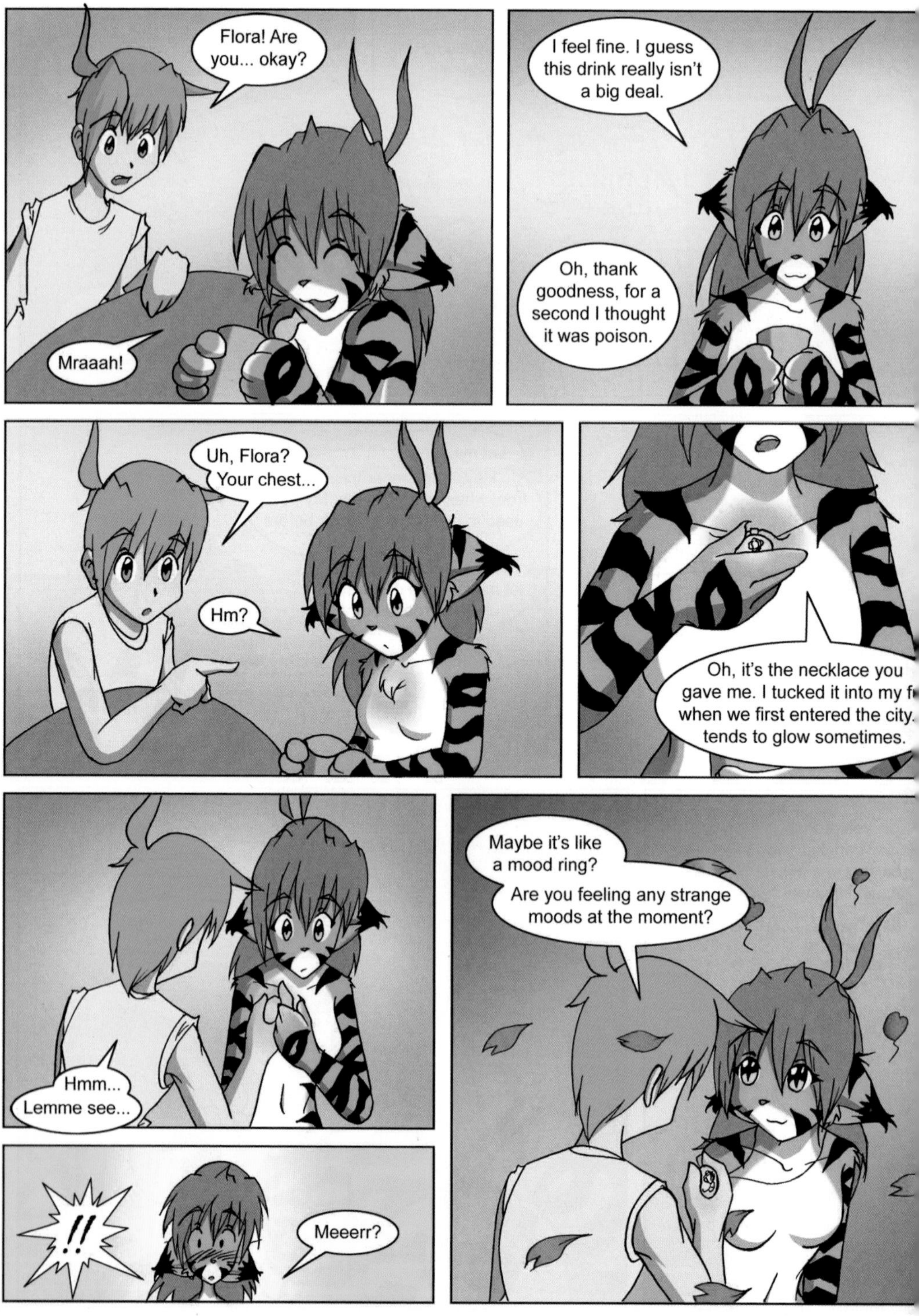
Flora! Are you... okay?
Mraaah!
I feel fine. I guess this drink really isn't a big deal.
Oh, thank goodness, for a second I thought it was poison.
Uh, Flora? Your chest...
Hm?
Oh, it's the necklace you gave me. I tucked it into my f
when we first entered the city.
tends to glow sometimes.
Hmm... Lemme see...
!!
Meeerr?
Maybe it's like a mood ring?
Are you feeling any strange moods at the moment?

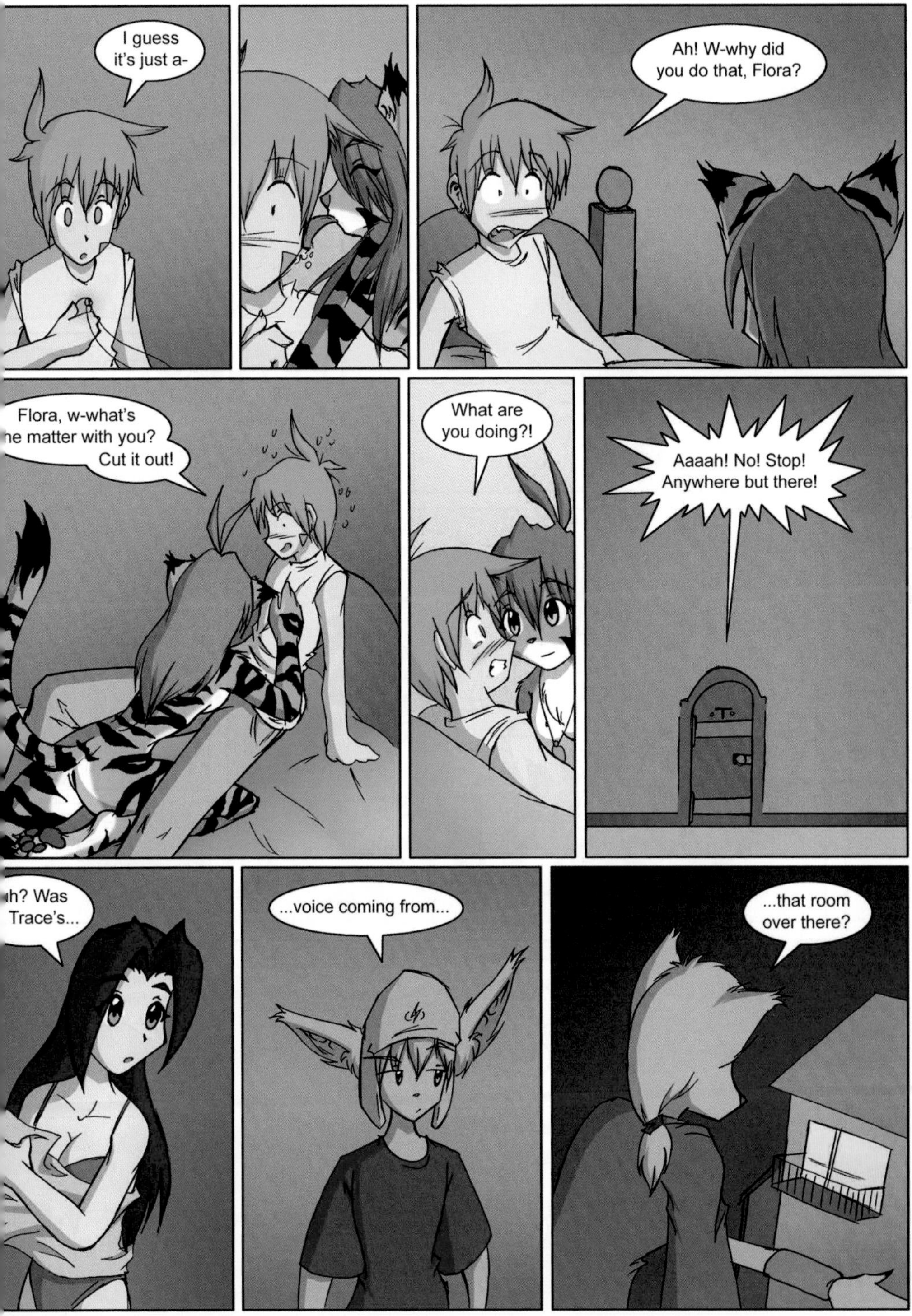
I guess it's just a-
Ah! W-why did you do that, Flora?
Flora, w-what's
he matter with you? Cut it out!
What are you doing?!
Aaaah! No! Stop! Anywhere but there!
h? Was Trace's...
...voice coming from...
...that room over there?

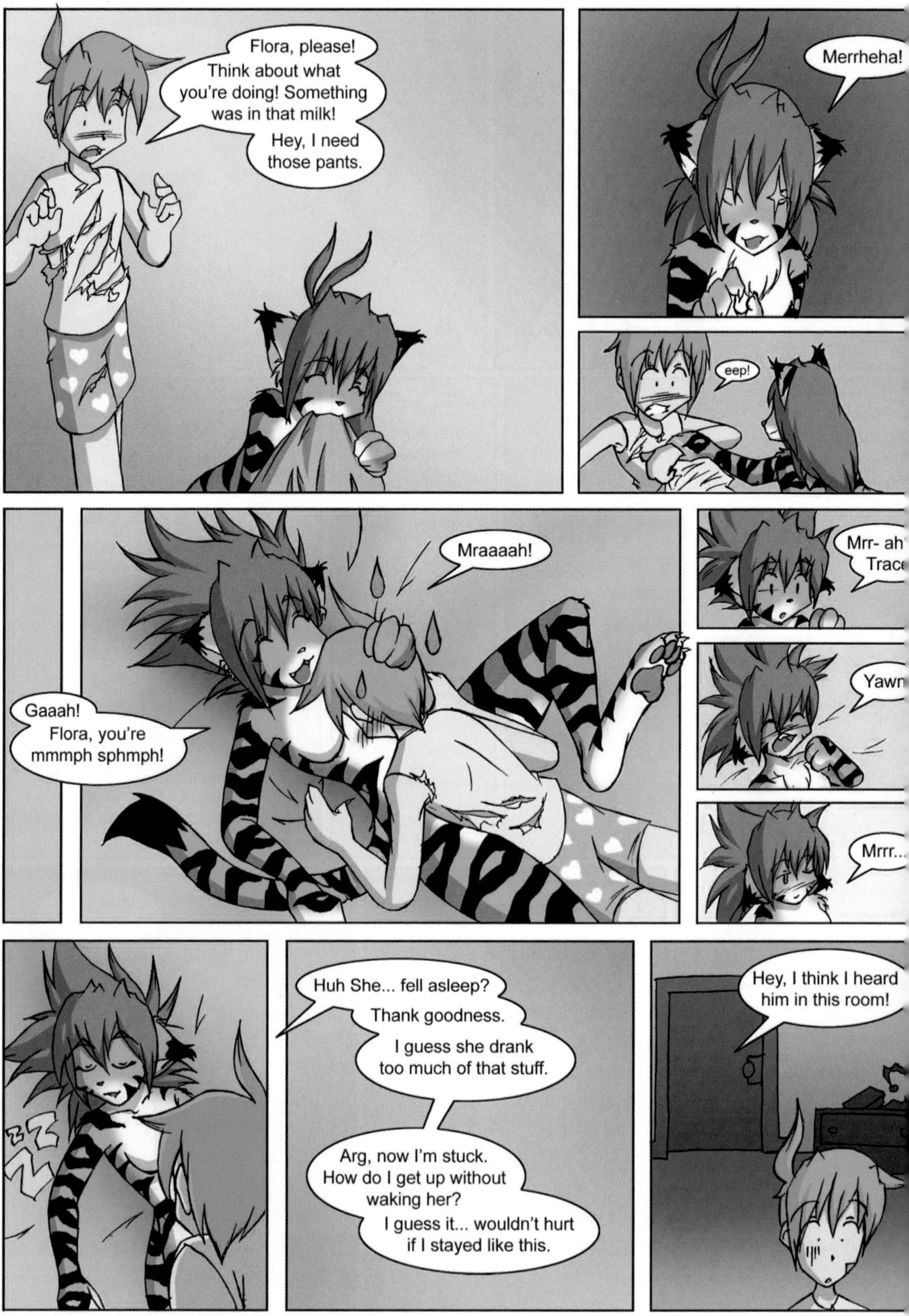
Flora, please! Think about what you're doing! Something was in that milk! Hey, I need those pants.
Merrheha!
eep!
Mraaaah!
Gaaah! Flora, you're mmmph sphmph!
Mrr- ah
Trac
Yawn
Mrrr...
Huh She... fell asleep? Thank goodness. I guess she drank too much of that stuff.
Arg, now I'm stuck. How do I get up without waking her? I guess it... wouldn't hurt if I stayed like this.
Hey, I think I heard him in this room!

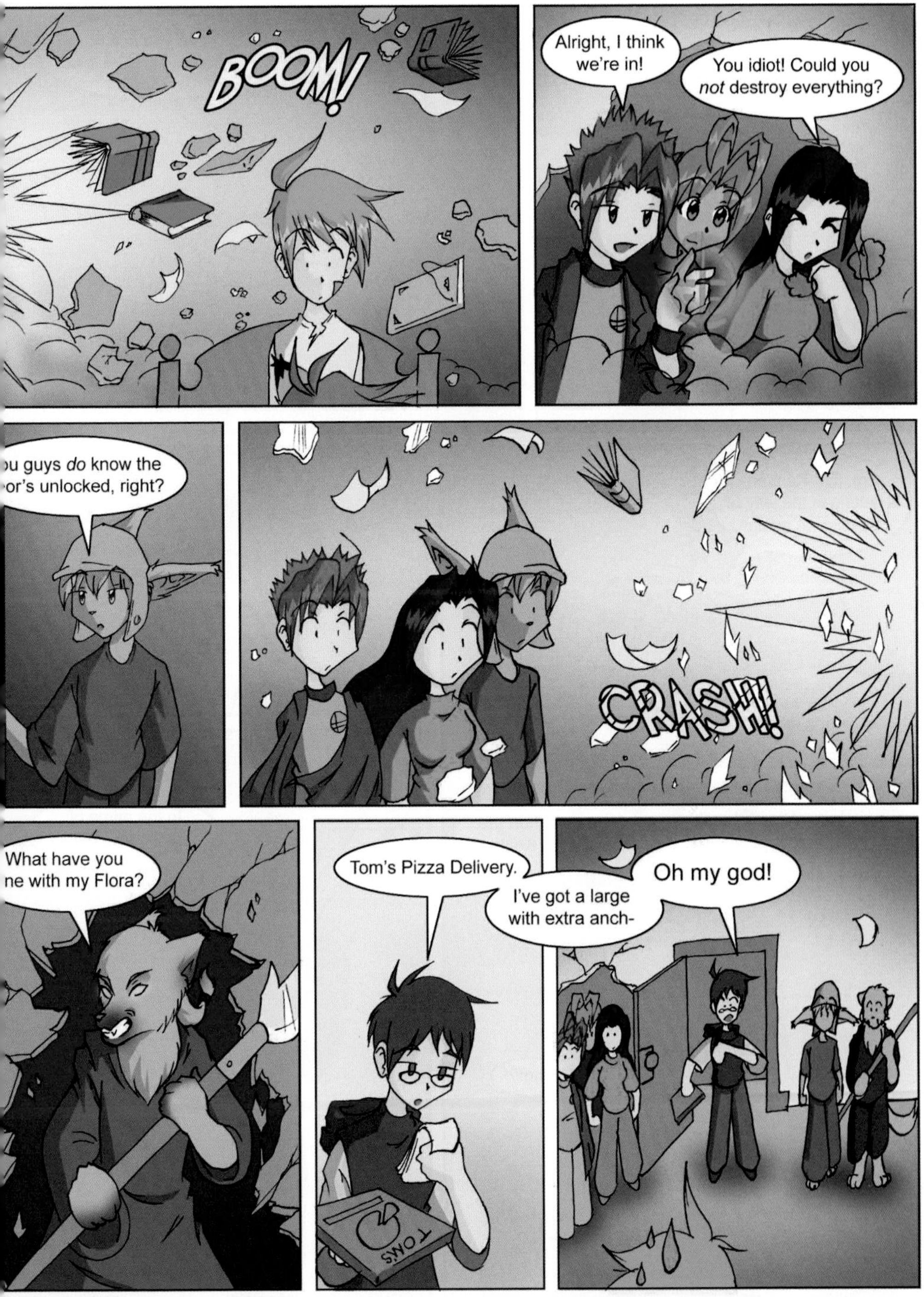
BOOM!
Alright, I think we're in!
You idiot! Could you *not* destroy everything?
ou guys *do* know the
or's unlocked, right?
CRASH!
What have you
ne with my Flora?
Tom's Pizza Delivery.
I've got a large with extra anch-
Oh my god!
TOM'S

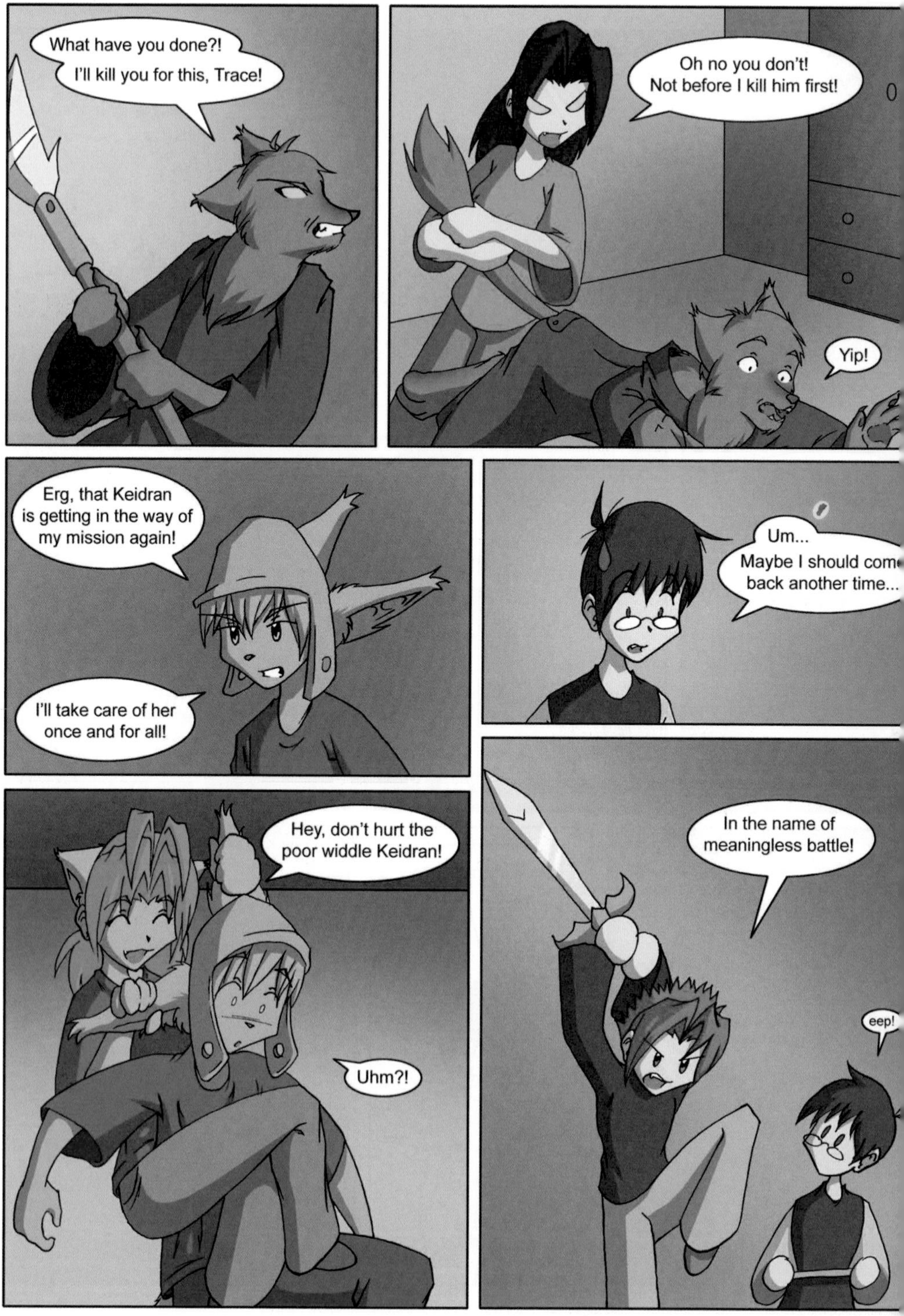
What have you done?!
I'll kill you for this, Trace!
Oh no you don't!
Not before I kill him first!
Yip!
Erg, that Keidran
is getting in the way of
my mission again!
I'll take care of her
once and for all!
Um...
Maybe I should com
back another time...
Hey, don't hurt the
poor widdle Keidran!
Uhm?!
In the name of
meaningless battle!
eep!

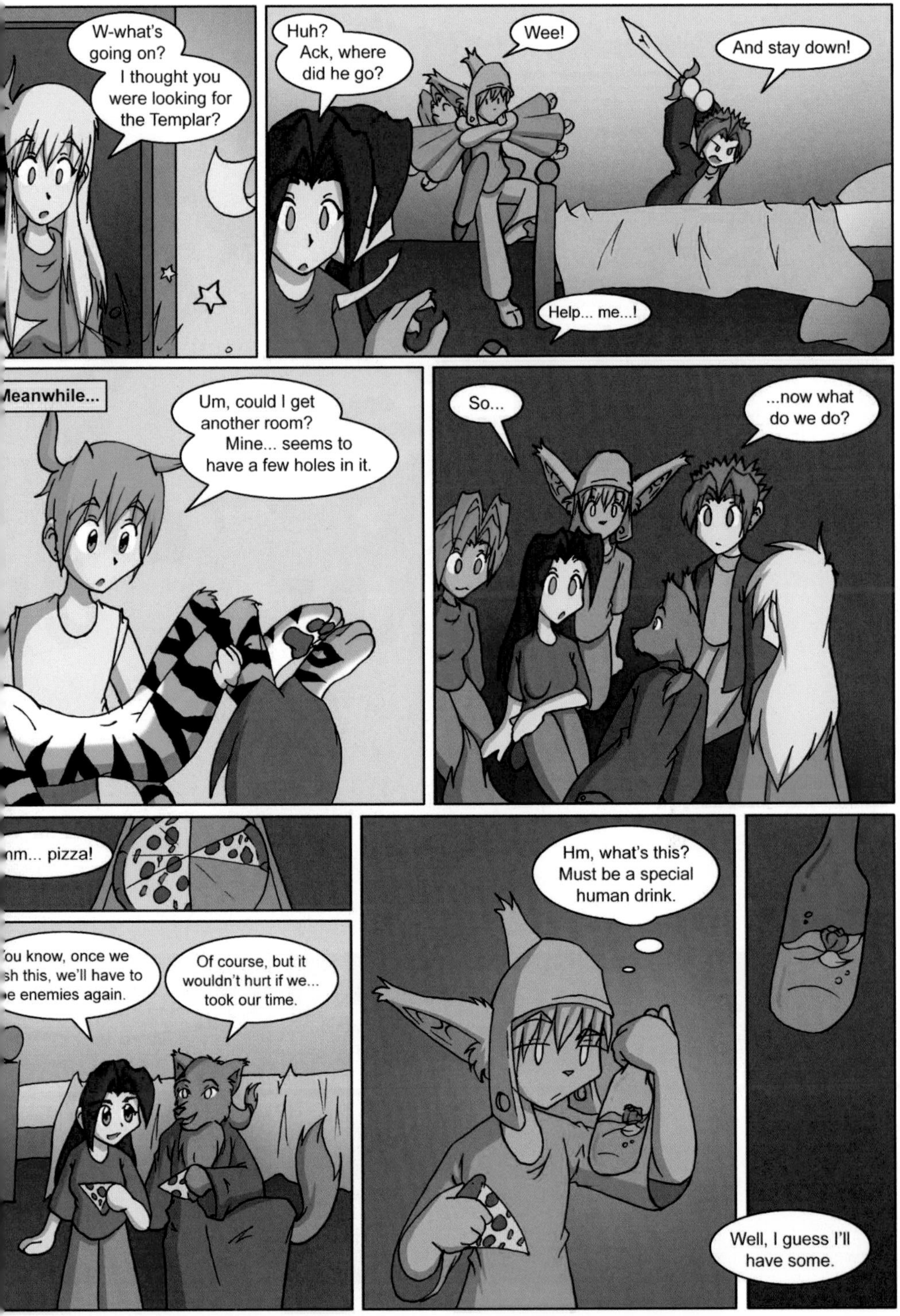
W-what's going on? I thought you were looking for the Templar?
Huh? Ack, where did he go?
Wee!
And stay down!
Help... me...!
Meanwhile...
Um, could I get another room? Mine... seems to have a few holes in it.
So...
...now what do we do?
nm... pizza!
ou know, once we sh this, we'll have to e enemies again.
Of course, but it wouldn't hurt if we... took our time.
Hm, what's this? Must be a special human drink.
Well, I guess I'll have some.

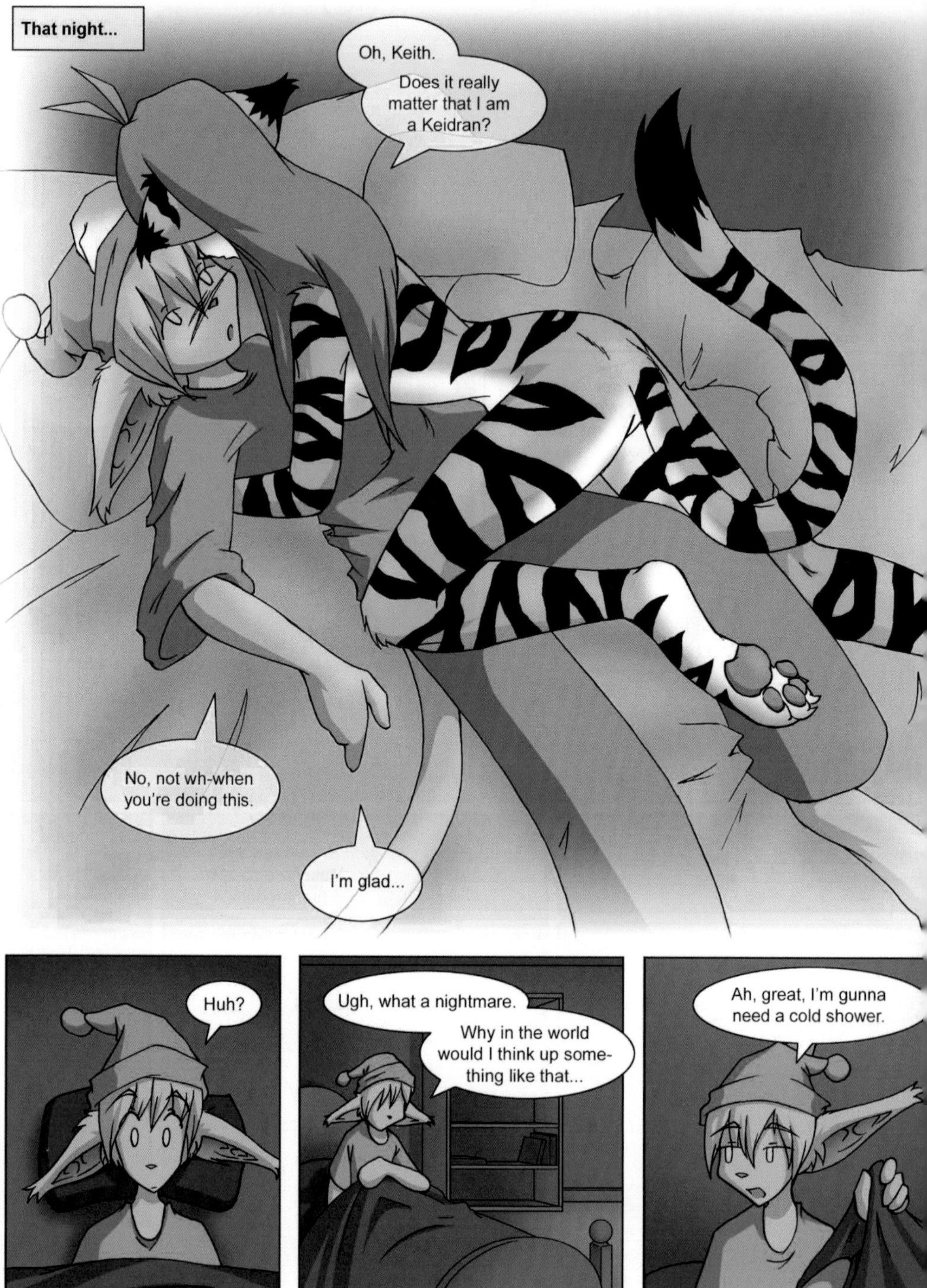
That night...
Oh, Keith.
Does it really matter that I am a Keidran?
No, not wh-when you're doing this.
I'm glad...
Huh?
Ugh, what a nightmare.
Why in the world would I think up some-thing like that...
Ah, great, I'm gunna need a cold shower.

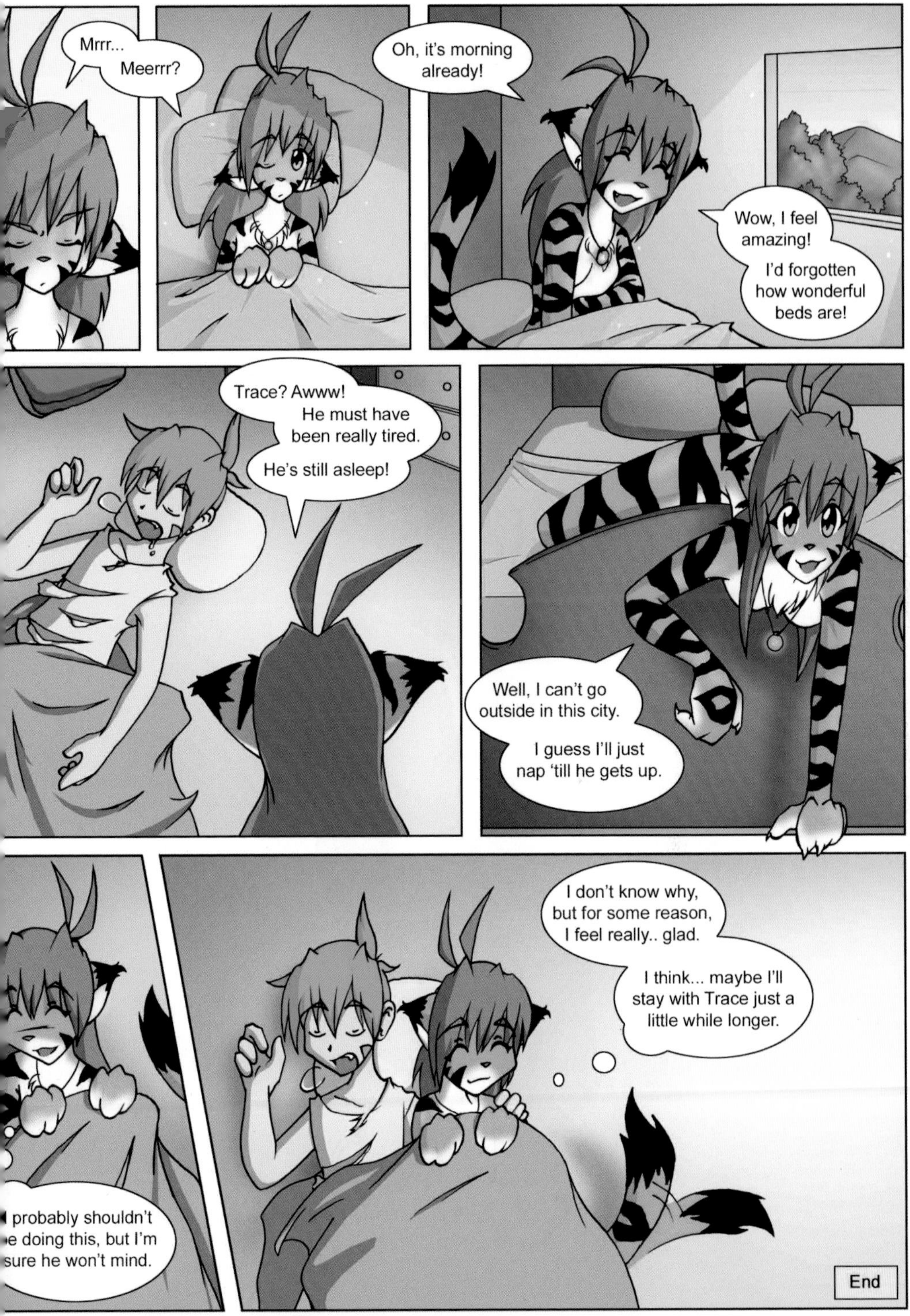
Mrrr... Meerrr?
Oh, it's morning already!
Wow, I feel amazing!
I'd forgotten how wonderful beds are!
Trace? Awww!
He must have been really tired.
He's still asleep!
Well, I can't go outside in this city.
I guess I'll just nap 'till he gets up.
probably shouldn't e doing this, but I'm sure he won't mind.
I don't know why, but for some reason, I feel really.. glad.
I think... maybe I'll stay with Trace just a little while longer.
End

TWOKINDS

Chapter Four

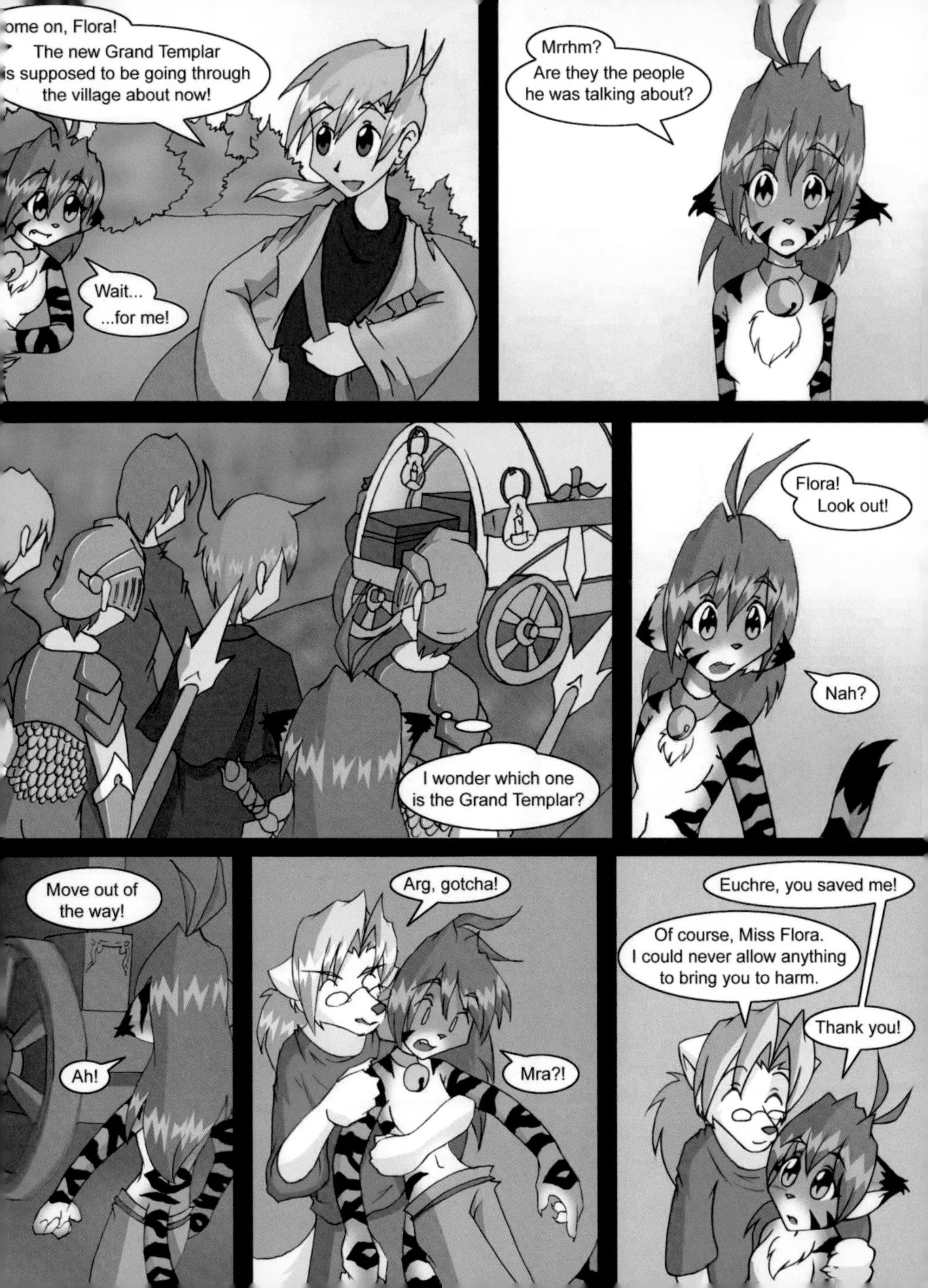
ome on, Flora! The new Grand Templar is supposed to be going through the village about now!
Wait... ...for me!
Mrrhm? Are they the people he was talking about?
I wonder which one is the Grand Templar?
Flora! Look out!
Nah?
Move out of the way!
Ah!
Arg, gotcha!
Mra?!
Euchre, you saved me!
Of course, Miss Flora. I could never allow anything to bring you to harm.
Thank you!

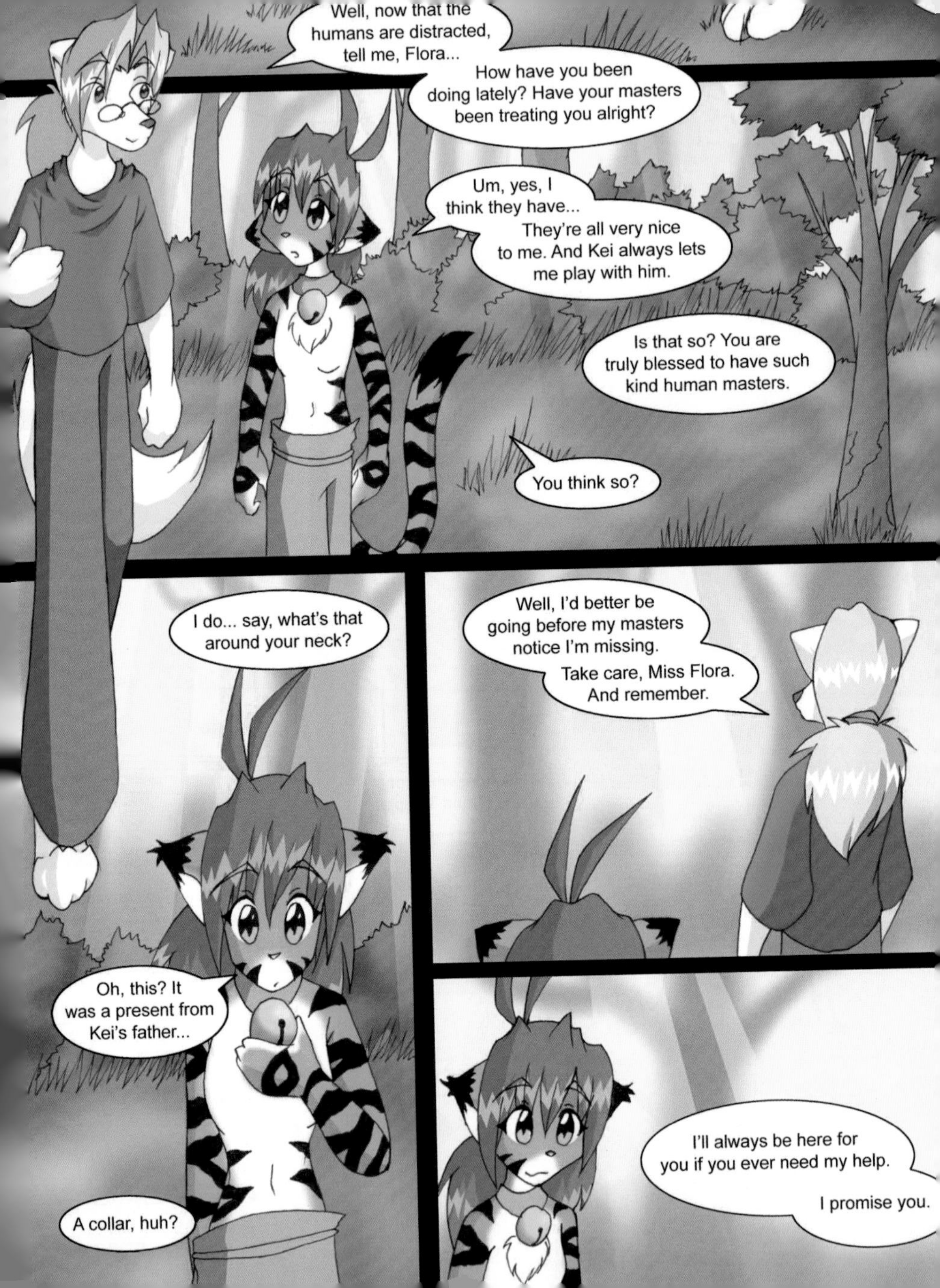
Well, now that the humans are distracted, tell me, Flora...
How have you been doing lately? Have your masters been treating you alright?
Um, yes, I think they have...
They're all very nice to me. And Kei always lets me play with him.
Is that so? You are truly blessed to have such kind human masters.
You think so?
I do... say, what's that around your neck?
Oh, this? It was a present from Kei's father...
A collar, huh?
Well, I'd better be going before my masters notice I'm missing.
Take care, Miss Flora. And remember.
I'll always be here for you if you ever need my help.
I promise you.

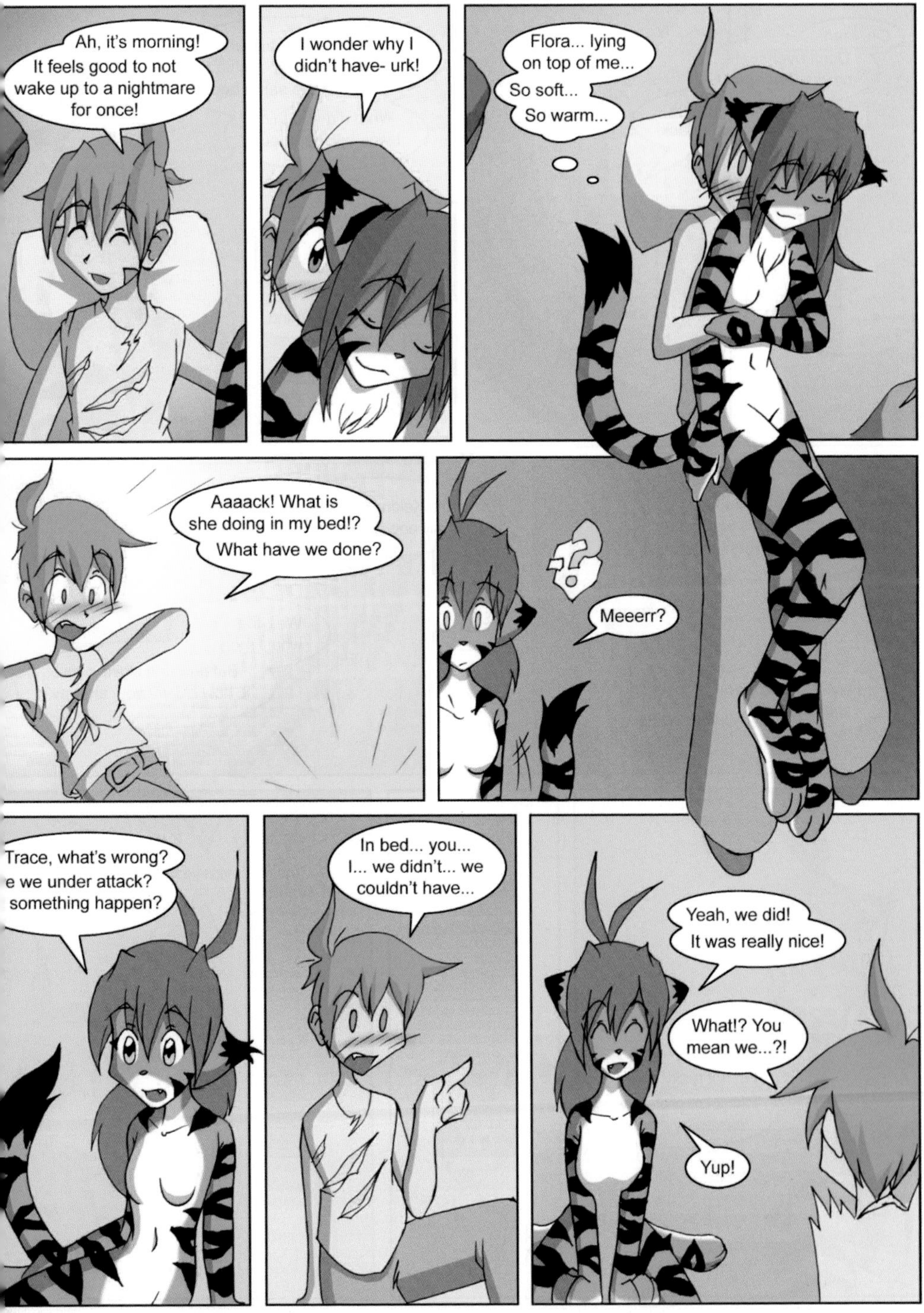
Ah, it's morning! It feels good to not wake up to a nightmare for once!
I wonder why I didn't have- urk!
Flora... lying on top of me...
So soft...
So warm...
Aaaack! What is she doing in my bed!? What have we done?
Meeerr?
Trace, what's wrong?
e we under attack?
something happen?
In bed... you... I... we didn't... we couldn't have...
Yeah, we did! It was really nice!
What!? You mean we...?!
Yup!

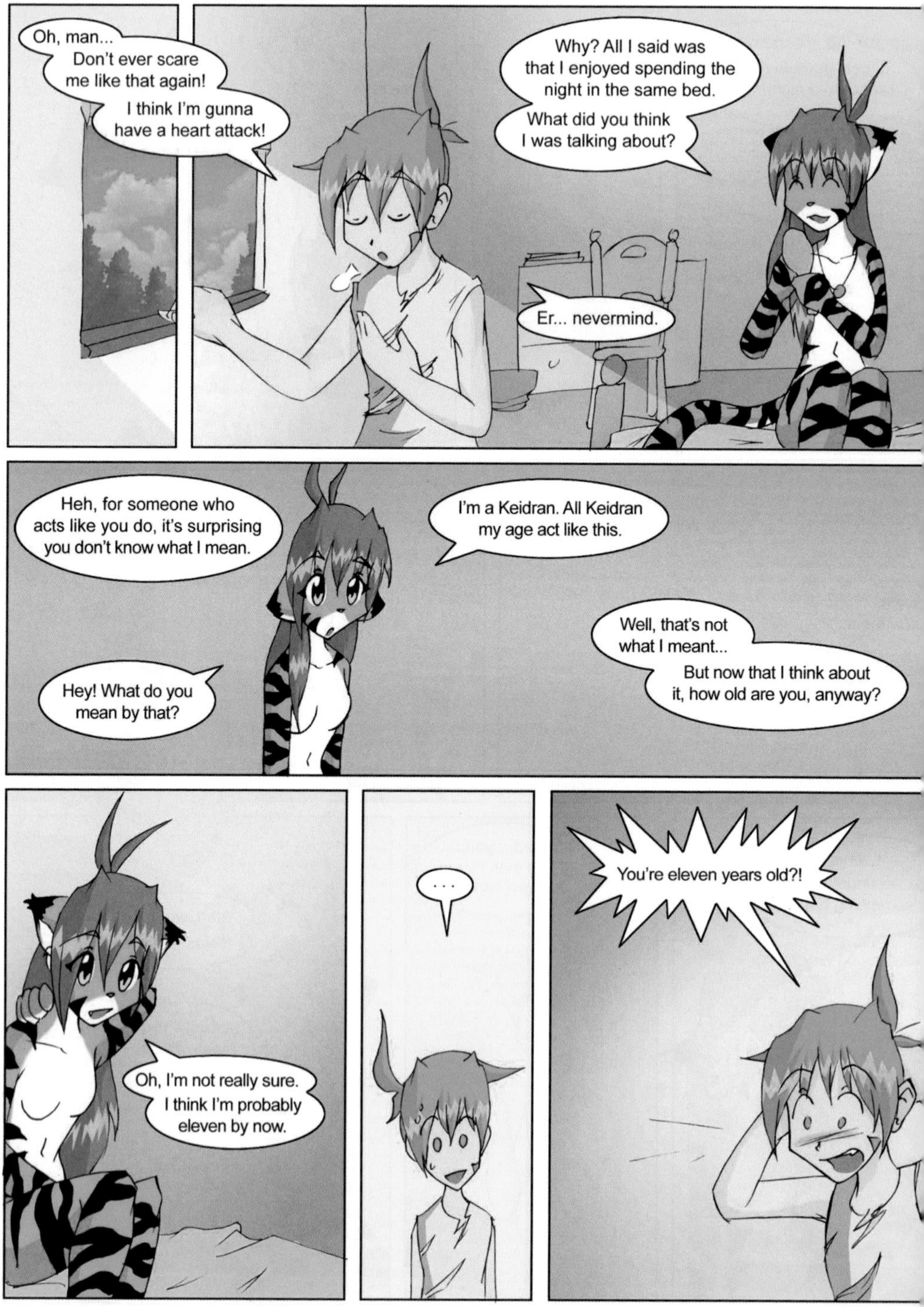
Oh, man...
Don't ever scare me like that again!
I think I'm gunna have a heart attack!
Why? All I said was that I enjoyed spending the night in the same bed.
What did you think I was talking about?
Er... nevermind.
Heh, for someone who acts like you do, it's surprising you don't know what I mean.
I'm a Keidran. All Keidran my age act like this.
Hey! What do you mean by that?
Well, that's not what I meant...
But now that I think about it, how old are you, anyway?
Oh, I'm not really sure.
I think I'm probably eleven by now.
...
You're eleven years old?!

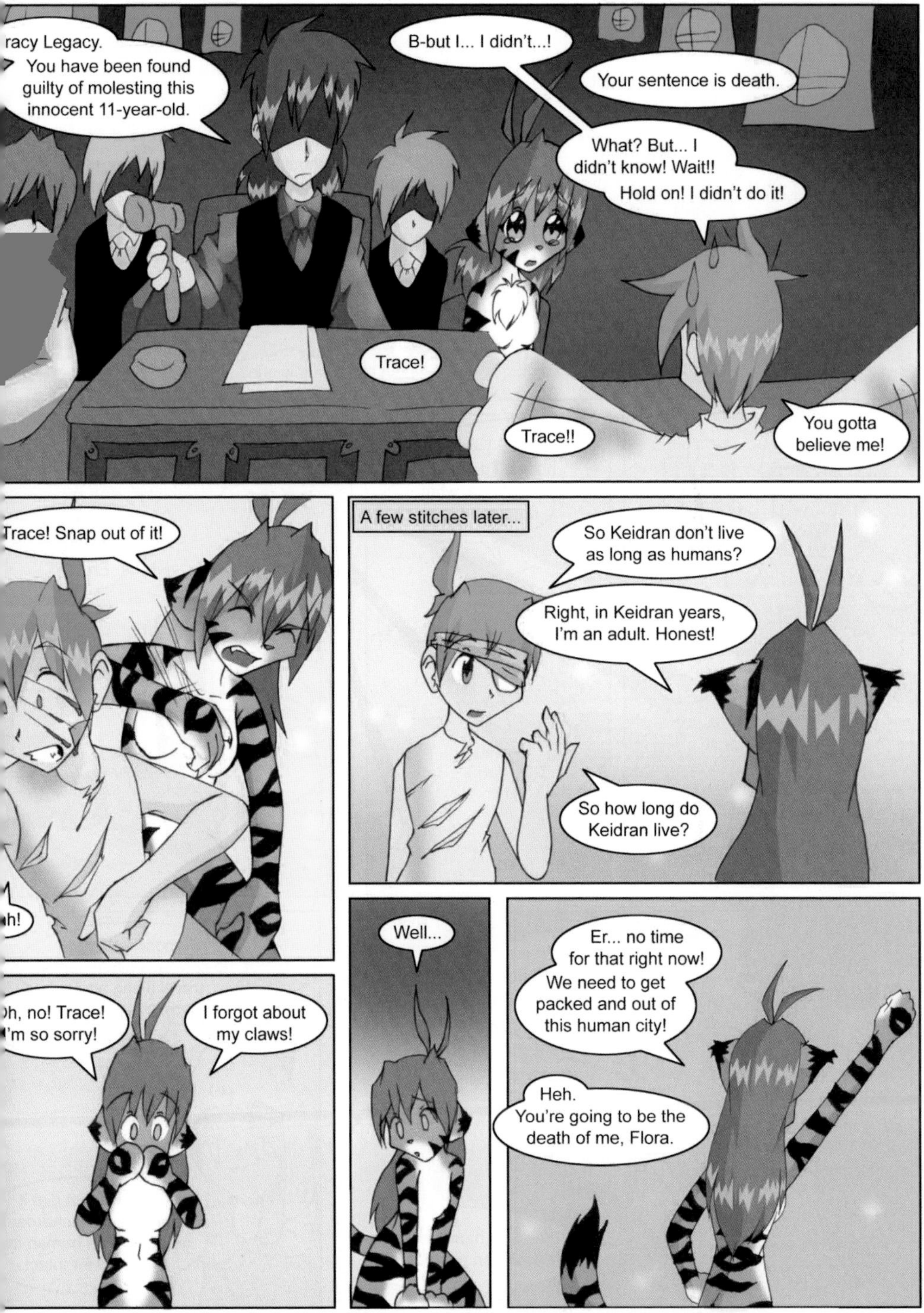
racy Legacy.
You have been found guilty of molesting this innocent 11-year-old.
B-but I... I didn't...!
Your sentence is death.
What? But... I didn't know! Wait!!
Hold on! I didn't do it!
Trace!
Trace!!
You gotta believe me!
Trace! Snap out of it!
h!
A few stitches later...
So Keidran don't live as long as humans?
Right, in Keidran years, I'm an adult. Honest!
So how long do Keidran live?
h, no! Trace! 'm so sorry!
I forgot about my claws!
Well...
Er... no time for that right now!
We need to get packed and out of this human city!
Heh. You're going to be the death of me, Flora.

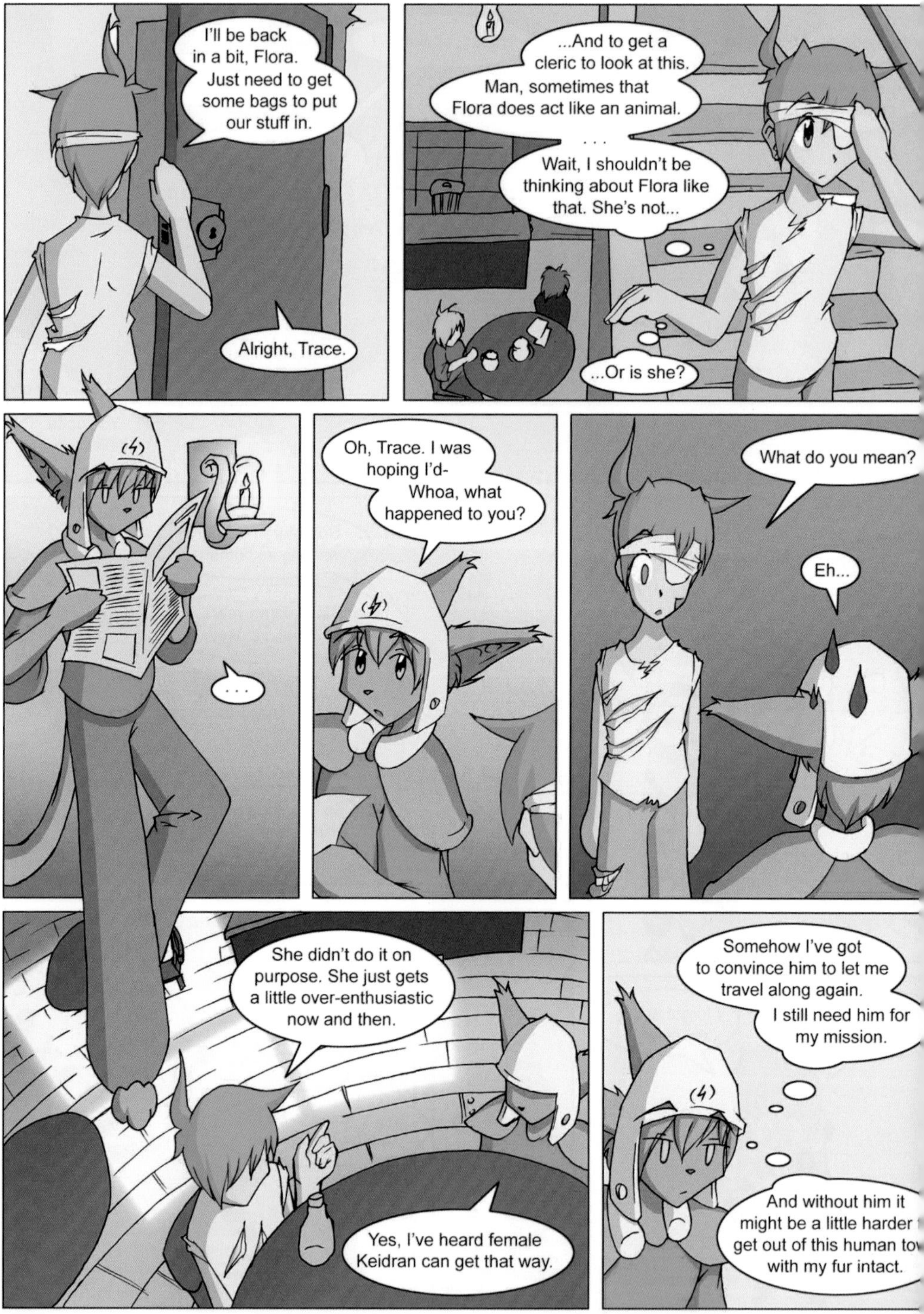
I'll be back in a bit, Flora. Just need to get some bags to put our stuff in.
Alright, Trace.
...And to get a cleric to look at this. Man, sometimes that Flora does act like an animal.
. . .
Wait, I shouldn't be thinking about Flora like that. She's not...
...Or is she?
. . .
Oh, Trace. I was hoping I'd- Whoa, what happened to you?
What do you mean?
Eh...
She didn't do it on purpose. She just gets a little over-enthusiastic now and then.
Yes, I've heard female Keidran can get that way.
Somehow I've got to convince him to let me travel along again. I still need him for my mission.
And without him it might be a little harder to get out of this human town with my fur intact.

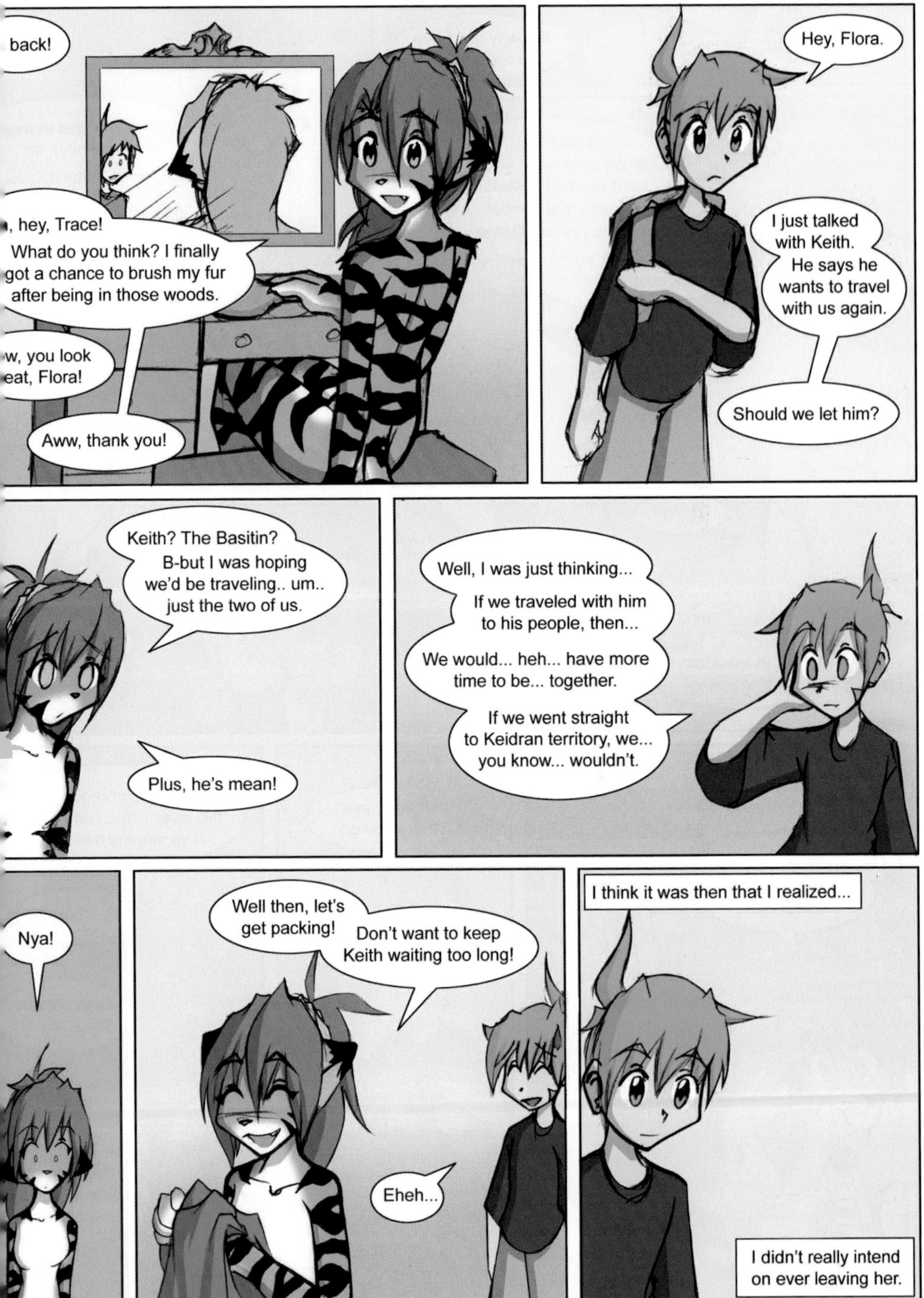
back!
, hey, Trace!
What do you think? I finally got a chance to brush my fur after being in those woods.
w, you look eat, Flora!
Aww, thank you!
Hey, Flora.
I just talked with Keith.
He says he wants to travel with us again.
Should we let him?
Keith? The Basitin?
B-but I was hoping we'd be traveling.. um.. just the two of us.
Plus, he's mean!
Well, I was just thinking...
If we traveled with him to his people, then...
We would... heh... have more time to be... together.
If we went straight to Keidran territory, we... you know... wouldn't.
Nya!
Well then, let's get packing!
Don't want to keep Keith waiting too long!
Eheh...
I think it was then that I realized...
I didn't really intend on ever leaving her.

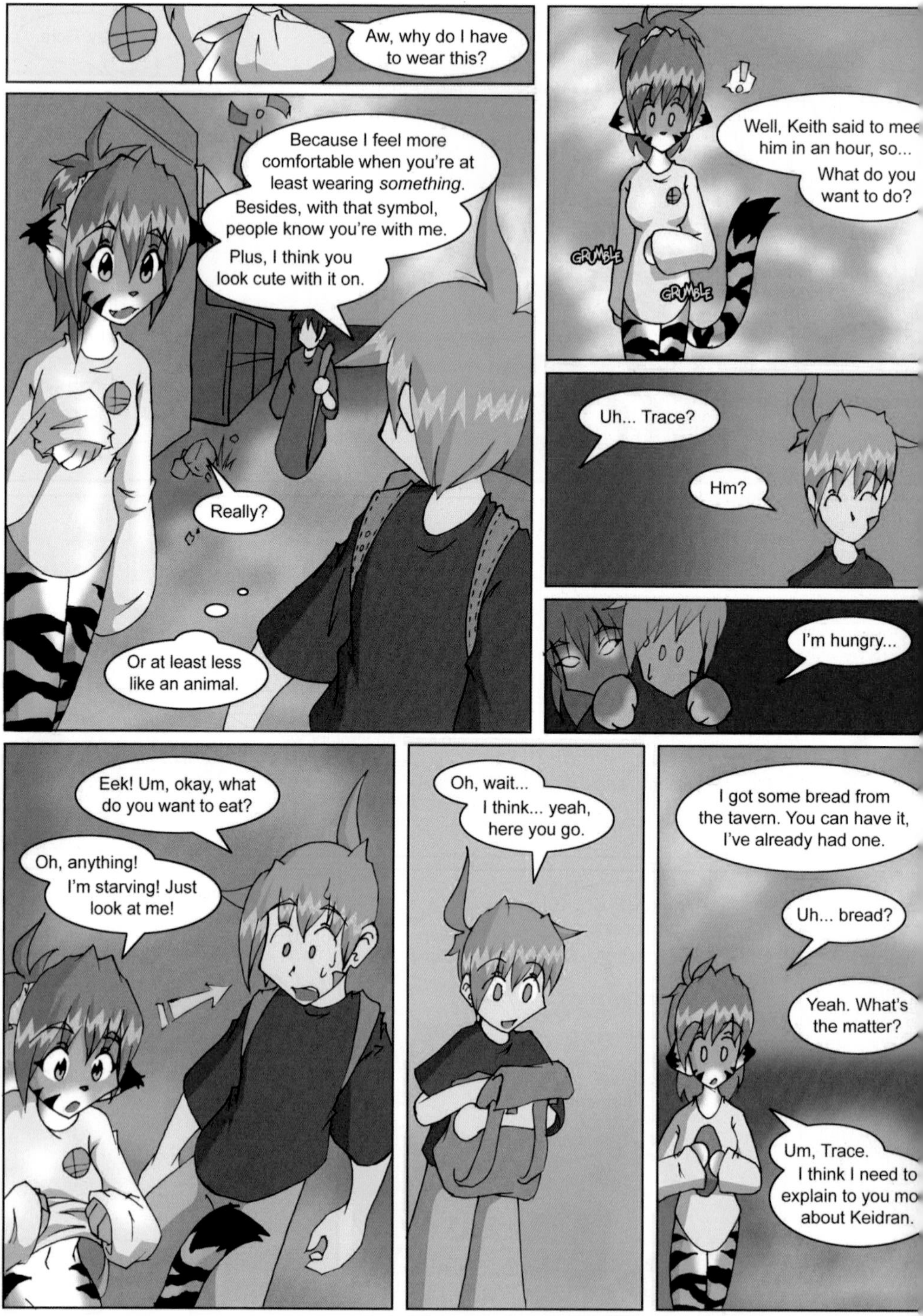
Aw, why do I have to wear this?
Because I feel more comfortable when you're at least wearing *something*.
Besides, with that symbol, people know you're with me.
Plus, I think you look cute with it on.
Really?
Or at least less like an animal.
!
Well, Keith said to mee him in an hour, so...
What do you want to do?
GRUMBLE
GRUMBLE
Uh... Trace?
Hm?
I'm hungry...
Eek! Um, okay, what do you want to eat?
Oh, anything! I'm starving! Just look at me!
Oh, wait... I think... yeah, here you go.
I got some bread from the tavern. You can have it, I've already had one.
Uh... bread?
Yeah. What's the matter?
Um, Trace. I think I need to explain to you mo about Keidran.

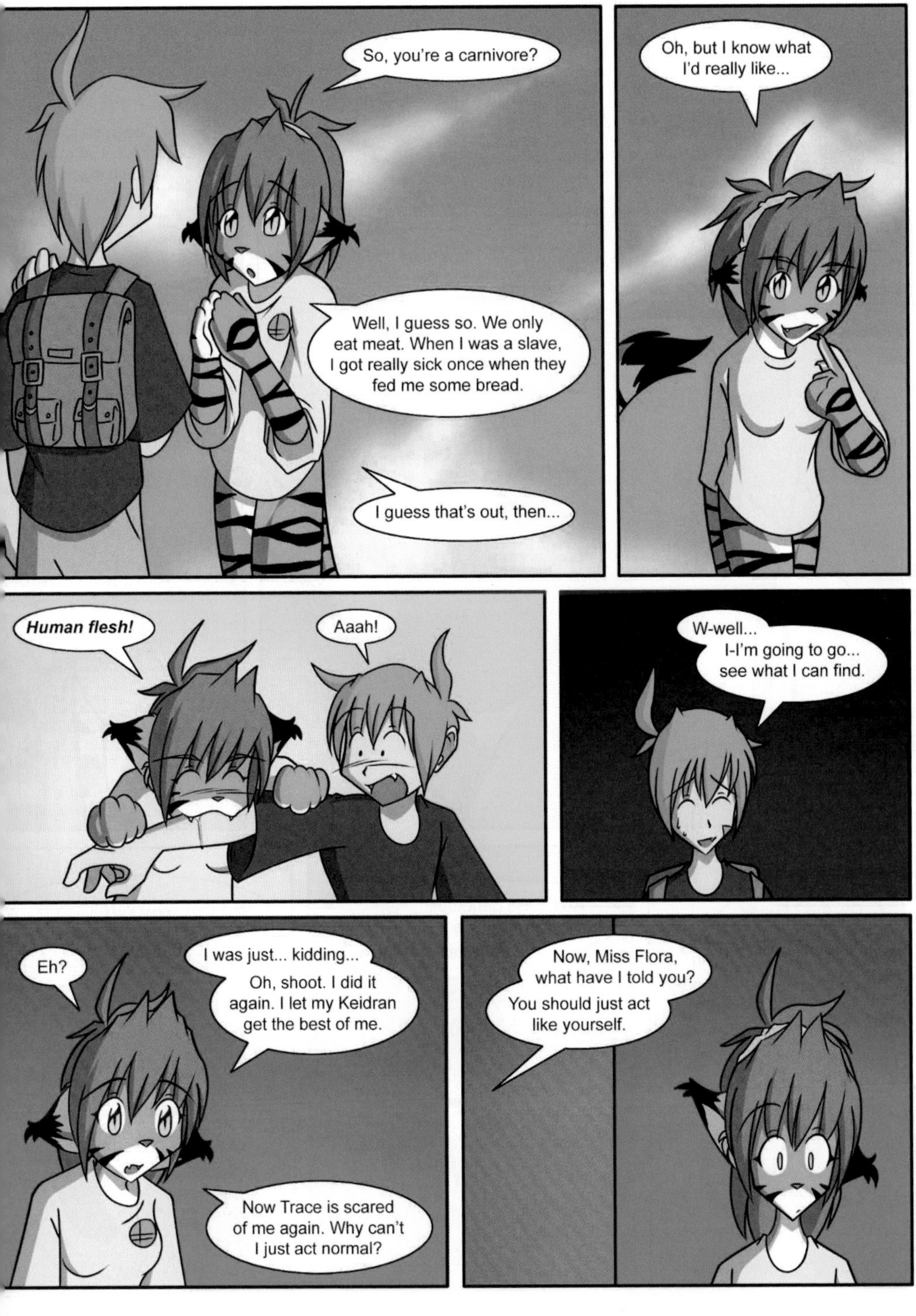
So, you're a carnivore?
Well, I guess so. We only eat meat. When I was a slave, I got really sick once when they fed me some bread.
I guess that's out, then...
Oh, but I know what I'd really like...
Human flesh!
Aaah!
W-well... I-I'm going to go... see what I can find.
Eh?
I was just... kidding...
Oh, shoot. I did it again. I let my Keidran get the best of me.
Now Trace is scared of me again. Why can't I just act normal?
Now, Miss Flora, what have I told you?
You should just act like yourself.

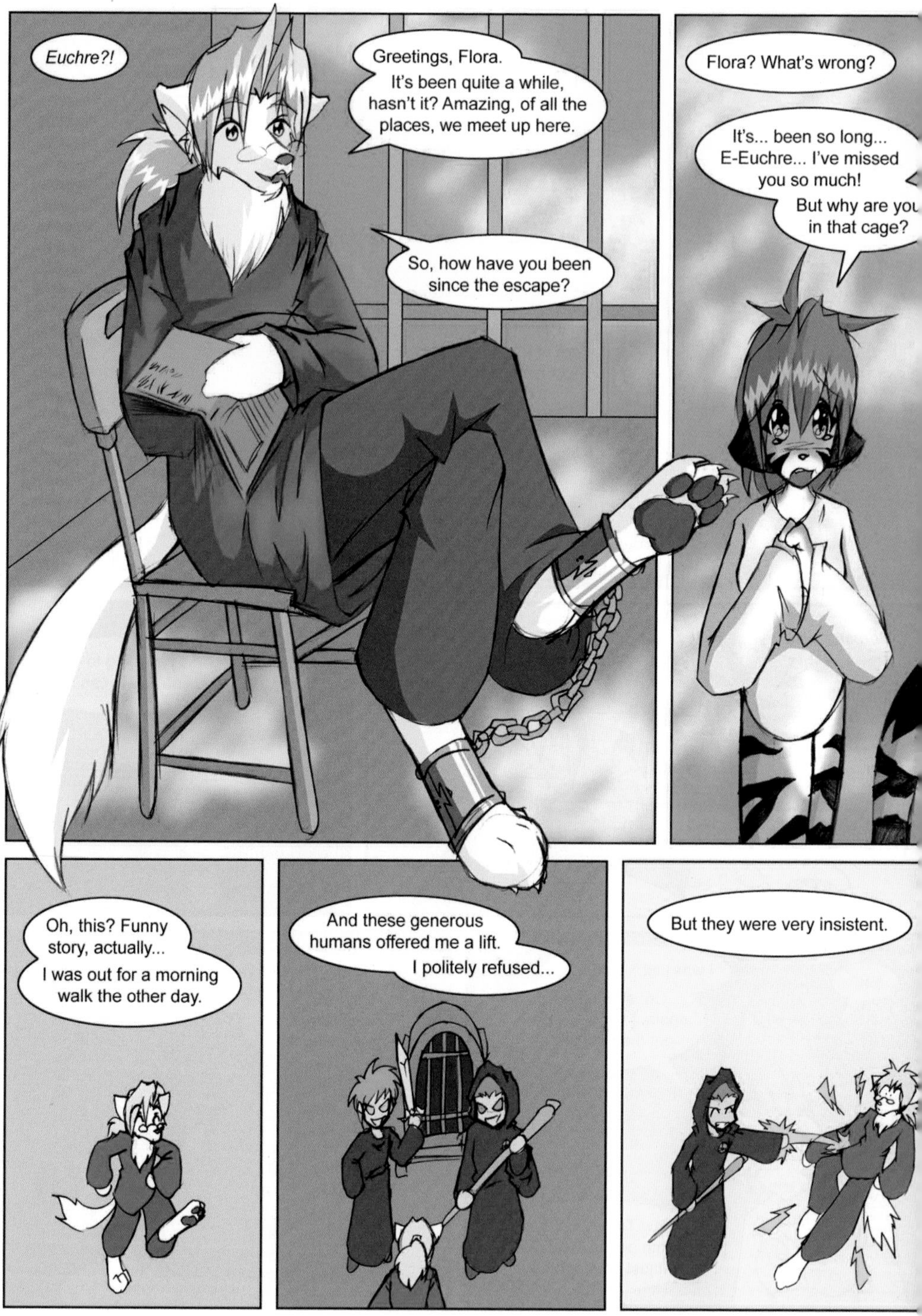
Euchre?!
Greetings, Flora.
It's been quite a while, hasn't it? Amazing, of all the places, we meet up here.
So, how have you been since the escape?
Flora? What's wrong?
It's... been so long... E-Euchre... I've missed you so much!
But why are you in that cage?
Oh, this? Funny story, actually...
I was out for a morning walk the other day.
And these generous humans offered me a lift.
I politely refused...
But they were very insistent.

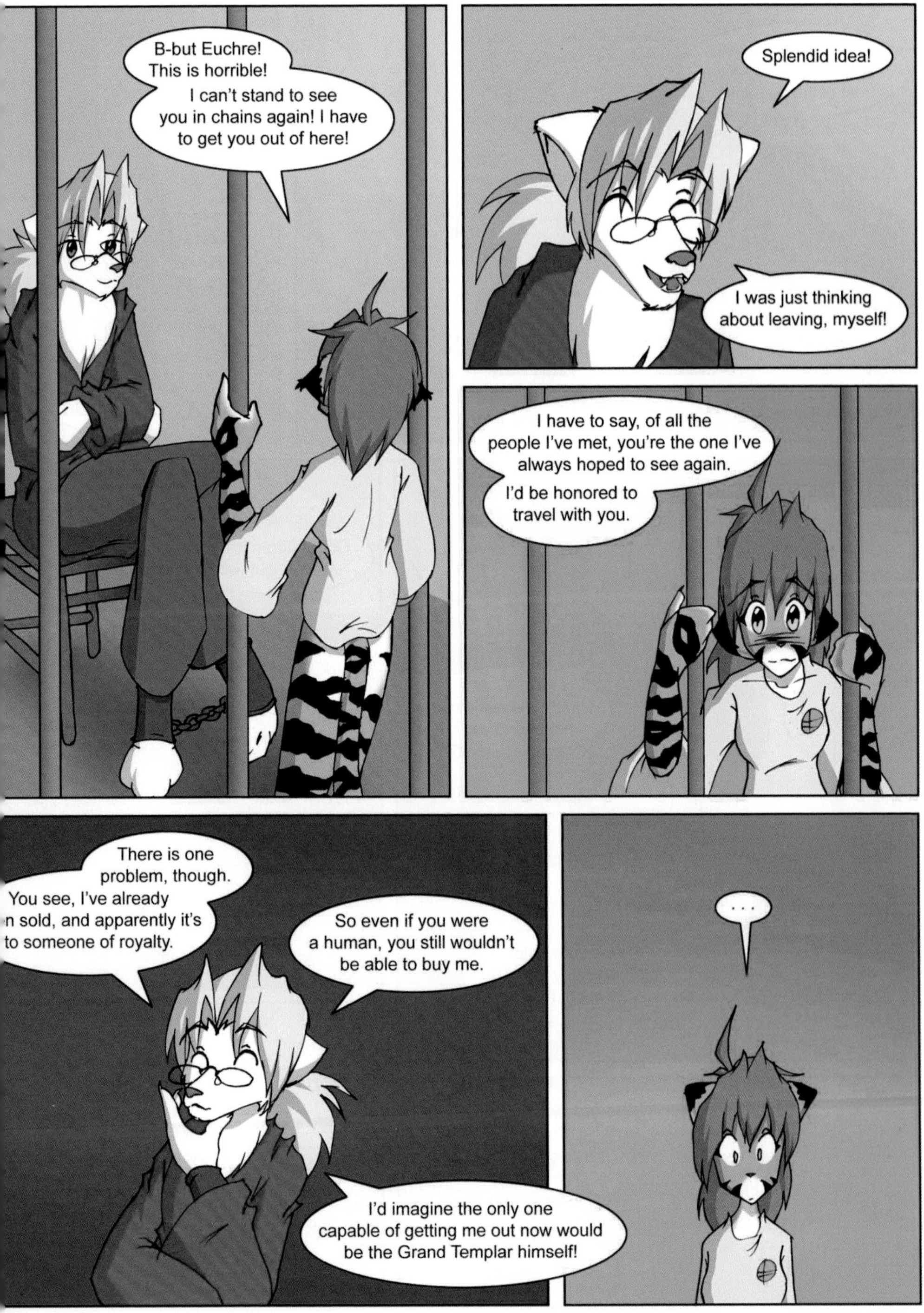
B-but Euchre! This is horrible!
I can't stand to see you in chains again! I have to get you out of here!
Splendid idea!
I was just thinking about leaving, myself!
I have to say, of all the people I've met, you're the one I've always hoped to see again.
I'd be honored to travel with you.
There is one problem, though.
You see, I've already n sold, and apparently it's to someone of royalty.
So even if you were a human, you still wouldn't be able to buy me.
I'd imagine the only one capable of getting me out now would be the Grand Templar himself!
. . .

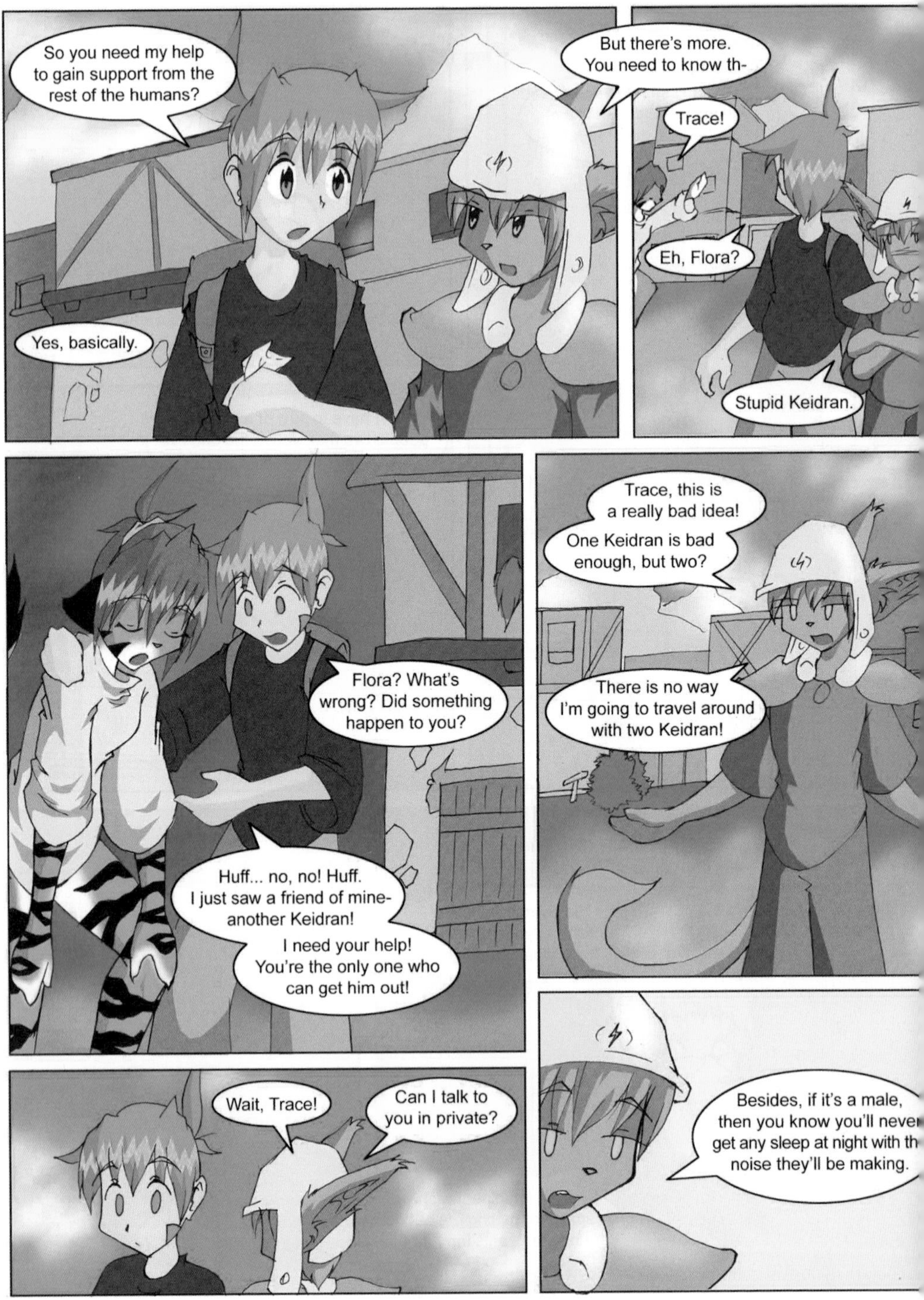

So you need my help to gain support from the rest of the humans?
Yes, basically.
But there's more. You need to know th-
Trace!
Eh, Flora?
Stupid Keidran.
Flora? What's wrong? Did something happen to you?
Huff... no, no! Huff. I just saw a friend of mine- another Keidran!
I need your help! You're the only one who can get him out!
Trace, this is a really bad idea!
One Keidran is bad enough, but two?
There is no way I'm going to travel around with two Keidran!
Wait, Trace!
Can I talk to you in private?
Besides, if it's a male, then you know you'll neve
get any sleep at night with th
noise they'll be making.

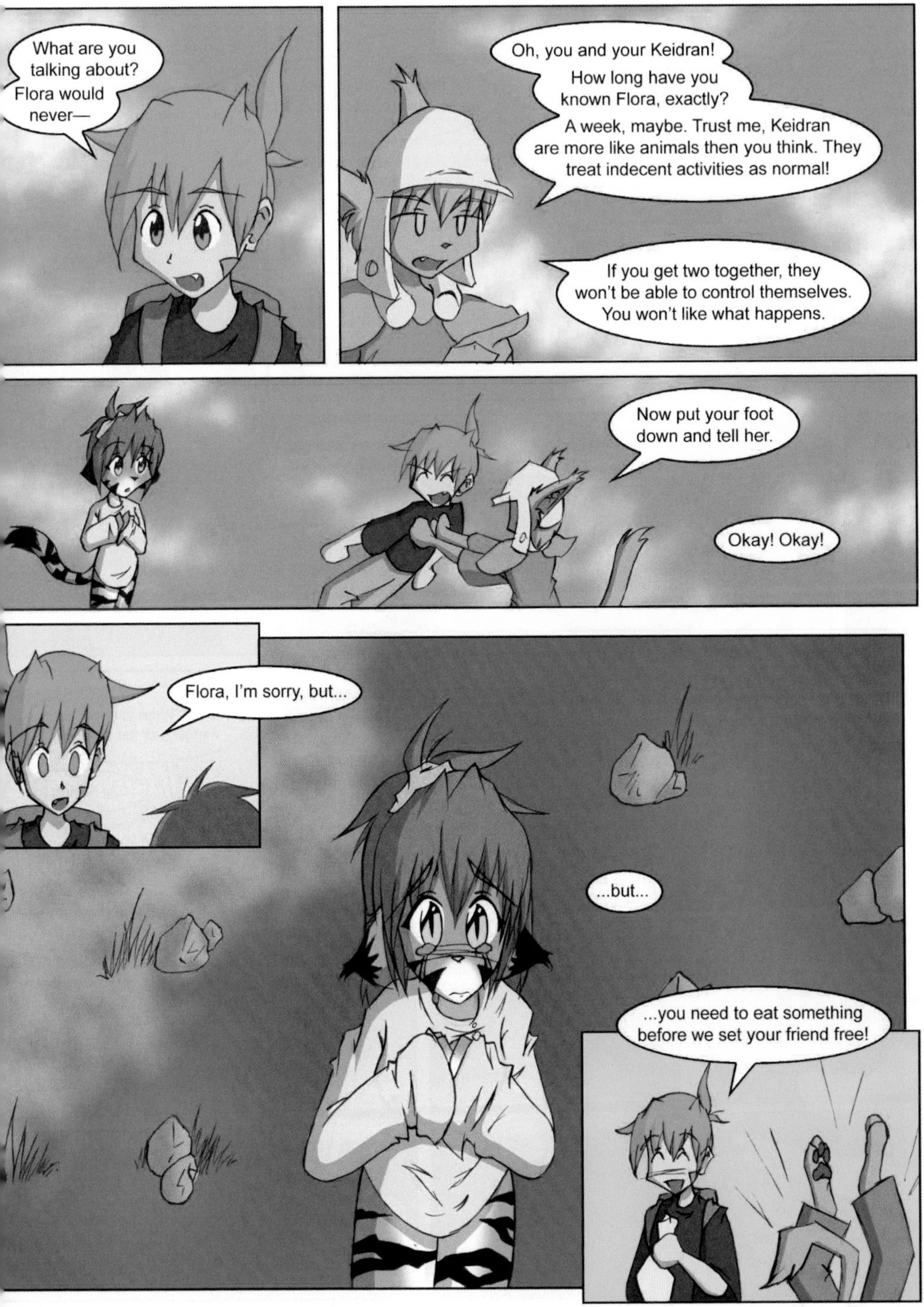
What are you talking about? Flora would never—
Oh, you and your Keidran!
How long have you known Flora, exactly?
A week, maybe. Trust me, Keidran are more like animals then you think. They treat indecent activities as normal!
If you get two together, they won't be able to control themselves. You won't like what happens.
Now put your foot down and tell her.
Okay! Okay!
Flora, I'm sorry, but...
...but...
...you need to eat something before we set your friend free!

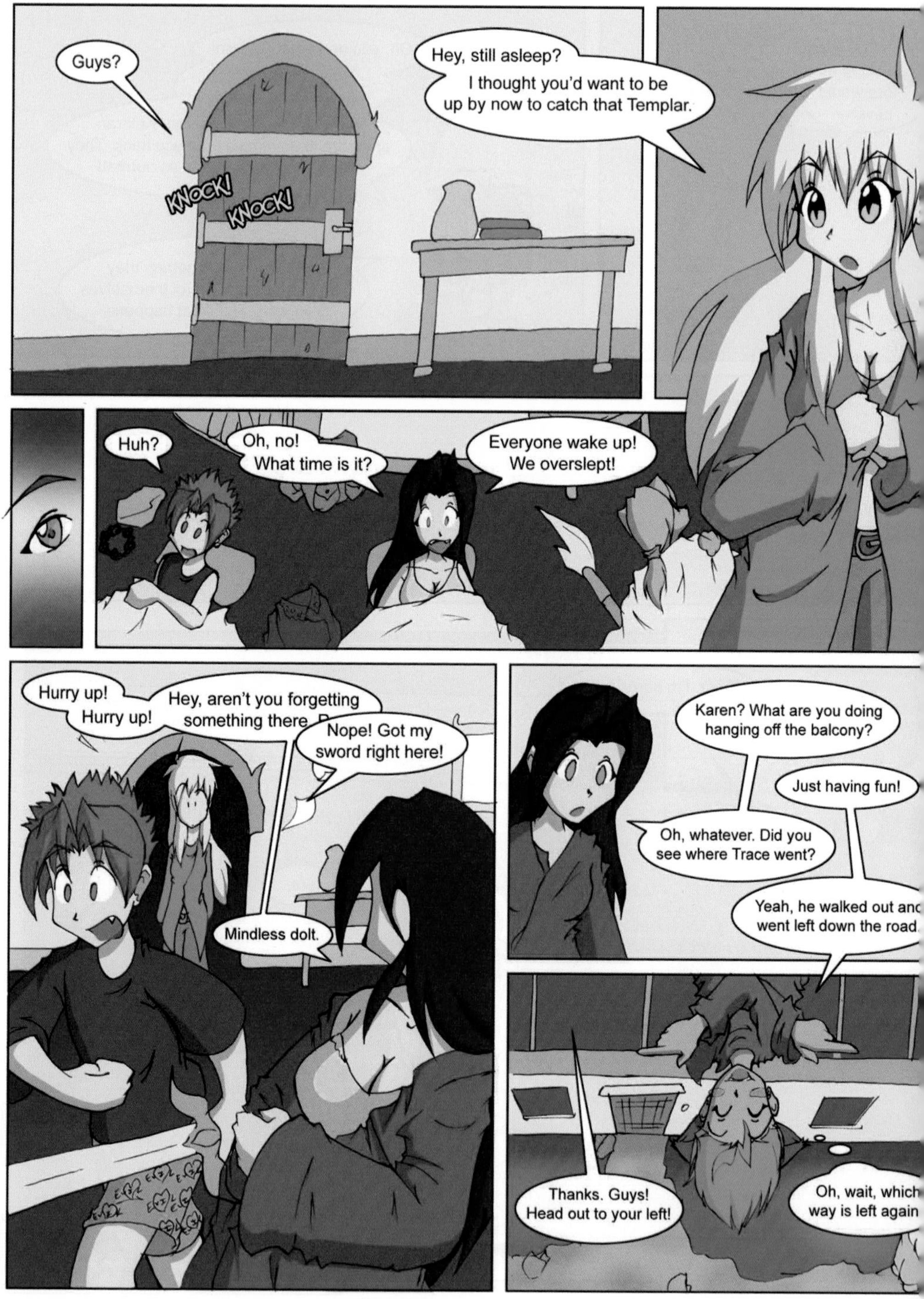
Guys?
KNOCK!
KNOCK!
Hey, still asleep?
I thought you'd want to be up by now to catch that Templar.
Huh?
Oh, no! What time is it?
Everyone wake up! We overslept!
Hurry up! Hurry up!
Hey, aren't you forgetting something there,
Nope! Got my sword right here!
Mindless dolt.
Karen? What are you doing hanging off the balcony?
Just having fun!
Oh, whatever. Did you see where Trace went?
Yeah, he walked out and went left down the road.
Thanks. Guys! Head out to your left!
Oh, wait, which way is left again

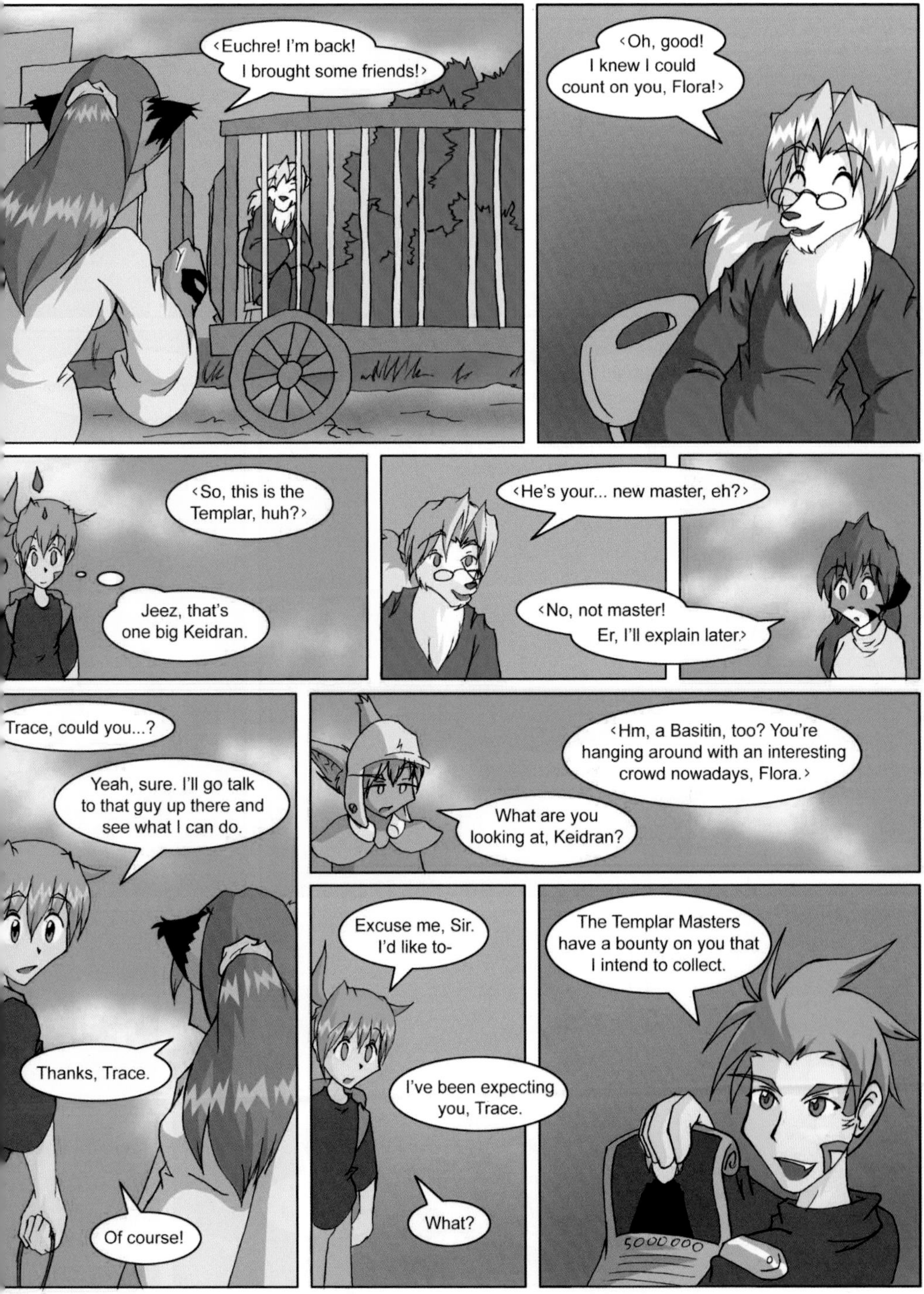
‹Euchre! I'm back! I brought some friends!›
‹Oh, good! I knew I could count on you, Flora!›
‹So, this is the Templar, huh?›
Jeez, that's one big Keidran.
‹He's your... new master, eh?›
‹No, not master! Er, I'll explain later›
Trace, could you...?
Yeah, sure. I'll go talk to that guy up there and see what I can do.
Thanks, Trace.
Of course!
‹Hm, a Basitin, too? You're hanging around with an interesting crowd nowadays, Flora.›
What are you looking at, Keidran?
Excuse me, Sir. I'd like to-
I've been expecting you, Trace.
What?
The Templar Masters have a bounty on you that I intend to collect.
5000000

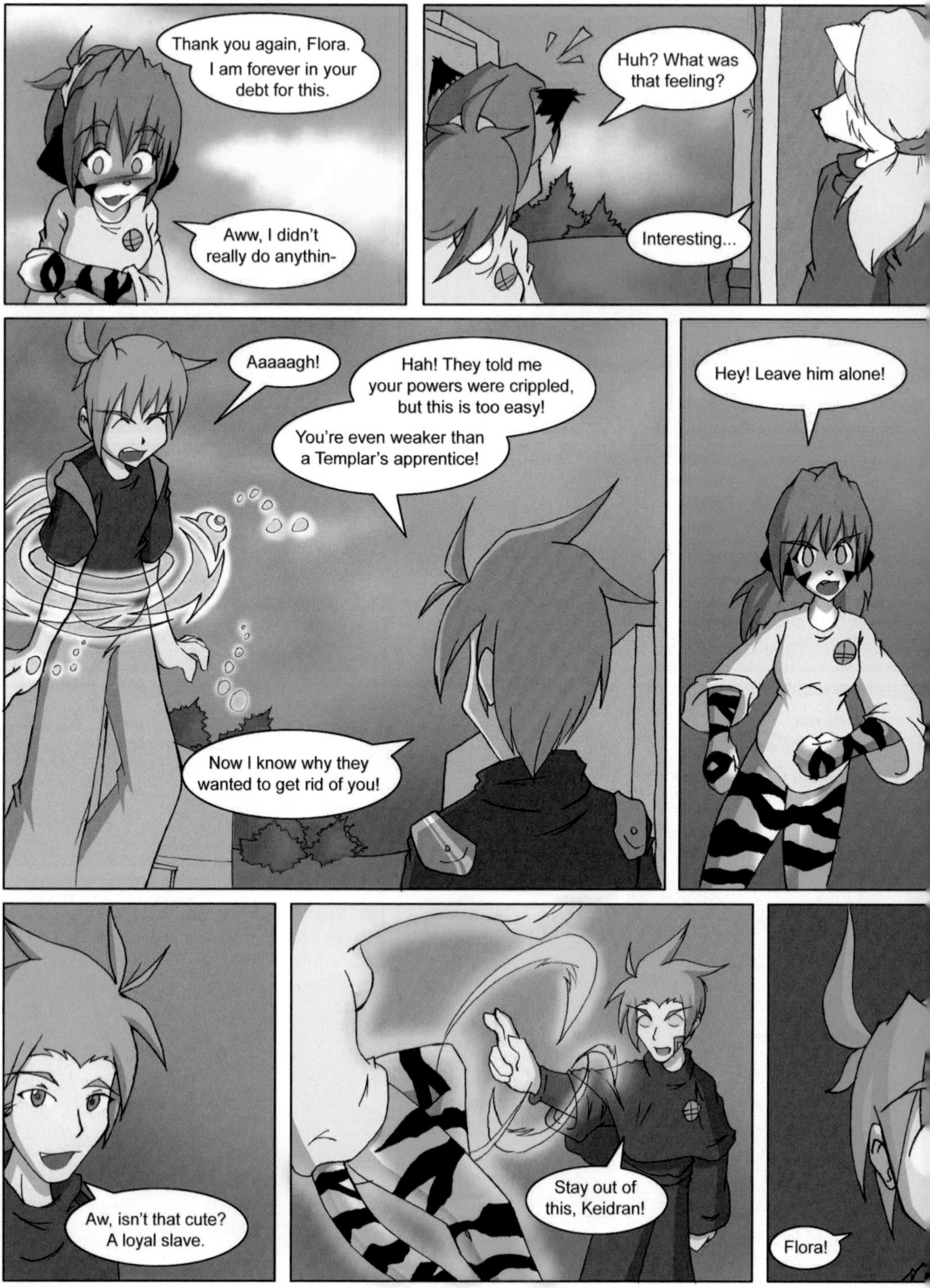

Thank you again, Flora. I am forever in your debt for this.
Aww, I didn't really do anythin-
Huh? What was that feeling?
Interesting...
Aaaaagh!
Hah! They told me your powers were crippled, but this is too easy!
You're even weaker than a Templar's apprentice!
Now I know why they wanted to get rid of you!
Hey! Leave him alone!
Aw, isn't that cute? A loyal slave.
Stay out of this, Keidran!
Flora!

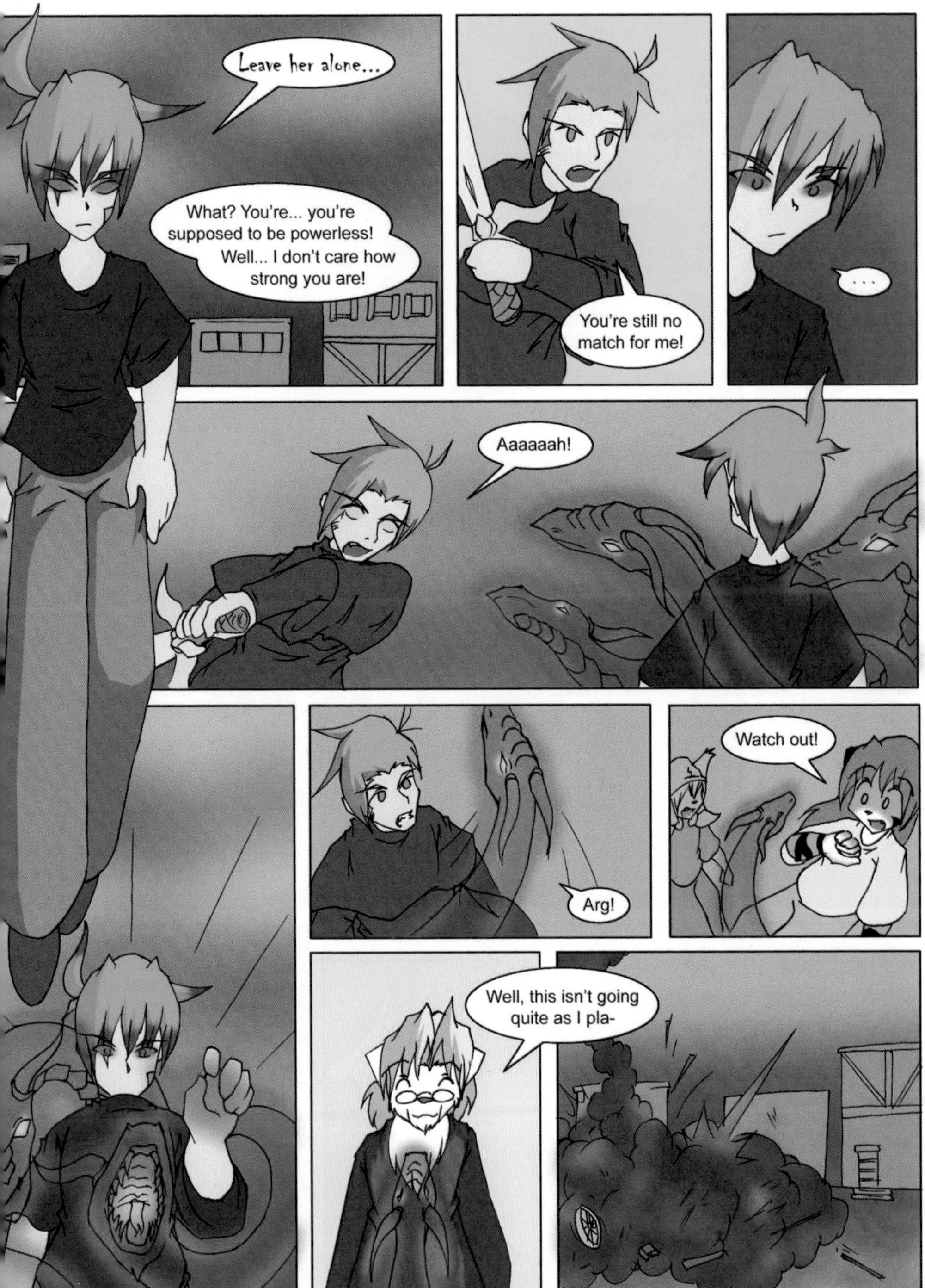
Leave her alone...
What? You're... you're supposed to be powerless!
Well... I don't care how strong you are!
You're still no match for me!
. . .
Aaaaaah!
Arg!
Watch out!
Well, this isn't going quite as I pla-

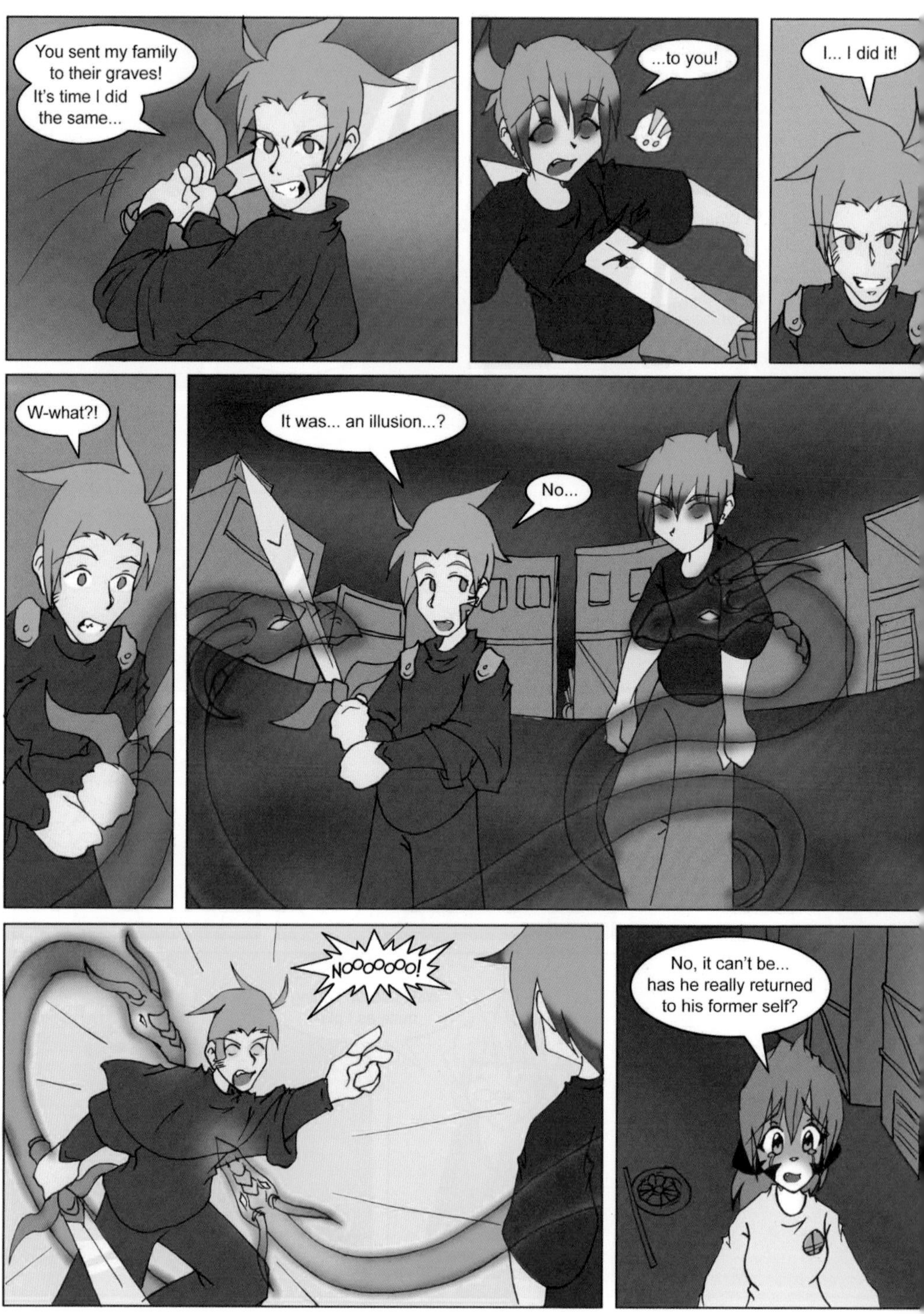
You sent my family to their graves! It's time I did the same...
...to you!
I... I did it!
W-what?!
It was... an illusion...?
No...
NOOOOOOOO!
No, it can't be... has he really returned to his former self?

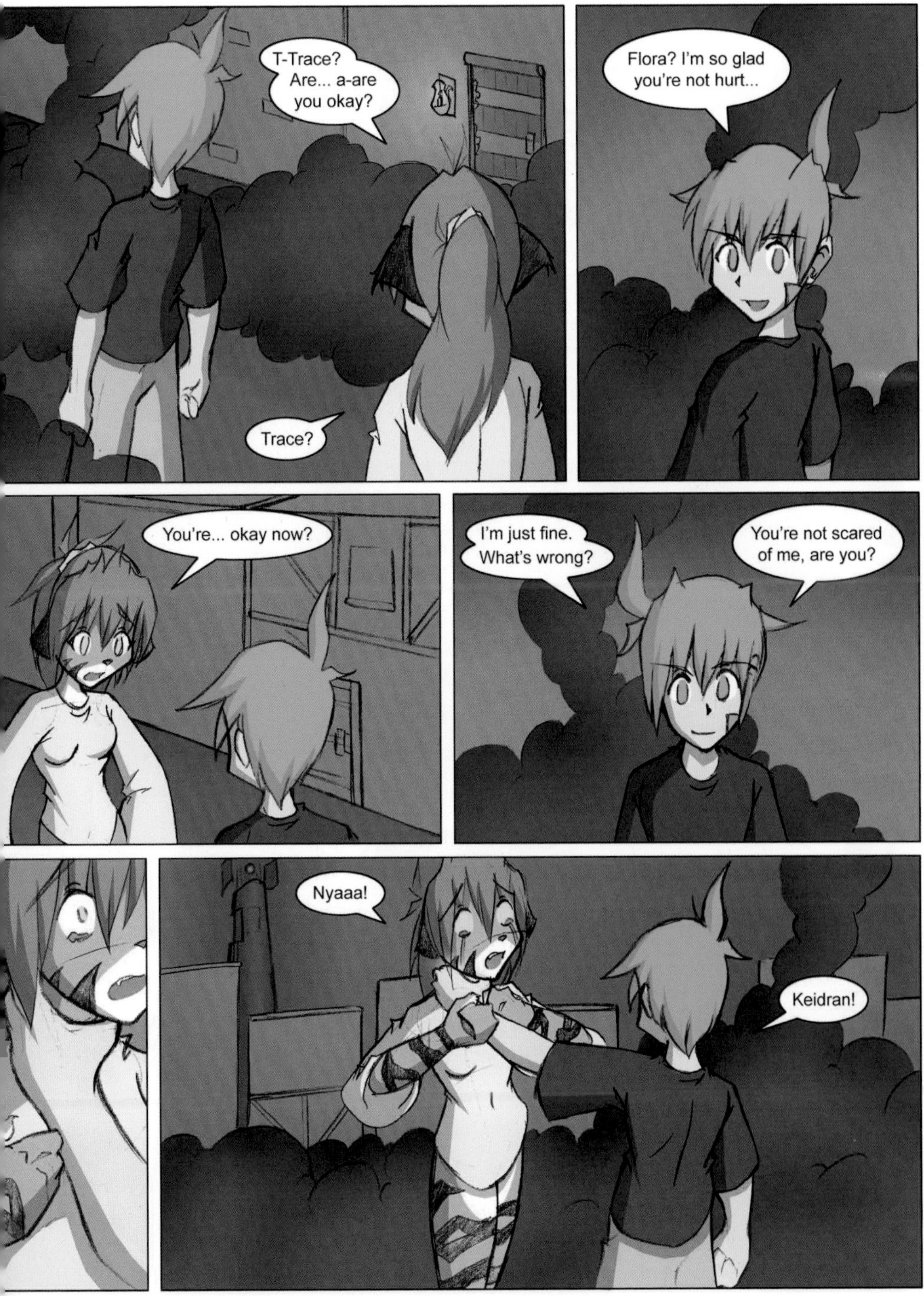
T-Trace?
Are... a-are
you okay?
Trace?
Flora? I'm so glad
you're not hurt...
You're... okay now?
I'm just fine.
What's wrong?
You're not scared
of me, are you?
Nyaaa!
Keidran!

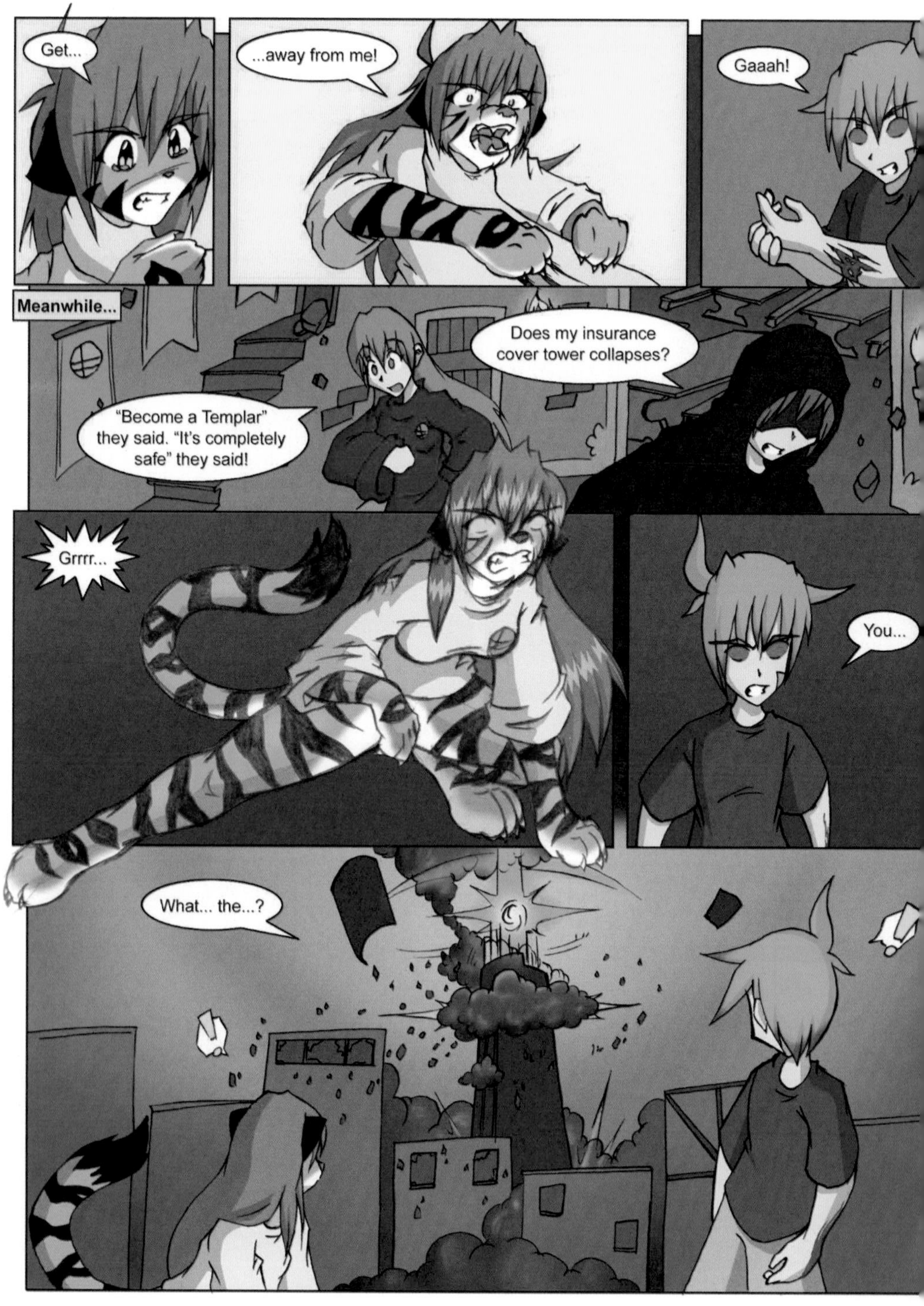
Get...
...away from me!
Gaaah!
Meanwhile...
Does my insurance cover tower collapses?
"Become a Templar" they said. "It's completely safe" they said!
Grrrr...
You...
What... the...?

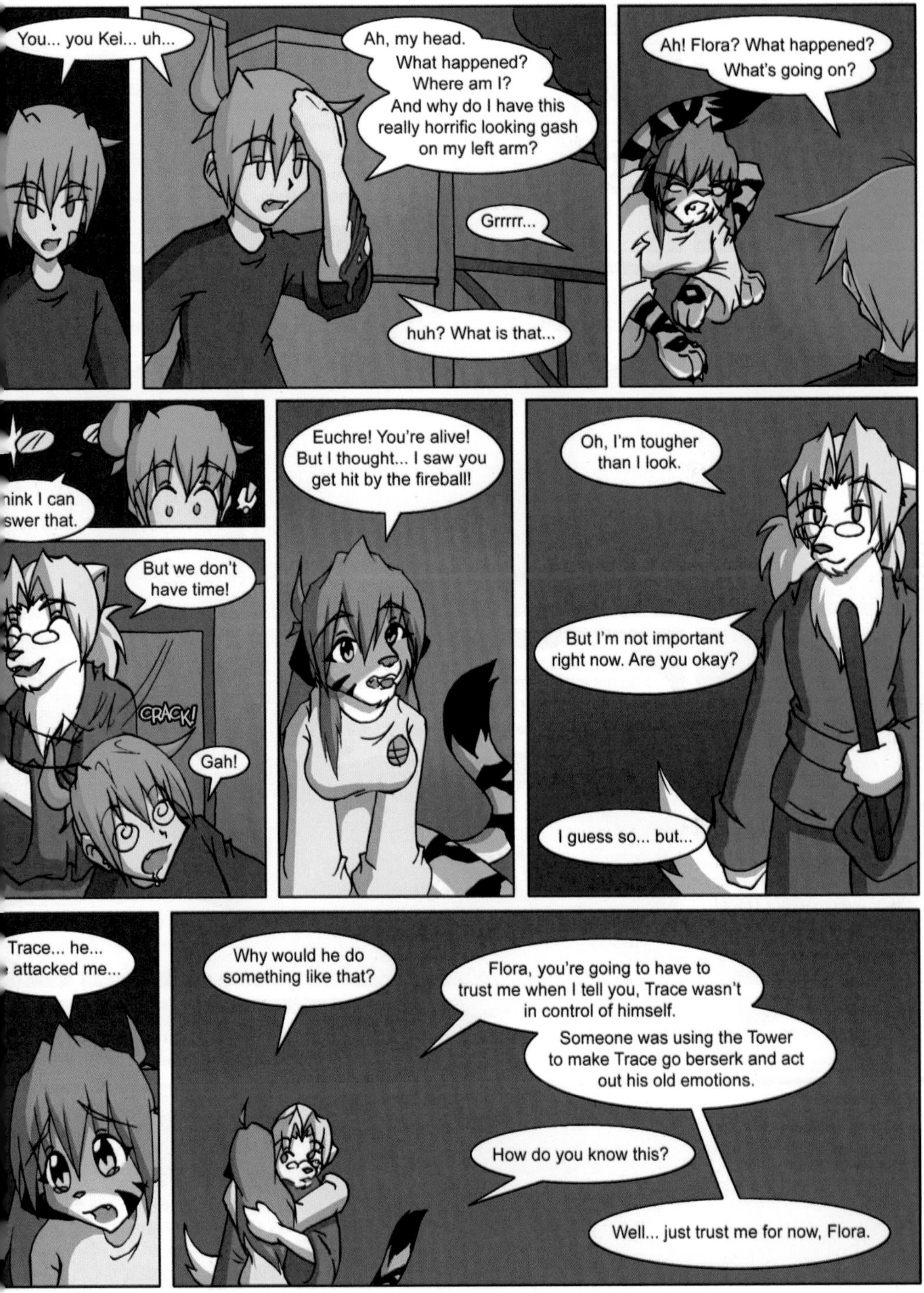
You... you Kei... uh...
Ah, my head.
What happened?
Where am I?
And why do I have this really horrific looking gash on my left arm?
Grrrrr...
huh? What is that...
Ah! Flora? What happened?
What's going on?
hink I can
swer that.
But we don't have time!
CRACK!
Gah!
Euchre! You're alive! But I thought... I saw you get hit by the fireball!
Oh, I'm tougher than I look.
But I'm not important right now. Are you okay?
I guess so... but...
Trace... he...
attacked me...
Why would he do something like that?
Flora, you're going to have to trust me when I tell you, Trace wasn't in control of himself.
Someone was using the Tower to make Trace go berserk and act out his old emotions.
How do you know this?
Well... just trust me for now, Flora.

Why would they want him to remember?

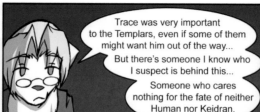

Trace was very important to the Templars, even if some of them might want him out of the way...

But there's someone I know who I suspect is behind this...

Someone who cares nothing for the fate of neither Human nor Keidran.

Ephemural!

Look what you've done! You've destroyed everything!

Oh? You don't like my plan?

Wrong! I do not involve myself with the petty quarrels of you Templar mortals.

I care not for Trace's fate!

Plan? You've destroyed my tower and nearly killed everyone *but* Trace!

You're plan is a failure.

There's only one thing I seek: balance! I am Neutrality.

I'm after... her.

Her? But she's just an ordinary Keidran...

I have foreseen that she will one day bring balance to the races of this world.

And betrayal is the key to spark the hatred to make it happen.

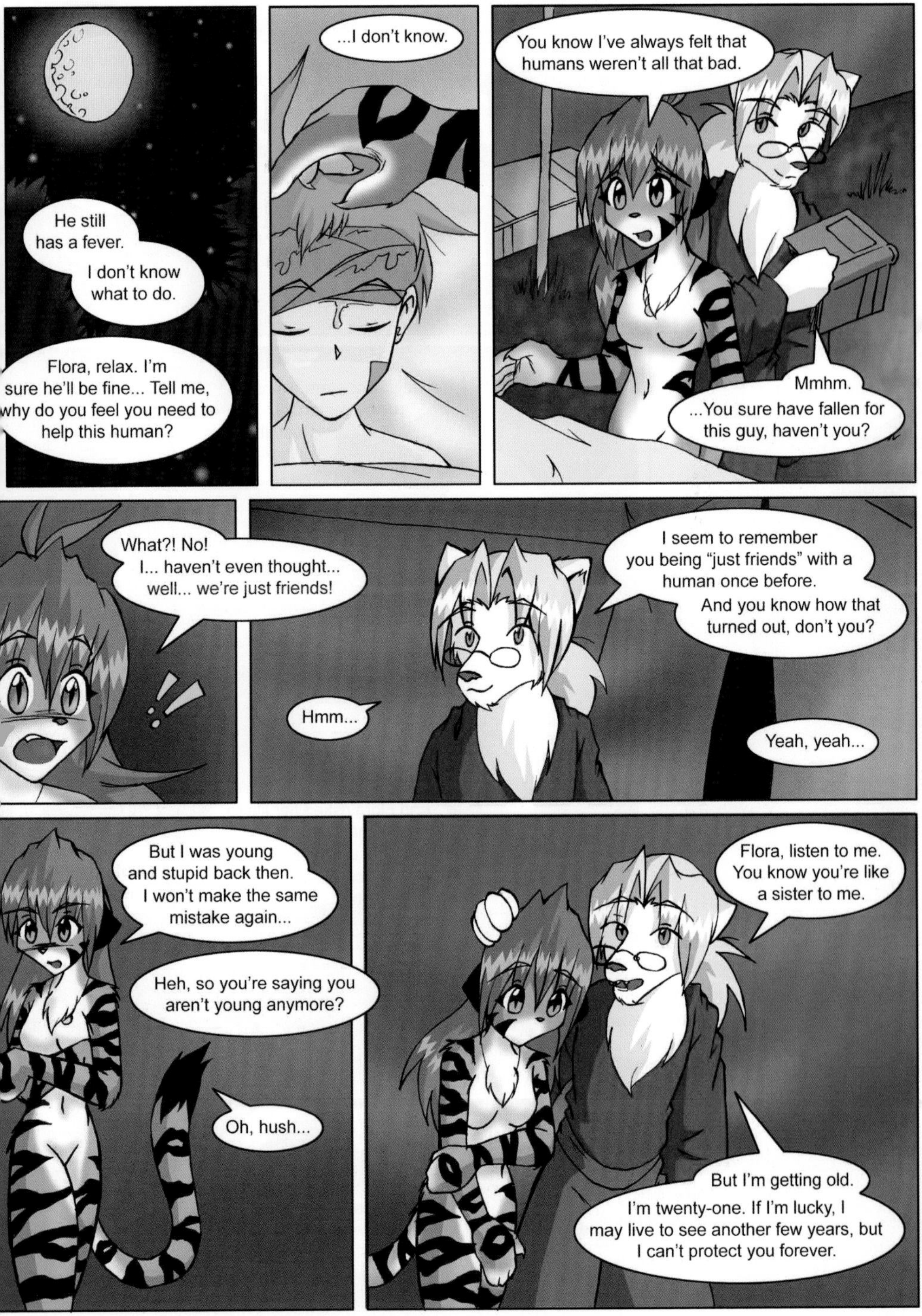
He still has a fever.
I don't know what to do.
Flora, relax. I'm sure he'll be fine... Tell me, why do you feel you need to help this human?
...I don't know.
You know I've always felt that humans weren't all that bad.
Mmhm.
...You sure have fallen for this guy, haven't you?
What?! No! I... haven't even thought... well... we're just friends!
Hmm...
I seem to remember you being "just friends" with a human once before.
And you know how that turned out, don't you?
Yeah, yeah...
But I was young and stupid back then.
I won't make the same mistake again...
Heh, so you're saying you aren't young anymore?
Oh, hush...
Flora, listen to me. You know you're like a sister to me.
But I'm getting old.
I'm twenty-one. If I'm lucky, I may live to see another few years, but I can't protect you forever.

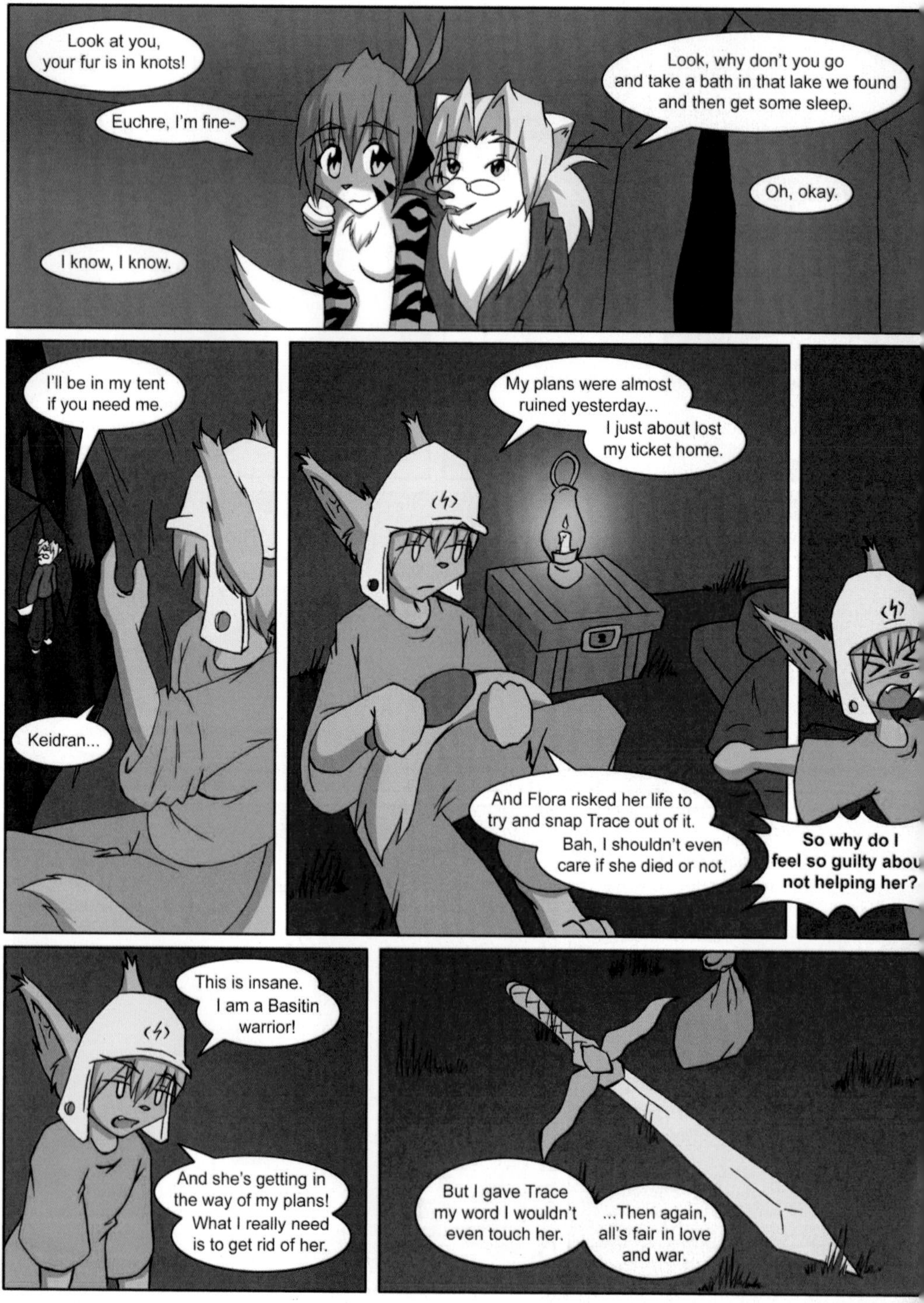
Look at you, your fur is in knots!
Euchre, I'm fine-
Look, why don't you go and take a bath in that lake we found and then get some sleep.
Oh, okay.
I know, I know.
I'll be in my tent if you need me.
Keidran...
My plans were almost ruined yesterday...
I just about lost my ticket home.
And Flora risked her life to try and snap Trace out of it.
Bah, I shouldn't even care if she died or not.
So why do I feel so guilty abou not helping her?
This is insane.
I am a Basitin warrior!
And she's getting in the way of my plans!
What I really need is to get rid of her.
But I gave Trace my word I wouldn't even touch her.
...Then again, all's fair in love and war.

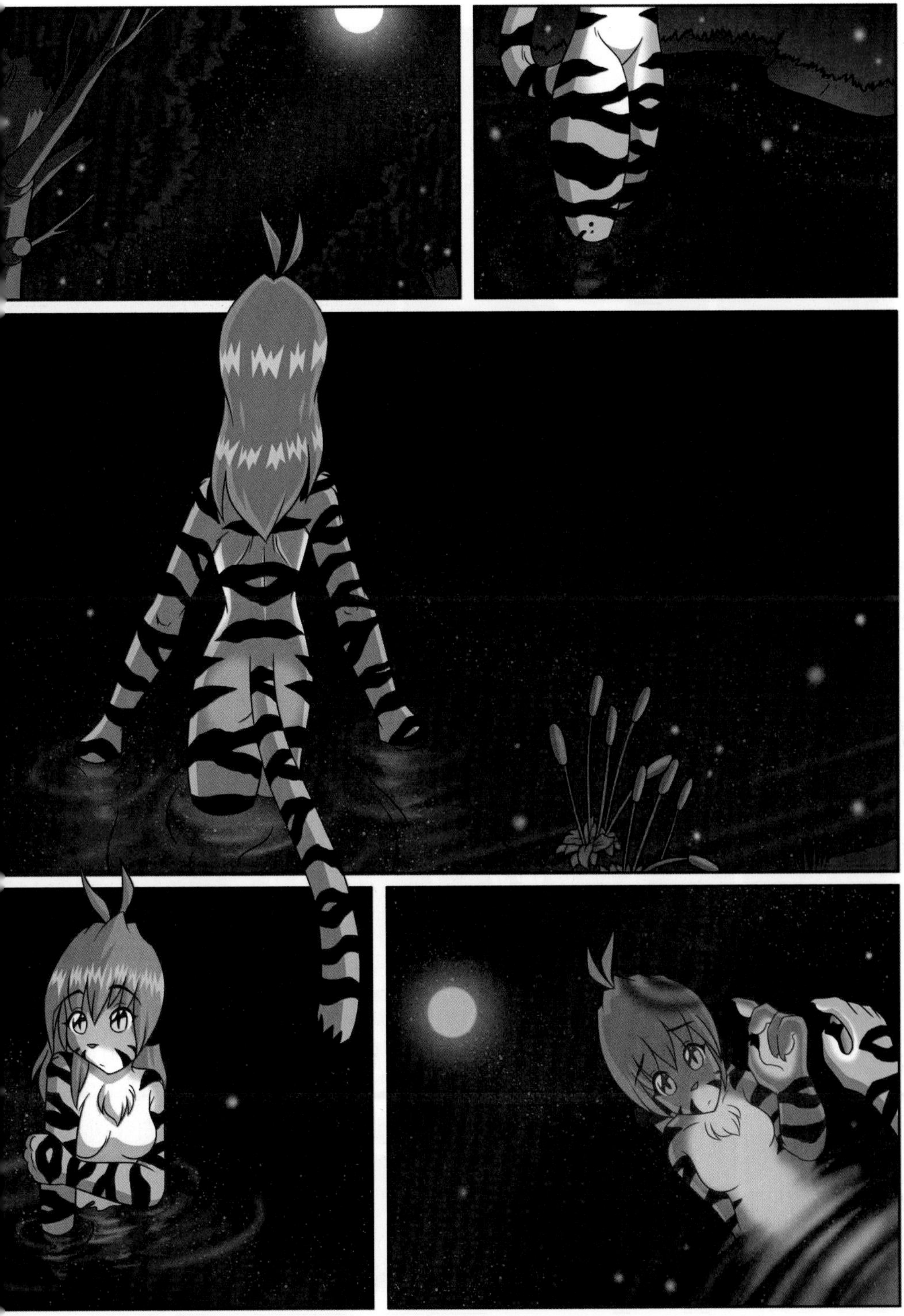

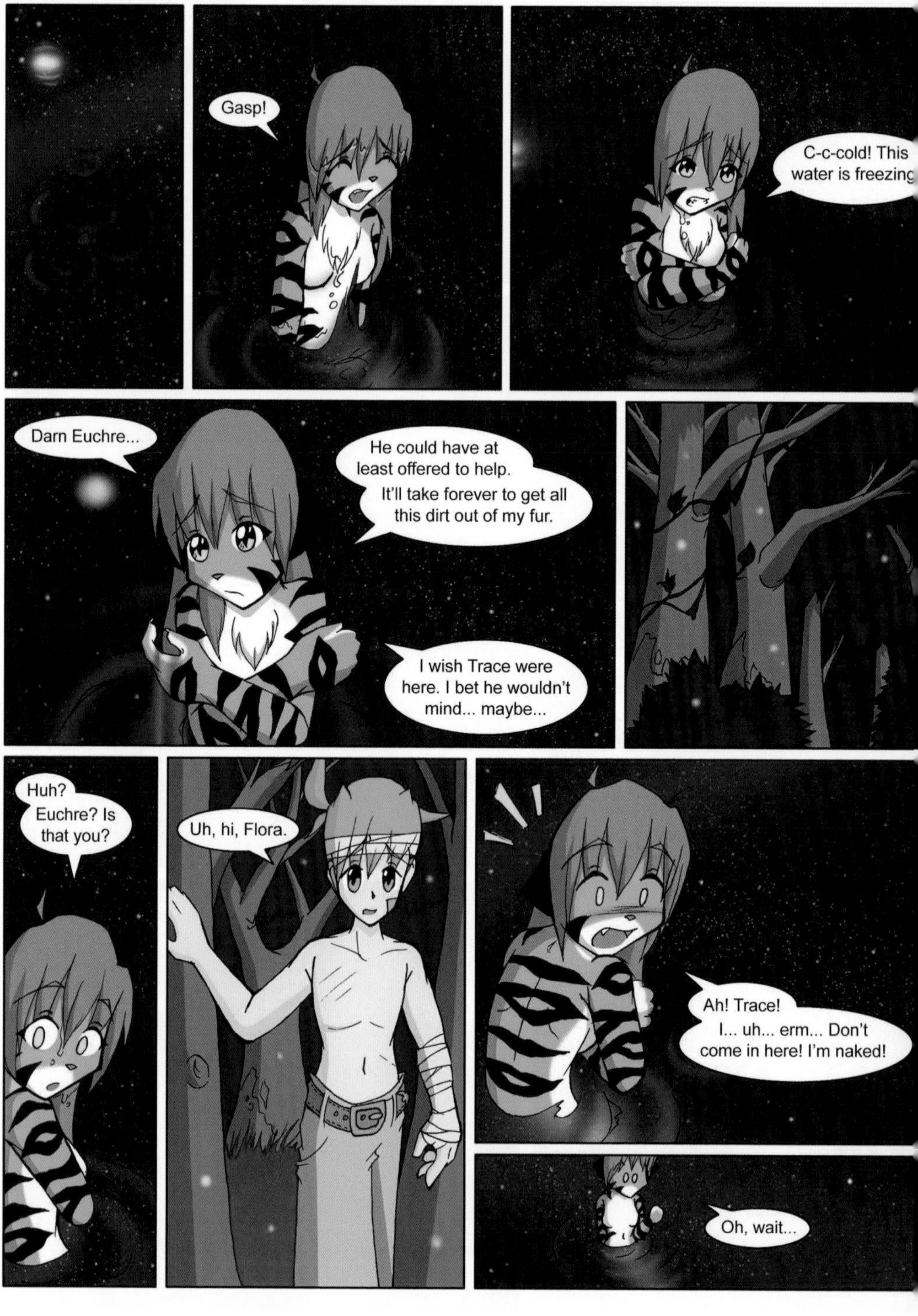
Gasp!
C-c-cold! This water is freezing
Darn Euchre...
He could have at least offered to help.
It'll take forever to get all this dirt out of my fur.
I wish Trace were here. I bet he wouldn't mind... maybe...
Huh? Euchre? Is that you?
Uh, hi, Flora.
Ah! Trace! I... uh... erm... Don't come in here! I'm naked!
Oh, wait...

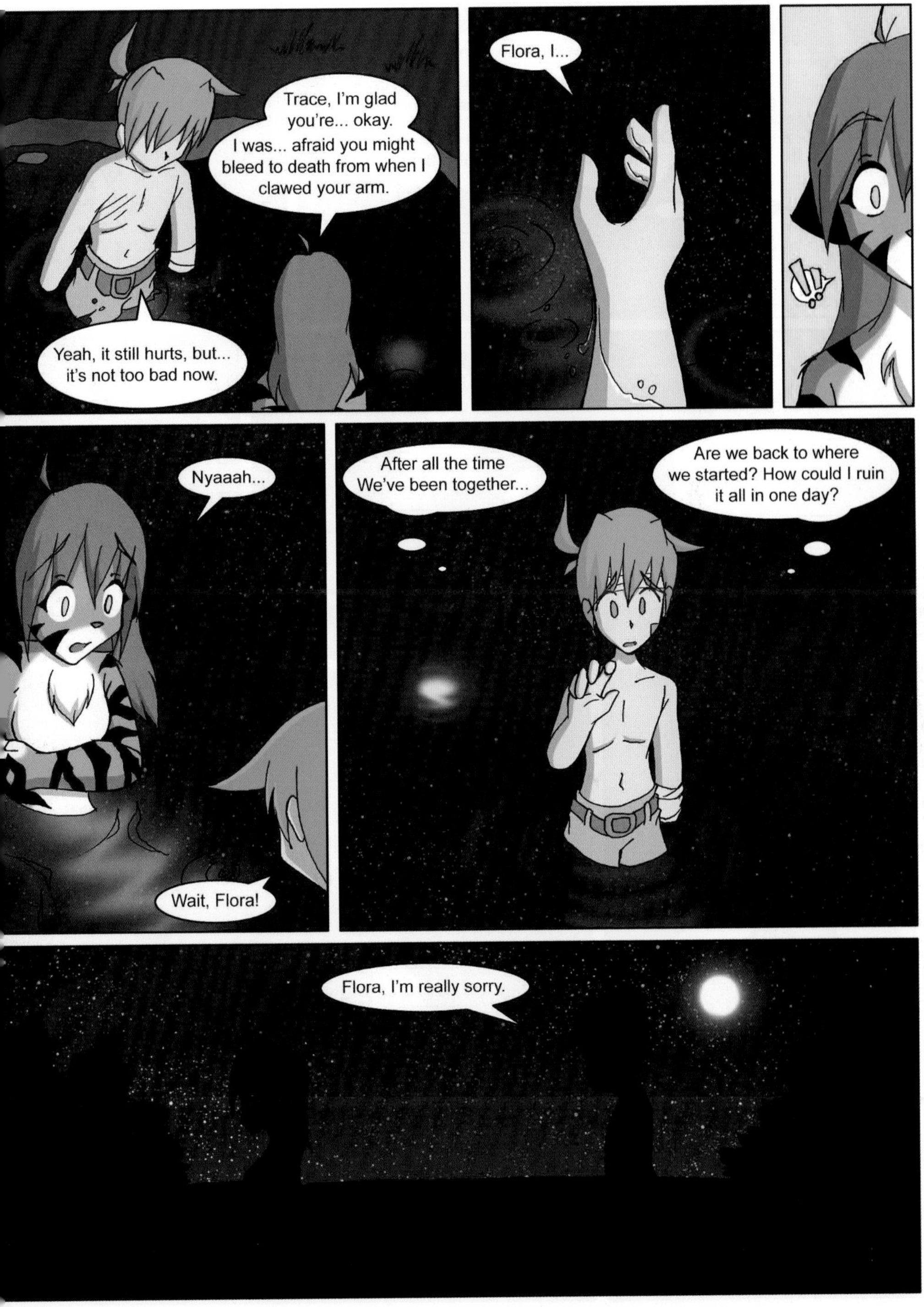

Trace, I'm glad you're... okay. I was... afraid you might bleed to death from when I clawed your arm.
Yeah, it still hurts, but... it's not too bad now.
Flora, I...
!!
Nyaaah...
Wait, Flora!
After all the time We've been together...
Are we back to where we started? How could I ruin it all in one day?
Flora, I'm really sorry.

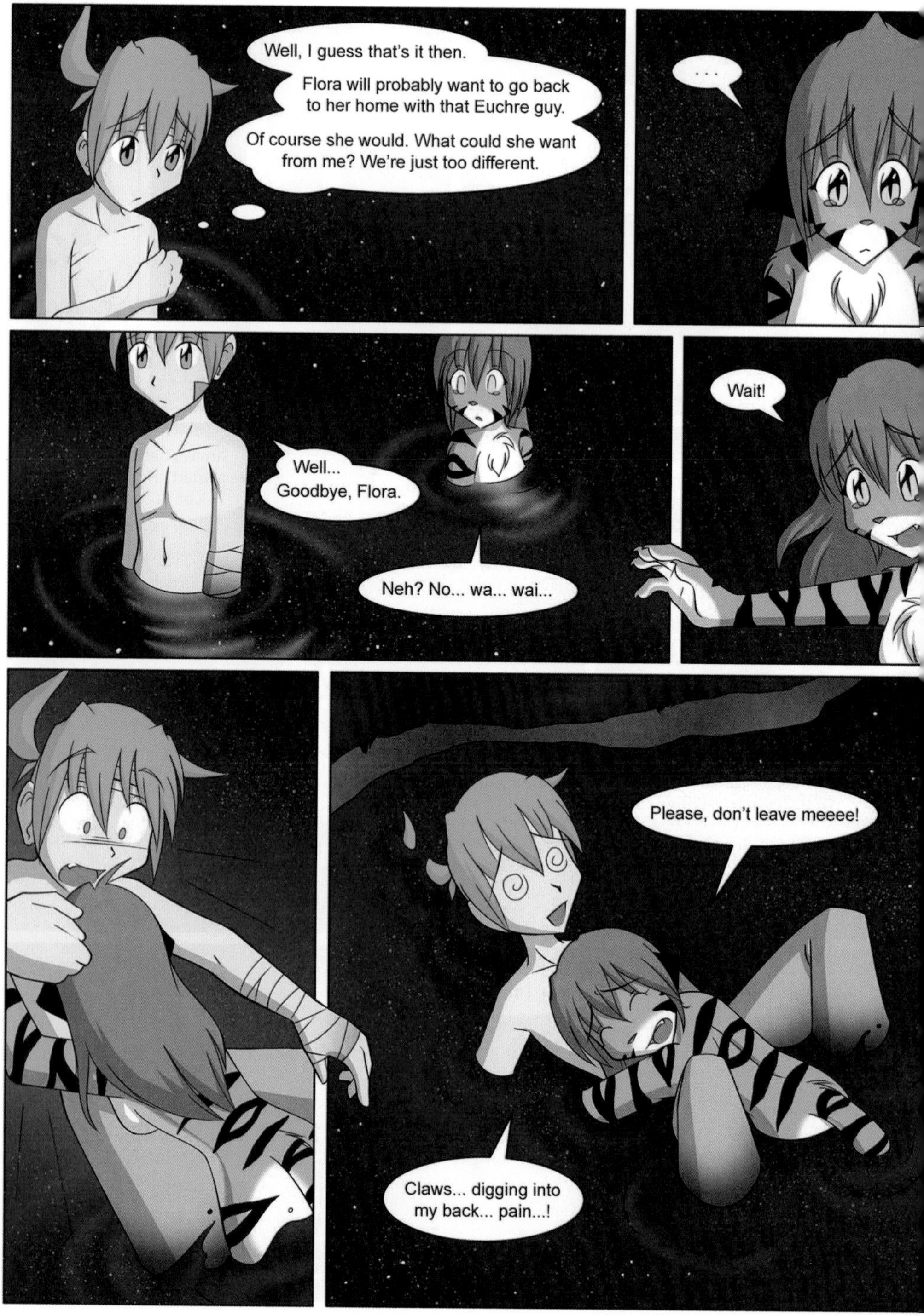
Well, I guess that's it then.
Flora will probably want to go back to her home with that Euchre guy.
Of course she would. What could she want from me? We're just too different.
. . .
Well... Goodbye, Flora.
Neh? No... wa... wai...
Wait!
Please, don't leave meeee!
Claws... digging into my back... pain...!

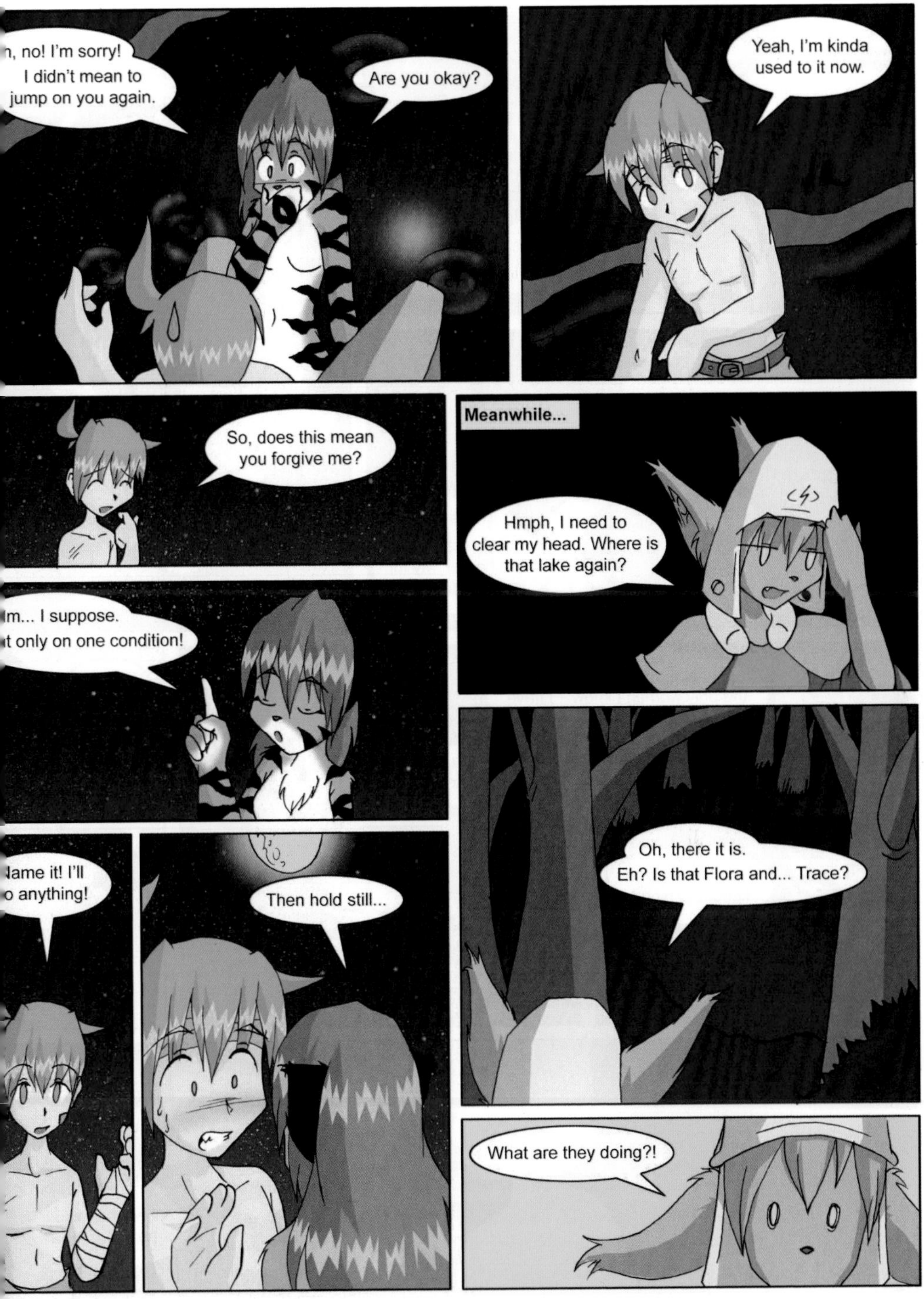

, no! I'm sorry! I didn't mean to jump on you again.
Are you okay?
Yeah, I'm kinda used to it now.
So, does this mean you forgive me?
Meanwhile...
Hmph, I need to clear my head. Where is that lake again?
m... I suppose. t only on one condition!
lame it! I'll o anything!
Then hold still...
Oh, there it is. Eh? Is that Flora and... Trace?
What are they doing?!

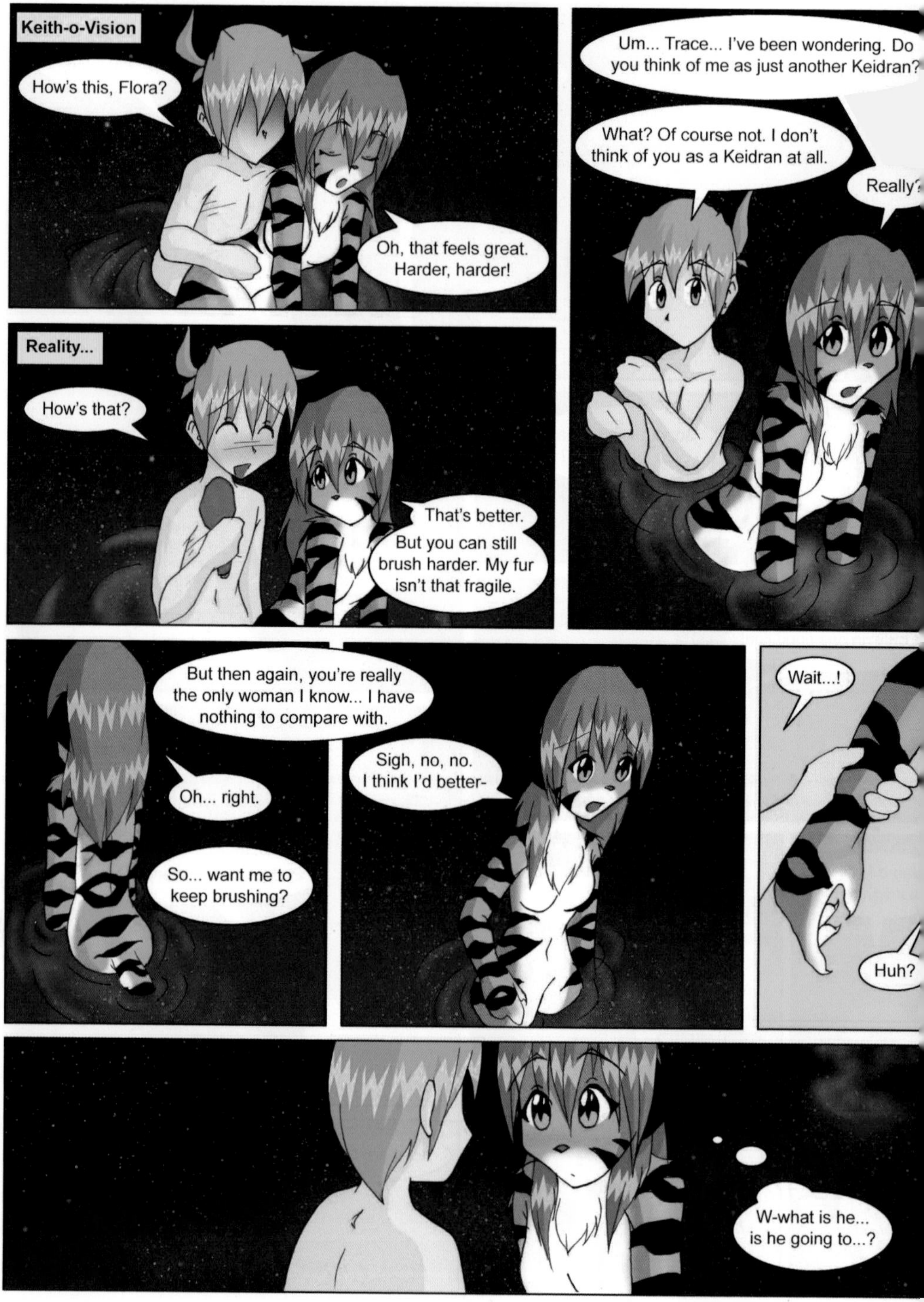
Keith-o-Vision
How's this, Flora?
Oh, that feels great. Harder, harder!
Reality...
How's that?
That's better.
But you can still brush harder. My fur isn't that fragile.
Um... Trace... I've been wondering. Do you think of me as just another Keidran?
What? Of course not. I don't think of you as a Keidran at all.
Really?
But then again, you're really the only woman I know... I have nothing to compare with.
Oh... right.
So... want me to keep brushing?
Sigh, no, no. I think I'd better-
Wait...!
Huh?
W-what is he... is he going to...?

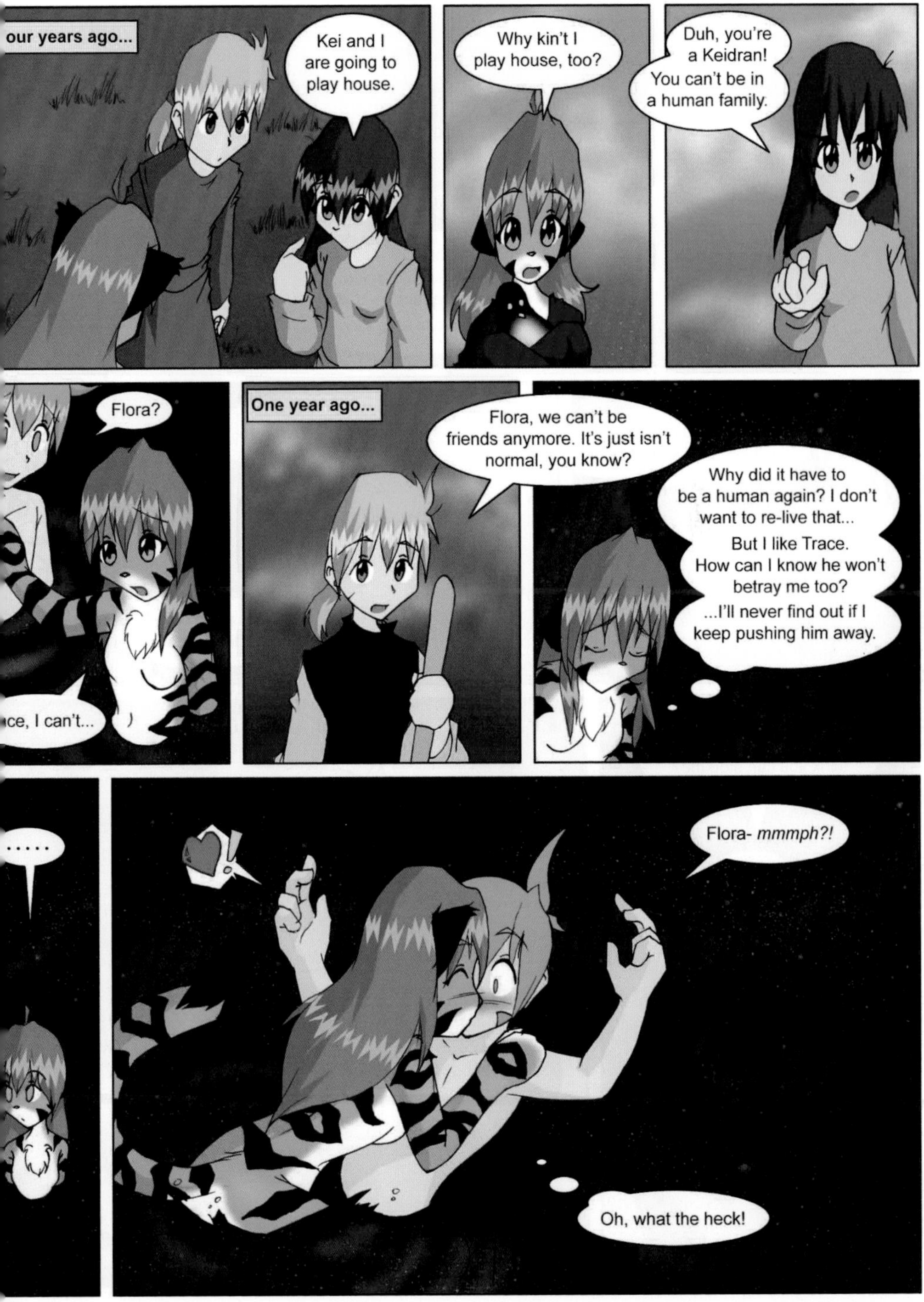
our years ago...
Kei and I are going to play house.
Why kin't I play house, too?
Duh, you're a Keidran! You can't be in a human family.
Flora?
ce, I can't...
One year ago...
Flora, we can't be friends anymore. It's just isn't normal, you know?
Why did it have to be a human again? I don't want to re-live that...
But I like Trace. How can I know he won't betray me too?
...I'll never find out if I keep pushing him away.
......
Flora- *mmmph?!*
Oh, what the heck!

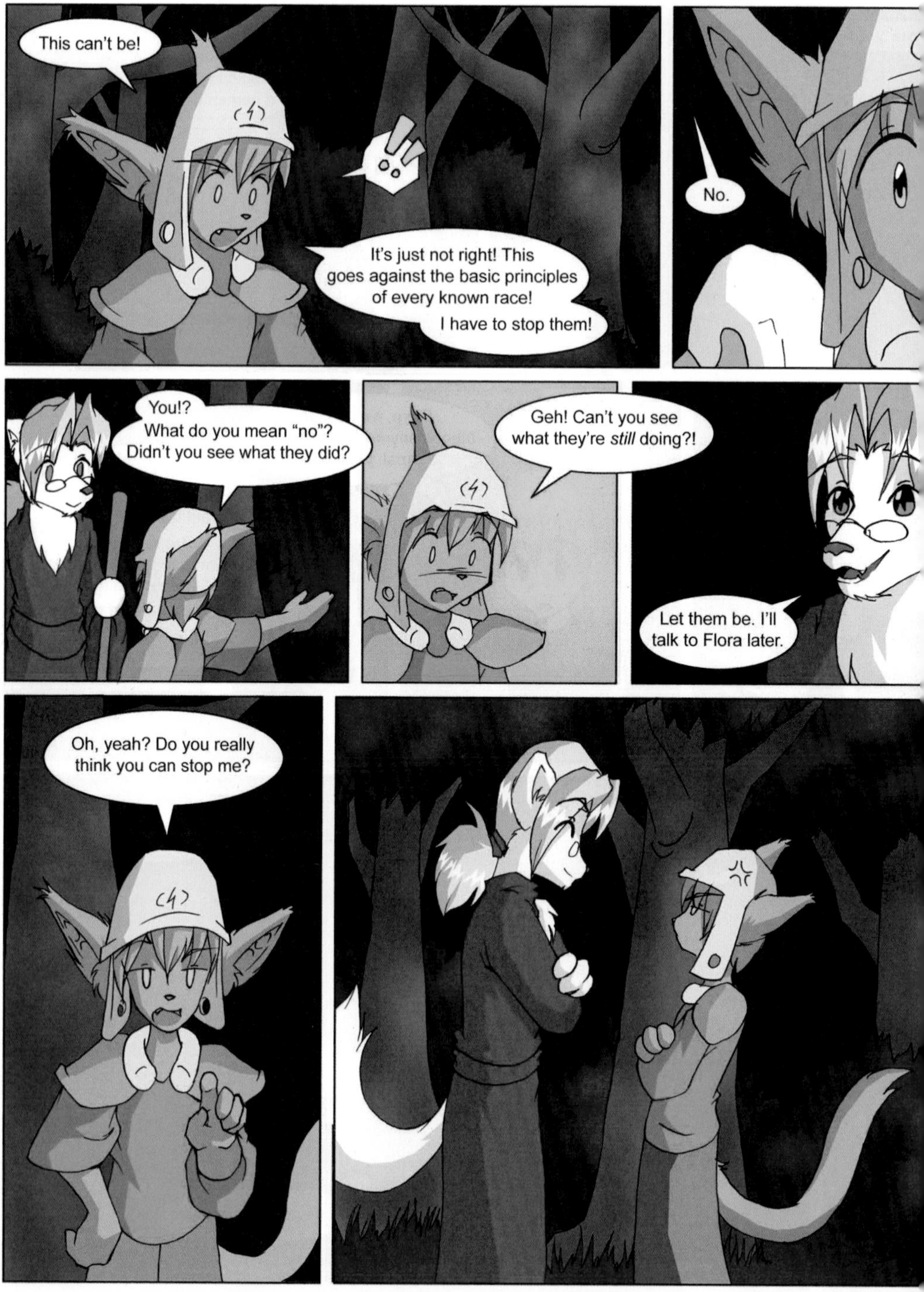
This can't be!
!
It's just not right! This goes against the basic principles of every known race!
I have to stop them!
No.
You!? What do you mean "no"? Didn't you see what they did?
Geh! Can't you see what they're *still* doing?!
Let them be. I'll talk to Flora later.
Oh, yeah? Do you really think you can stop me?

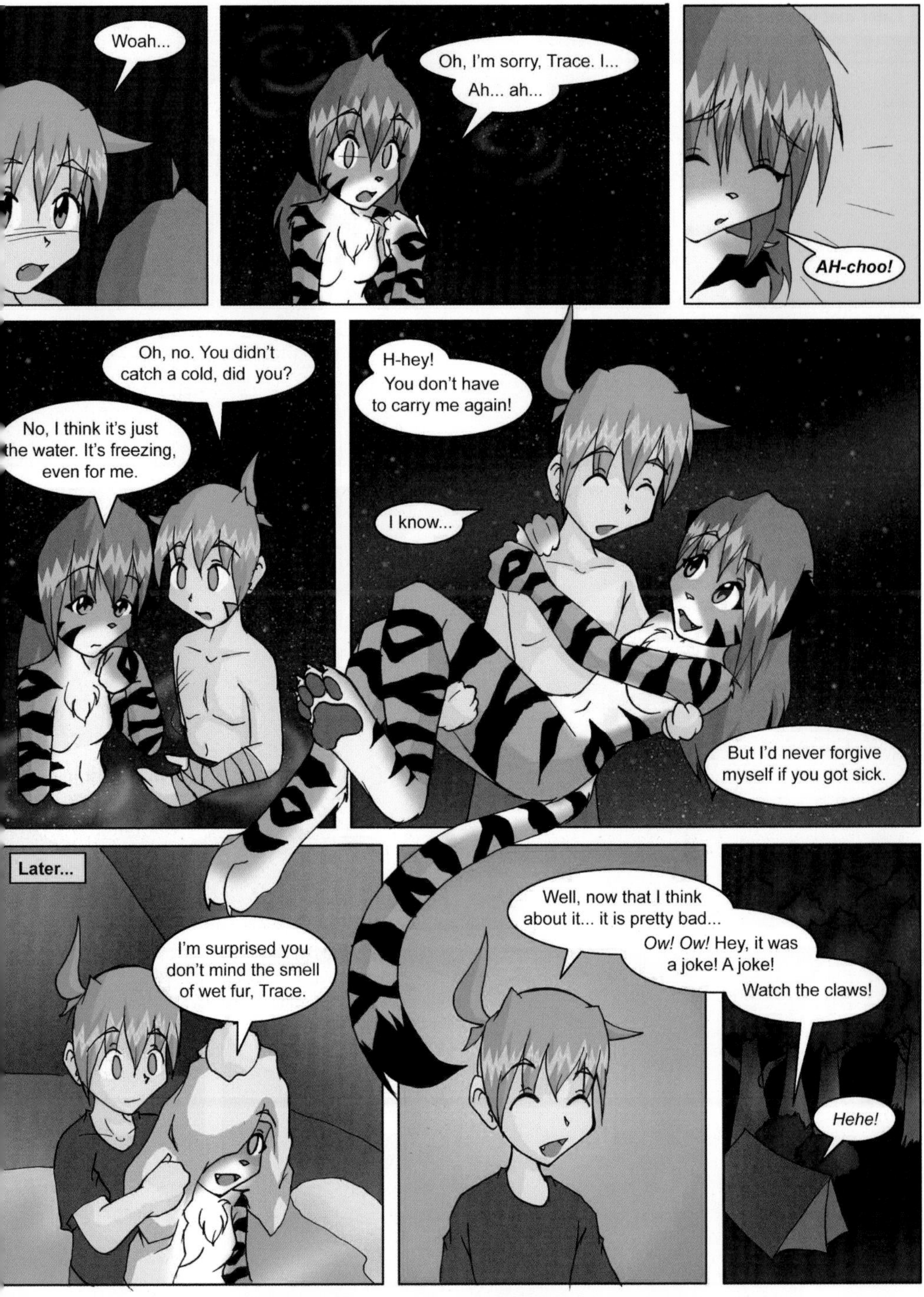
Woah...
Oh, I'm sorry, Trace. I...
Ah... ah...
AH-choo!
Oh, no. You didn't catch a cold, did you?
No, I think it's just the water. It's freezing, even for me.
H-hey! You don't have to carry me again!
I know...
But I'd never forgive myself if you got sick.
Later...
I'm surprised you don't mind the smell of wet fur, Trace.
Well, now that I think about it... it is pretty bad...
Ow! Ow! Hey, it was a joke! A joke!
Watch the claws!
Hehe!

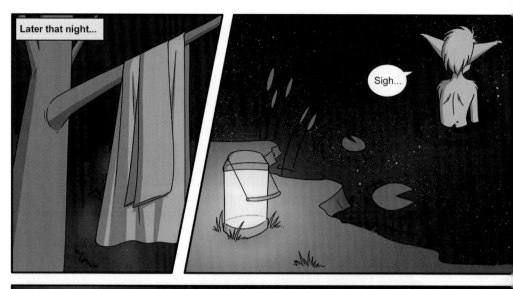

Sigh...

Damn Keidran.

How dare that wolf threaten me, a Basitin warrior? Their kind is nothing but trouble...

If it weren't for my mission, I'd get rid of them all right now.

But for now, I must endure their company. At least I have moments like this to myself.

Keith?

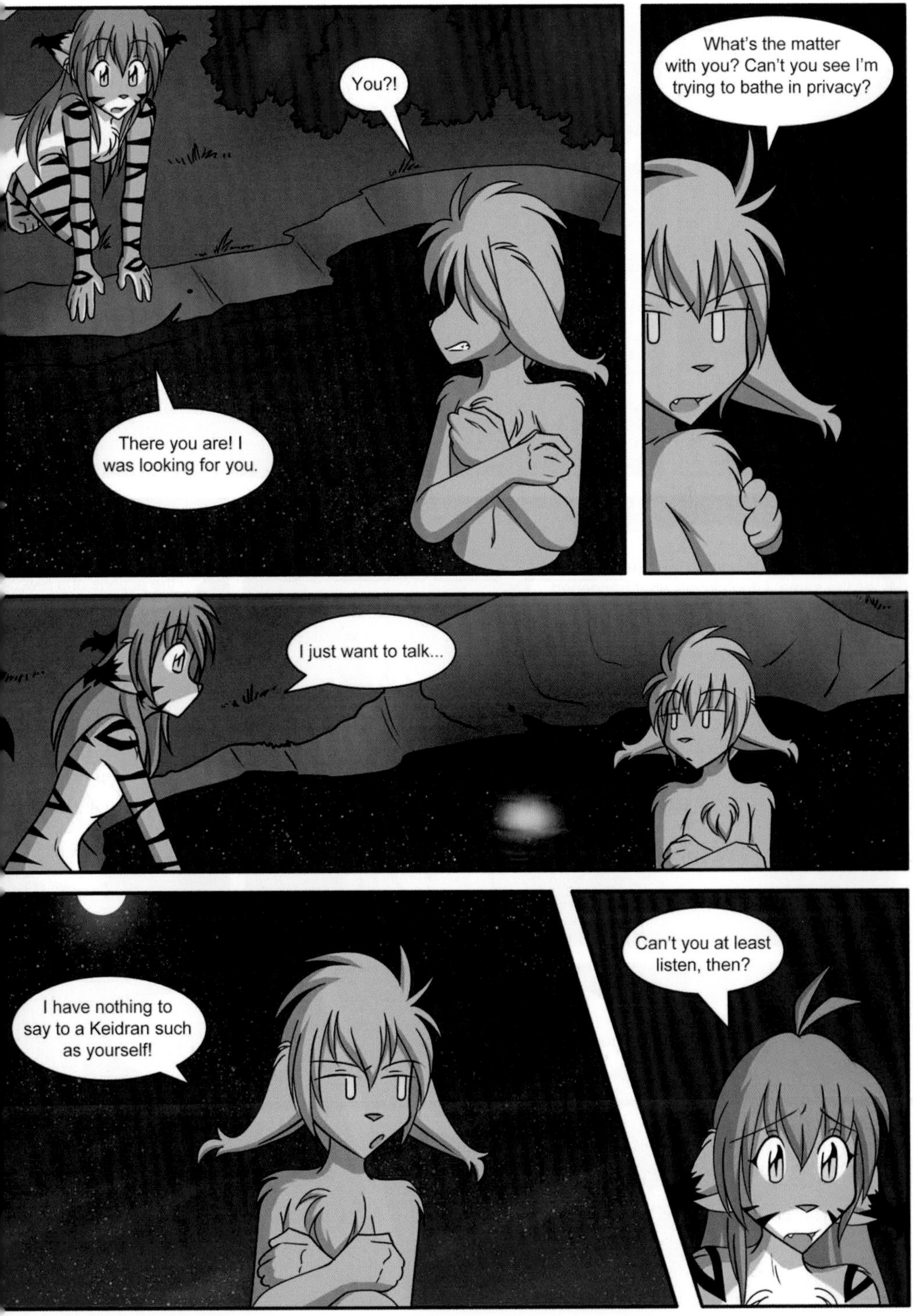
You?!
There you are! I was looking for you.
What's the matter with you? Can't you see I'm trying to bathe in privacy?
I just want to talk...
I have nothing to say to a Keidran such as yourself!
Can't you at least listen, then?

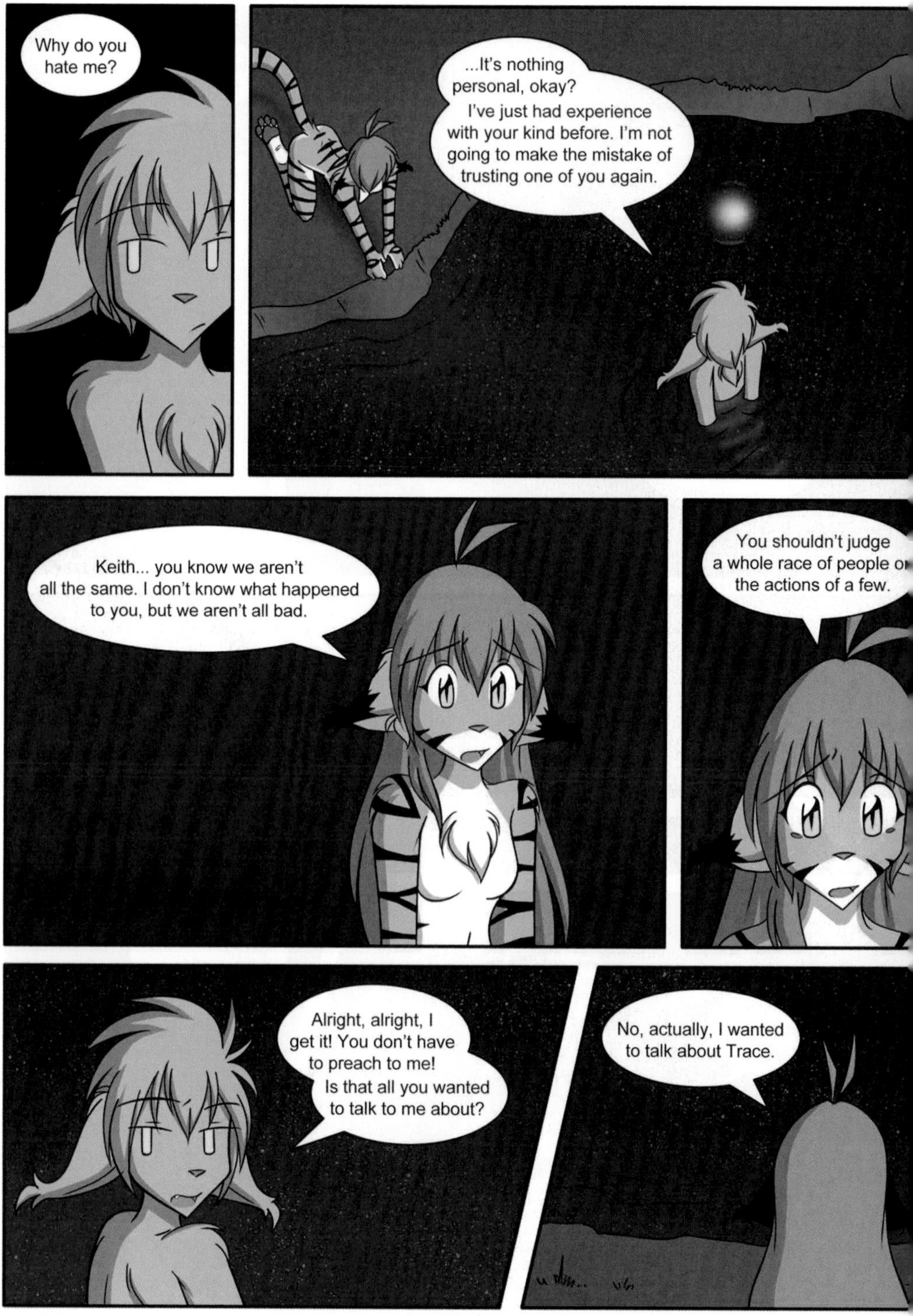
Why do you hate me?
...It's nothing personal, okay?
I've just had experience with your kind before. I'm not going to make the mistake of trusting one of you again.
Keith... you know we aren't all the same. I don't know what happened to you, but we aren't all bad.
You shouldn't judge a whole race of people o the actions of a few.
Alright, alright, I get it! You don't have to preach to me!
Is that all you wanted to talk to me about?
No, actually, I wanted to talk about Trace.

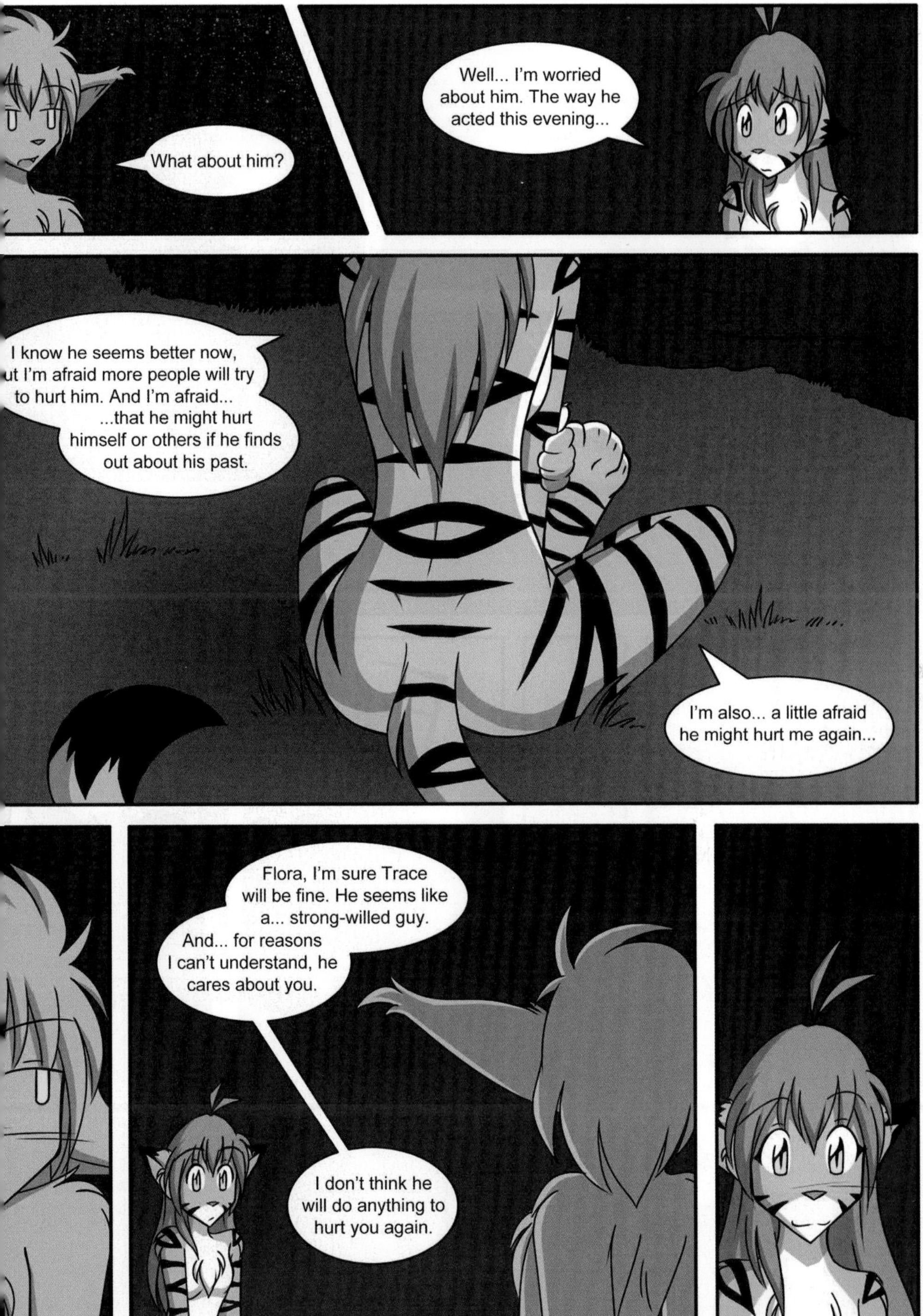
What about him?
Well... I'm worried about him. The way he acted this evening...
I know he seems better now, ut I'm afraid more people will try to hurt him. And I'm afraid... ...that he might hurt himself or others if he finds out about his past.
I'm also... a little afraid he might hurt me again...
Flora, I'm sure Trace will be fine. He seems like a... strong-willed guy.
And... for reasons I can't understand, he cares about you.
I don't think he will do anything to hurt you again.

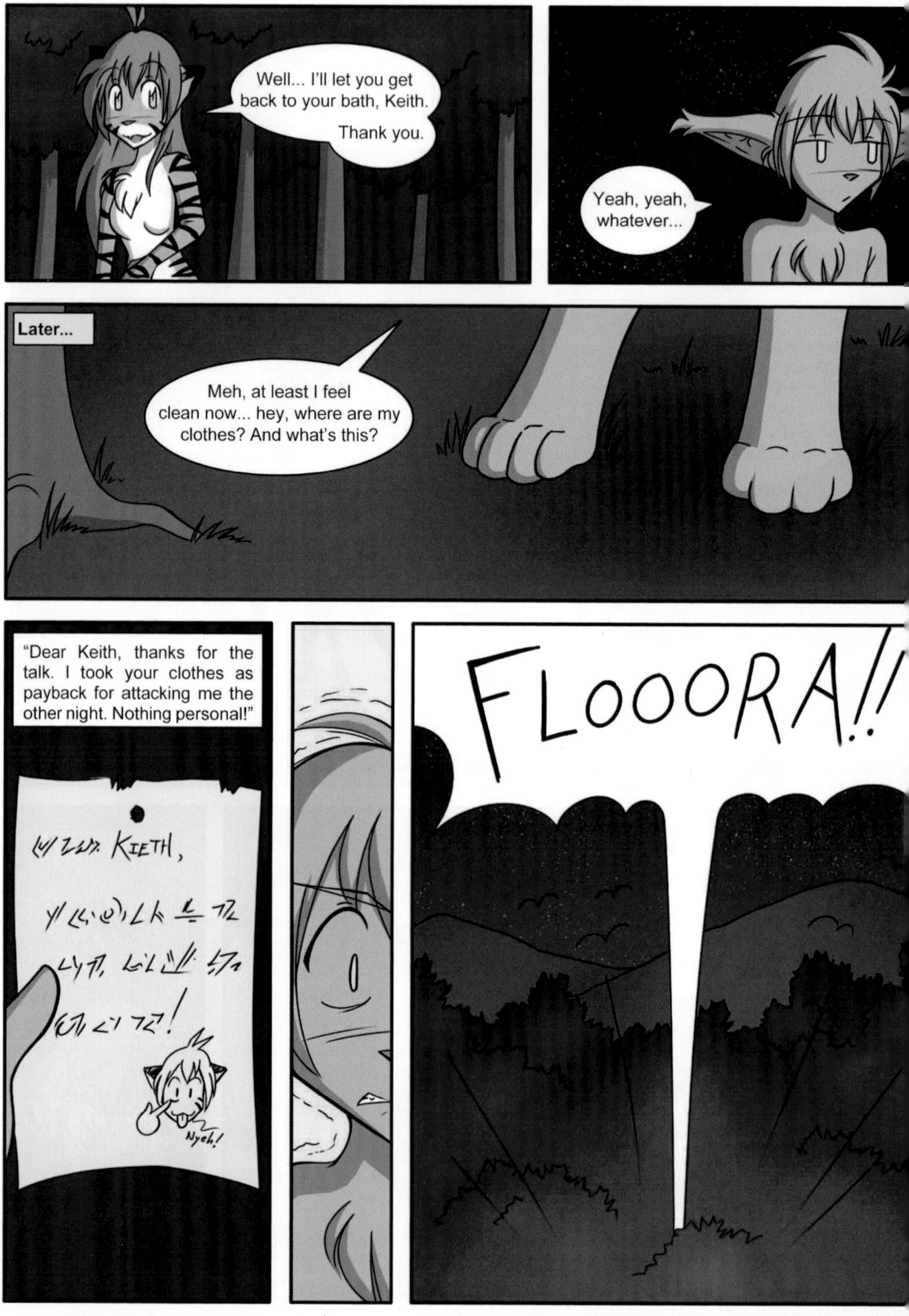

Well... I'll let you get back to your bath, Keith.
Thank you.
Yeah, yeah, whatever...
Later...
Meh, at least I feel clean now... hey, where are my clothes? And what's this?
"Dear Keith, thanks for the talk. I took your clothes as payback for attacking me the other night. Nothing personal!"
KIETH,
Nyeh!
FLOOORA!!